Reckless Charm

Ivy Lane

Published by Ivy Lane, 2024.

This is a work of fiction. Similarities to real people, places, or events are entirely coincidental.

RECKLESS CHARM

First edition. October 26, 2024.

Copyright © 2024 Ivy Lane.

ISBN: 979-8227521651

Written by Ivy Lane.

Chapter 1: The Whispering Hills

The sun dipped low over the rolling Tennessee hills as I stood on the wraparound porch of my grandmother's farmhouse, the scent of honeysuckle heavy in the air. It had been a year since I'd left Boston, running from the life I thought I wanted. I wasn't ready to face the city again, or the career that had swallowed me whole. Here, I could breathe. But then, he appeared—Clayton Davis, the man I hadn't seen in over a decade, the boy who used to make me laugh until my sides hurt. He wasn't a boy anymore. The sight of him, leaning against his truck, sent a jolt through me. We weren't kids anymore, and everything felt too complicated now.

Clayton was a kaleidoscope of contrasts. The rugged lines of his jaw and the way his faded flannel shirt clung to his muscular frame spoke of hard work and determination, but there was a softness in his hazel eyes, a warmth that drew me in, unraveling the walls I'd built around myself. I'd spent the last year wrestling with my own demons, battling the memory of a life I thought I wanted—a life filled with board meetings, deadlines, and the suffocating air of corporate ambition. Here, among the whispering hills, everything felt like a forgotten dream, and he was a fragment of that past I had buried deep.

As he walked towards me, his boots crunching on the gravel path, I felt my heart race. What would I say? Would I pretend the years hadn't passed, that I wasn't just a little more broken than before? His smile was disarming, a reminder of lazy summer days spent climbing trees and stealing kisses behind the barn. "Carmen?" he said, his voice rich and warm, wrapping around me like the Southern sun. "Is that really you?"

"Clayton," I replied, trying to sound casual, but the name slipped out with a breathiness that betrayed me. I couldn't help but laugh, a nervous sound that echoed in the stillness. "What brings you back to Whispering Hills?"

His laughter, deep and genuine, filled the space between us. "My mom's been trying to convince me to visit more often. I guess I finally caved." He gestured vaguely behind him, and I noticed the familiar old pickup truck, its rusty charm still intact. It felt like a symbol of all the things I had left behind and the unexpected return of those memories.

"Your mom always did love this place," I said, glancing back at the farmhouse, the weathered wood and peeling paint telling stories of summers gone by. "And what about you? You still playing guitar in that bar downtown?" The question slipped from my lips before I could think better of it, dredging up memories of smoky rooms and late-night serenades.

He shrugged, a flicker of vulnerability passing over his face. "Not so much anymore. Life has a way of changing plans, doesn't it?" The weight of unspoken words hung between us, and I wondered what had shaped his journey while I was busy crafting my own.

The gentle rustle of leaves whispered secrets in the fading light, and I found myself stepping closer, pulled in by an invisible thread. "I can't believe it's been this long," I murmured, a mix of nostalgia and regret swirling in my chest. We had shared so many moments—our dreams, our laughter—before life took us in different directions.

"I know," he said, tilting his head slightly as if studying me. "You left for the big city, and I got stuck in this little town." The hint of melancholy in his voice made my heart ache. "But honestly? I'm kind of glad you're back."

"Glad?" The word surprised me, a simple notion that held so much weight. "Why's that?"

"I don't know," he said, running a hand through his tousled hair. "Maybe because this place always felt more alive when you were around. And maybe because I've missed you." The last part hung in the air, both vulnerable and courageous, a testament to the boy he once was and the man he had become.

The evening sky darkened, shades of orange and purple mingling in a breathtaking display. I could hear the distant call of crickets, their serenade urging the night to come alive. "Missed me?" I echoed, the words tasting foreign on my tongue. "Why would you miss me?"

His laughter was low, almost sheepish. "Well, you were a pretty big deal back then. You always knew how to lighten the mood. Remember that time we snuck into the old quarry?"

How could I forget? The thrill of the adventure, the way we dared each other to jump, and the sheer joy of feeling invincible for a moment. "You were such a chicken," I teased, nudging him lightly.

"Hey! I'll have you know that I made that jump," he protested, crossing his arms dramatically. "You were the one who climbed back down, scared out of your mind."

"Only because you dared me!" I shot back, unable to stifle the laughter bubbling up.

His eyes sparkled with mischief, the playful banter flowing between us like the sweet tea we'd sipped on those long-ago summer afternoons. The easy rhythm of our conversation enveloped me, reminding me that perhaps not all of the past was a burden. Maybe some parts still held the magic of possibility.

But just as I felt myself slipping into that comfort, the tension returned, uninvited. The memories, tinged with the bittersweet aftertaste of lost dreams and paths not taken, threatened to pull me under. How could I reconcile the carefree girl I had been with the woman I was now? I took a step back, caught between longing and uncertainty, the shadows of my choices looming larger than the warmth of the sun setting behind the hills.

As the last rays of daylight faded, leaving a dusky glow in their wake, I felt the weight of the moment settle around us. Time felt suspended, charged with unspoken words and hidden truths. I could either embrace this unexpected reunion, or I could retreat into the safety of my carefully constructed walls.

But what if there was a third option? What if this moment was the catalyst I needed to uncover not just the past, but also the promise of what could be? With that thought simmering in my mind, I dared to look into his eyes again, ready to explore the uncharted territory of our newfound connection.

The moment lingered, a fragile thread of connection stretching between us, charged with the weight of unspoken possibilities. I could feel my heart thrumming like a runaway train, caught between the thrill of rekindling an old flame and the trepidation of what that flame might ignite. Clayton shifted slightly, his hands shoved deep into his pockets, an uncertain smile playing at the corners of his lips. "So, what have you been up to? Besides avoiding the chaos of city life?"

I tilted my head, weighing my response carefully. "Oh, you know, the usual. Finding myself in the hills, exploring the fine art of porch sitting, and avoiding any serious adult responsibilities." My teasing tone matched his, but the undercurrent of truth tugged at me. "It's been... refreshing, to say the least."

"Refreshing sounds nice," he mused, his gaze drifting to the horizon where the last embers of sunlight flickered. "I think I could use a bit of that myself." He glanced back at me, his eyes glinting with curiosity. "What's next for you, Carmen? Planning on staying in Whispering Hills forever?"

The question hung between us, thickening the air. I wanted to laugh it off, to play the part of the carefree wanderer, but the truth lingered in my throat like an unbidden sob. "I don't know, honestly. I just needed to escape for a bit. Boston felt like a prison, and this place..." I gestured broadly to the familiar fields and trees, the ghosts of my childhood dancing among them. "This place feels like home. A place where I can breathe without the weight of expectation."

"Expectation can be a heavy burden," he replied, his voice low, resonating with understanding. The earnestness in his tone pulled at my heartstrings, reminding me of the boy who once offered comfort in the chaos of life's uncertainties.

I opened my mouth to respond, but just then, a cacophony of sounds erupted from the backyard, shattering our moment. Laughter, loud and unrestrained, pierced the air, pulling me back into the present. I turned to see a group of children racing across the yard, their faces flushed with joy, innocent and free. One of them, a little girl with pigtails, caught sight of me and sprinted over, her arms outstretched like she was about to fly.

"Aunt Carmen!" she squealed, launching herself into my embrace. "You're back! You promised to teach me how to make your famous cookies!"

The interruption was a jolt, but the warmth of her embrace melted away any lingering tension. "Of course I did, Zoe! But we have to make them extra special this time. You'll need to show me your secret ingredient."

"I will! I will!" she exclaimed, her eyes shining with excitement. The chatter of the other kids faded into the background as I let myself be swept into the whirlwind of her energy, an anchor in the storm of uncertainty that had been swirling around me since Clayton's arrival.

As the children gathered around, I caught Clayton watching me, a bemused smile on his face. "Looks like you've found your fan club," he teased, his voice tinged with admiration. "The cookies must be legendary."

"Only because of my secret ingredient," I replied, winking at Zoe, who was already bouncing on her toes in anticipation. "You know what they say: sugar and spice make everything nice."

"Is that really all it is? I always thought it was just a lot of love," Clayton interjected, stepping closer, drawn into the cheerful chaos. "And maybe some of that homegrown charm."

Zoe, oblivious to the adult conversation, chimed in, "You should come and help us, Mr. Clayton! We need a strong helper to mix the batter!"

Clayton raised an eyebrow, clearly amused. "Oh, I don't know if I'm qualified for that task. I might just end up eating all the dough."

"Then it's settled! You'll help us make cookies, and then we can eat them!" Zoe declared with the authority of a miniature dictator.

Laughter bubbled up between us, and suddenly, the weight of the earlier conversation felt lighter. It was impossible to resist her infectious enthusiasm, especially when it seemed to bridge the gap between the past and the present. "Alright, I'm in," he relented, feigning reluctance as he knelt to Zoe's level. "But I warn you, I'm an expert at sneaking extra chocolate chips into everything."

"Perfect!" she squealed, grabbing his hand and pulling him toward the kitchen. "Let's go!"

As I followed, a smile still tugging at my lips, I caught a glimpse of Clayton's glance over his shoulder, a playful glint in his eyes. There was a spark there, one that hinted at possibilities I hadn't dared to explore. In this vibrant chaos, perhaps there was room for something more—something unexpected, just waiting to unfold.

The kitchen was a lively mess, a world of flour clouds and sugar sprinkles. Zoe had gathered her little friends, and soon, the space was filled with giggles and squeals as they set to work, their tiny hands eager to dive into the mixing bowl. I found myself swept into their enthusiasm, rolling up my sleeves and guiding them through the motions of cookie-making.

"More flour, Aunt Carmen! More flour!" Zoe commanded, her serious little face a delightful contrast to the mischief dancing in her eyes.

"Is that really necessary?" I shot back playfully, my own laughter bubbling to the surface. "I thought we were making cookies, not a snowstorm!"

Clayton watched us with an amused expression, a hint of nostalgia in his gaze as he began to help the kids shape the cookie dough. "I think the more flour, the better. Nothing says 'fun' like a little chaos in the kitchen."

With every whisk of the bowl, every sprinkle of flour, the memories came flooding back—long nights spent cooking with my grandmother, laughter echoing off the walls of this very kitchen, the scent of warm cookies wrapping us in comfort. In this moment, surrounded by laughter and love, the burdens of adulthood began to slip away.

The joy was palpable, and as I glanced at Clayton, I felt a shift—a tentative bridge forming between the past and the present. There was something about this chaotic beauty that whispered promises of a brighter tomorrow. Perhaps I could stay here longer than I thought, wrapped in the embrace of laughter and warmth, crafting new memories to cherish.

Just then, as I reached for a handful of chocolate chips, the door creaked open, revealing my grandmother's silhouette. She stepped into the kitchen, her eyes sparkling with delight. "Well, I see the cookie crew is hard at work!" she declared, a knowing smile playing on her lips. "Just don't forget to save me some!"

The energy in the room shifted, a welcome warmth radiating from her presence. I caught a glimpse of Clayton's smile, his easy charm igniting a flicker of hope deep within me. Maybe this reunion was more than just a chance encounter. Maybe it was the beginning of something beautifully unpredictable, a reminder that life could be both messy and magical, just like the cookies we were about to bake.

As my grandmother joined the fray in the kitchen, her presence turned the playful chaos into something even warmer, like the first rays of dawn breaking through the night. She rolled up her sleeves, her hands already dusted with flour as she began directing the children, her voice a soothing melody among the din of laughter. "Now, now, let's not forget the secret to the perfect cookie: a little bit of patience and a whole lot of love," she said, her eyes twinkling with wisdom and joy.

Clayton leaned over the counter, feigning seriousness as he pretended to weigh out ingredients on an imaginary scale. "And a dash of mischief, right?" he quipped, shooting me a playful wink. "I think that's what we're missing. Who needs measuring cups when you can just eyeball it?"

Zoe, totally captivated by his antics, giggled, bouncing on her toes. "You're funny, Mr. Clayton! I want to measure like that!"

Before I could respond, a loud crash echoed from the other side of the kitchen. My grandmother turned, her eyes wide, as a bowl tipped precariously from the edge of the counter, sending flour and sugar cascading to the floor like a culinary explosion. "Oh dear! Not my flour!" she exclaimed, her voice a mix of shock and amusement.

Amid the laughter and the chaos, Clayton jumped to action, grabbing a handful of paper towels and rushing to help. "See? This is what happens when you bring a bunch of cookie amateurs into the kitchen!" he joked, wiping up the mess with exaggerated determination.

I couldn't help but chuckle, the sound bubbling up effortlessly. It felt so refreshing to laugh like this, to lose myself in the moment. "At this rate, we'll need to rename our cookies 'Whispering Hills' Disaster Cookies,'" I joked, tossing a playful look at Clayton, who was still on the floor, surrounded by the remnants of our baking catastrophe.

"Or maybe 'Flour Power' cookies," he shot back, the gleam in his eyes making my heart flutter in ways I wasn't quite prepared for.

As we cleaned up the mess together, the conversation flowed easily, a blend of witty banter and gentle teasing that felt both familiar and new. The world outside faded, the sun sinking lower in the sky, casting a warm, golden light that filtered through the kitchen window. The air was filled with the scent of sugar and spice, mixed with the undeniable spark of a connection rekindling after years apart.

Zoe and her friends, engrossed in their baking duties, had become our little audience. "What's it like in Boston, Aunt Carmen?" Zoe asked, her curiosity shining bright. "Do you miss it?"

"I do, but it's a different kind of life there," I said, reflecting for a moment on the city's relentless pace. "It's like being in a race, always trying to keep up. But here," I gestured around the cozy kitchen, "it feels like time takes a break. Like we can actually breathe."

Clayton nodded, his expression thoughtful. "I get that. Sometimes, it's hard to remember what we really want when everything is moving so fast." He paused, looking at me with a sincerity that made my breath hitch. "And sometimes, you just need to come home."

Home. The word hung in the air, heavy with possibility. I glanced at my grandmother, who was expertly rolling out the dough, and then back at Clayton, a flicker of understanding passing between us. Home was more than just a place; it was a feeling, a refuge.

As the children finished shaping the cookies and the smell of baking began to fill the air, I felt an unexpected thrill run through me. This was what I had been missing—this sense of belonging, the warmth of connection.

Clayton moved closer, leaning against the counter, and I could feel the electricity in the space between us. "You know, Carmen, you have a gift for bringing joy wherever you go," he said, his voice low, sincere. "It's like you carry sunshine in your pocket."

"Maybe it's the cookies," I replied, unable to suppress the grin that spread across my face. "Or maybe it's the company."

Before he could respond, the oven timer beeped, slicing through the tension with a jarring beep. Zoe squealed in delight, racing to open the oven door, her face alight with anticipation.

"Cookies are ready!" she cried, and the room erupted in cheers, the earlier mishaps forgotten in the face of freshly baked treats. As the golden cookies tumbled onto the cooling rack, I couldn't help but feel a surge of warmth swell in my chest.

"Who's ready to taste?" I called, the question met with an enthusiastic chorus of "Me!" from the kids. Clayton stepped back, letting the children gather around, their tiny hands reaching for the warm, gooey delights.

"Just remember," I warned playfully, "they might be hot! You wouldn't want to burn your tongues before you can tell how delicious they are!"

Clayton leaned against the counter, watching the children with a smile that seemed to reflect the joy I felt in that moment. "You're a natural at this," he remarked, his voice soft yet teasing. "Maybe you missed your calling in Boston. You could've been a world-famous cookie maker instead of whatever you were doing."

"I don't know," I laughed, allowing the moment to wash over me. "I think I prefer my role as a humble cookie guru, training the next generation of baking enthusiasts."

As laughter filled the kitchen, I caught Clayton's gaze again, a momentary understanding flaring between us. Just as the atmosphere shifted, becoming cozy and full of promise, the phone rang, its shrill tone cutting through our laughter like a knife.

"Who could that be?" I wondered aloud, glancing at the kitchen's wall clock, noting the hour.

Zoe, still clutching a cookie, bounced over to grab the phone from the wall. "I'll get it!" she chirped, her excitement palpable as she dashed off to answer the call.

I watched her scamper away, but a strange tension gripped me. A nagging feeling settled in my gut, an instinct that warned something wasn't right. Clayton must have felt it too; his brow furrowed slightly as he exchanged glances with me.

"What's wrong?" I asked, my voice lowering as I noticed the shift in his demeanor.

"I don't know. Just a feeling." He straightened, a frown forming on his lips. "We should be careful. Sometimes, calls come with news we aren't ready for."

Before I could respond, Zoe returned, her face pale, the phone still cradled in her tiny hands. "Aunt Carmen, it's for you."

My heart raced as I stepped forward, the warmth of the kitchen suddenly feeling cold against my skin. "For me? Who is it?"

Zoe hesitated, her eyes wide with worry. "It's... it's someone from Boston."

The air thickened with unspoken fears, and I could feel the weight of the moment pressing down on me. I took the phone from her, my pulse quickening as I raised it to my ear. "Hello?"

The voice on the other end was clipped, formal. "Ms. Kleszcz? This is Eric from your old firm. We need to discuss a matter that requires your immediate attention."

The joy of baking, the laughter of children, and the warmth of reconnection faded away, replaced by the stark reality of my past crashing into my present. "What is it?" I asked, my voice steadier than I felt.

"It's about your position... and an urgent situation that has arisen."

My heart dropped, an icy tendril of dread snaking through me. I glanced at Clayton, his expression mirroring my own apprehension.

The familiarity of the kitchen, the laughter, the cookies—everything I had found solace in seemed to slip through my fingers like grains of sand.

"Carmen?" Eric's voice broke through my thoughts. "Are you still there?"

I took a deep breath, the world around me growing smaller, the stakes suddenly much higher. "I'm here," I managed, my voice trembling slightly. "What's going on?"

"Something has come to light that changes everything," he said, the gravity of his words settling like a storm cloud overhead. "We need you back in Boston."

I glanced at Clayton, who was now standing directly across from me, his expression a mix of concern and confusion. The warmth of the kitchen felt distant, replaced by the chill of uncertainty. "What do you mean, changes everything?" I asked, my voice barely above a whisper.

"Just... please, come as soon as you can. We can't discuss this over the phone."

Before I could respond, he hung up, leaving me holding the phone, the gravity of his words echoing in the silence. The kitchen, once a sanctuary, now felt like a battleground where decisions had to be made. As I looked at Clayton, his brow furrowed, I could sense the impending storm, and I knew this was just the beginning.

Chapter 2: Collision of Worlds

He walked up the steps like he owned them, every inch the confident, easy-going rancher. "Lana," he said, his voice low and familiar. My name had never sounded quite like that on anyone else's lips. "You're back."

The moment lingered, suspended in the air, as though the universe had decided to hold its breath. I stood frozen in the doorway, a swirl of emotions turning in my gut like a storm brewing over the plains. The wooden floor beneath my feet felt like it might buckle under the weight of my uncertainty. I didn't know what to say. How could I explain that I wasn't just back for a visit but running away from everything that had fallen apart in Boston?

The truth hung between us, unspoken, like a delicate thread waiting to snap. His dark hair caught the afternoon sunlight, making it gleam, and I couldn't help but remember the way he used to run his fingers through it when he was deep in thought. There was something raw and unyielding in his gaze, a clarity that sliced through the haze of my muddled thoughts. I had spent years believing I could hide my fears behind well-placed smiles and rehearsed lines, yet here he was, standing before me, his presence a mirror reflecting all my vulnerabilities.

But the way his eyes searched mine told me that he could see right through me, just as he always had. I felt exposed, naked in the warmth of his scrutiny, and I wondered if my carefully constructed walls were as transparent to him as they felt to me. Yet, he hadn't reached out before now. Why?

"Thought you'd gone for good," he said, stepping closer. The space between us crackled with a tension that both excited and terrified me. "You used to say you needed the city. New York was calling your name. Boston was just a pit stop, right?"

His smile was a charming lopsided thing, one I used to chase in my memory when the city felt too gray, too heavy. But now, in the stillness of this familiar porch, it felt like a flash of summer amid a winter storm.

"Plans change," I managed to say, my voice barely above a whisper.

"Is that so?" he replied, raising an eyebrow, the hint of a smirk dancing on his lips. "Seems like a whole lot of running away if you ask me."

I huffed a laugh that was half-choked. "What if I'm just... rediscovering my roots?" I tried to sound light, but the weight of my past loomed behind me, whispering of failures and lost opportunities.

He leaned against the railing, arms crossed, effortlessly at ease despite the storm brewing inside me. "You've always been good at that, haven't you? Disappearing to find yourself."

A muscle in my jaw tightened at his words. Did he think I was weak? That I couldn't face my choices? I straightened my shoulders, catching a glimpse of the wildflowers blooming in the garden—each one a burst of color defying the harshness of the world around it. "I came back because... because I needed a break, okay? The city wasn't what I thought it would be."

"Or maybe it's what you thought it would be, and it scared you," he challenged, his tone teasing yet sharp enough to slice through the layers I had wrapped around my heart.

I shook my head, the movement dismissive but also desperate, as if I could physically shake away the memories that clung to me like cobwebs. "It wasn't fear. It was just... exhausting. All the noise, the expectations, the constant hustle." I gestured toward the fields stretching behind him, the vastness of sky and earth unfolding like a story waiting to be told. "This is peaceful. I missed this."

For a moment, he held my gaze, the air between us thick with unsaid words. The ranch was a patchwork of golden fields and sprawling barns, a world that felt like a cocoon—a safe haven from the chaos that had engulfed me. The sun dipped low, casting long shadows across the porch, and I felt the day inching toward twilight, as if urging me to decide who I was going to be in this new chapter.

"I can't be the only reason you're back," he finally said, his voice dropping to a conspiratorial whisper. "I mean, let's be real. No one runs away to the sticks unless there's a story behind it."

His words hung in the air like a challenge. Did he really want to know the truth? To dig into the wreckage I had left behind? The thought of exposing my vulnerabilities sent a fresh wave of anxiety through me. But here was this man—this rancher, my childhood friend—offering a lifeline in a world that had felt unbearably lonely.

"Fine," I said, my bravado rising. "You want a story? I'll give you one."

"Good," he replied, leaning closer, eyes bright with curiosity. "I'm all ears."

The porch creaked under the weight of unshed truths, and I took a breath, pulling in the sweet scent of freshly cut grass mingled with the faint, comforting aroma of hay. Each inhale felt like a step toward unearthing my reality, a step away from the stifling confines of the city that had once held my dreams captive.

I glanced at him, searching for a flicker of judgment in his gaze, but instead, I found only encouragement. "I lost my job," I said, the words tumbling out before I could catch them. "They said I was too ambitious for a company that didn't want to grow. They wanted me to fit into a mold, and I didn't. I thought ambition was something to be proud of."

He nodded slowly, a knowing expression crossing his face. "It's tough to be the square peg in a round hole."

"Yeah, and then... my apartment flooded, and my landlord raised the rent," I continued, my voice gaining momentum as the tale unfolded. "It felt like a sign. So, I packed up and came here, thinking I could clear my head."

"Sounds more like a series of unfortunate events," he said, his lips curling into that signature grin that made my heart race. "But honestly, who needs a fancy apartment when you can have a view like this?" He swept his arm toward the sprawling landscape, the horizon painted in hues of orange and lavender.

In that moment, I felt a flicker of hope igniting in my chest. Maybe coming back was the best decision I had made. Or maybe it was just a pause before I figured out my next move. Whatever it was, the collision of worlds—the city I was running from and this quiet ranch life—was a spark igniting a new journey.

He leaned against the railing, the late afternoon sun casting a warm glow that softened the edges of his rugged features. "You know," he said, glancing toward the horizon, "the land has a way of healing you. It's like it knows what you need, even when you don't."

I studied him, marveling at the ease with which he navigated life in this place. To him, the open fields, the rolling hills, and the whispering winds were all old friends. But to me, they felt foreign, almost intimidating in their vastness. "I don't know if I'm broken enough to be healed," I replied, my voice catching slightly.

"Then maybe you're just a little dented," he quipped, a teasing lilt to his words. "I mean, everyone gets dented now and then, right? Even cars get a scratch or two and keep on going."

I couldn't help but chuckle, despite the heaviness in my chest. "So you're saying I'm like a vintage car? That's charming."

"Vintage? Definitely. But I'm more inclined to think of you as a classic—one of those cars everyone wants but only a few can handle." His gaze was unwavering, a playful challenge swirling in his deep brown eyes.

A sudden flush of warmth crept up my neck. "What if I'm more of a lemon?" I countered, folding my arms defensively.

"Lana, you're no lemon. Maybe just a little rusty around the edges," he shot back, that lopsided smile resurfacing. "But I've got a can of oil, and I'm more than happy to lend it to you."

His banter was a welcome distraction, wrapping me in a comforting blanket of familiarity. I took a breath, letting the tension ease just a fraction. "I appreciate the offer, but I'm not sure how much grease I can take."

"Enough to keep the gears turning," he said, his voice lowering, almost conspiratorial. "So, tell me, what are you really hoping to find out here?"

I hesitated, the question lingering in the air like an unwelcome gust of wind. "I don't know," I admitted finally. "Maybe some clarity? Or just a moment to breathe without the weight of expectations."

"You mean those highfalutin city folks? The ones with their fancy coffee orders and suits?" He leaned in closer, eyes sparkling with mischief. "What's wrong with just a good ol' cup of coffee made in a pot on the stove?"

"That sounds suspiciously like something my grandmother would say," I replied, laughing softly. "And just as comforting."

"Exactly! See, you're already on the right track. Let's start with some simple things. You need to reclaim your roots. I can show you the best spots around here—the hidden gems, the places that make you feel alive."

His enthusiasm was infectious, like sunlight streaming through dark clouds. "You mean there are places out here that don't involve staring at cows?"

"Hey now, don't knock the cows. They're great listeners," he shot back, feigning offense. "But yes, I promise there are waterfalls, hiking trails, and a diner that makes the best pie this side of the Mississippi."

"Pie?" I raised an eyebrow, my curiosity piqued. "Now you're speaking my language."

"Then it's settled. You and I are going to embark on a culinary adventure—an exploration of the local cuisine, starting with pie." He paused, his expression turning serious. "But you have to promise me something."

"What's that?"

"No running away again. You have to actually stick around long enough to enjoy the pie."

I swallowed hard, the weight of his words settling over me. The thought of staying felt daunting, like taking a leap off a cliff without knowing if the water below was deep enough to catch me. "I can't promise anything," I said, my voice wavering. "Not yet."

He nodded slowly, the challenge in his eyes replaced with something softer, more understanding. "Fair enough. Just know that this place—this life—is waiting for you whenever you're ready."

As if on cue, a faint whinny echoed from the barn, drawing our attention. I turned to see a chestnut horse sticking its head over the wooden fence, its big, curious eyes sparkling with mischief. "And I promise you, that horse is ready for a friend," he said, chuckling. "Can't say the same for my dad, though. He's been a little grumpy ever since you left."

"Grumpy?" I laughed, picturing his father, a stocky man with hands as big as shovels and a heart to match. "I can't imagine that. He always had a way of making me feel like family."

"Yeah, well, family means a lot to him, and he was pretty disappointed when you didn't come back after college. I think he was holding out for a grandchild to spoil."

The thought was absurd yet oddly sweet, igniting a long-dormant warmth in my chest. "No pressure, right?"

"Not at all," he said, his tone lightening again. "Just some friendly expectations. Anyway, are you ready to meet the horses?"

"Ready as I'll ever be," I replied, forcing myself to step into the unknown. I followed him toward the barn, my heart thumping like a drum echoing through a canyon.

As we walked, I let the charm of the ranch wash over me, the sweet smell of hay mingling with the earthy scent of leather and wood. The barn loomed ahead, its weathered red paint flaking in places, revealing the sturdy gray boards beneath. The gentle whinny of the horse mingled with the soft clinking of metal and the rustle of hay, creating a symphony of rural life that felt both foreign and achingly familiar.

"Meet Ginger," he said, gesturing toward the horse that had been calling to us. She was a lively creature, her coat gleaming like polished copper in the fading sunlight.

"Ginger?" I echoed, kneeling to scratch her nose, the warmth of her breath brushing against my palm. "I can see why you'd name her that. She's a real firecracker."

"Just like you," he quipped, leaning casually against the barn door, arms crossed, watching me with a hint of admiration. "You've always had a spark."

I blushed at his words, feeling something inside me flutter—a mix of nostalgia and possibility. "Flattery will get you everywhere, you know."

"Good to know," he replied, a playful glint in his eye. "Because I have a feeling you're going to need a lot more of it if you're going to stick around and embrace the simple life."

"Guess we'll see about that," I replied, my heart racing at the prospect of diving back into this world, this life I had once known so well. But just as I began to feel the pull of hope, a sudden uncertainty swelled inside me. What if I couldn't find my place here again? What if this was just a temporary escape, and the chaos of my old life followed me like a shadow?

Before I could dwell too much on the darkness, he stepped closer, the sunlight illuminating the edges of his face. "And if you ever feel overwhelmed, you can just shout. I'm pretty good at calming things down—especially with pie."

"Pie, huh? You really have a one-track mind."

"I mean, it's a solid strategy." He smirked, and for a moment, the worries that had haunted me felt like a distant memory. In his presence, I could almost believe that maybe, just maybe, I could reclaim my roots and find a way to heal. The dance of uncertainty lingered, but so did the vibrant possibility of what could be.

He leaned against the railing, a lazy smile playing at the corners of his mouth as he took in the landscape behind me. The golden fields rolled away in a patchwork quilt of amber and green, punctuated by the vibrant blue sky, and the horizon stretched infinitely, a reminder of the vastness that had once felt both exhilarating and terrifying. "You know, if I didn't know better, I'd think you were here to escape the city," he teased, his eyes sparkling with mischief.

I forced a laugh, the sound brittle and too bright in the tranquil setting. "What, me? Running from the thrill of urban life? Hardly." But the truth was, the city had become a cacophony of shattered dreams and relentless pressures. Each day in Boston had felt like a fog, heavy and unyielding, pressing down on my chest until the air turned thick and suffocating. The ranch, with its simple beauty and rugged charm, offered a stark contrast that tugged at my heart. I felt like a wayward child, drawn back to a childhood sanctuary, where the troubles of the world seemed to dissolve like morning mist under the rising sun.

He stepped closer, the warmth of his presence wrapping around me like a familiar blanket. "Then what brings you back? You know we don't bite," he said with a playful lilt, his hands resting casually on his hips, showcasing the strength in his arms. "Not much, anyway."

A shiver ran through me, a mix of nostalgia and something more potent. How could he so easily lighten the weight on my shoulders? I looked away, feigning interest in the fluttering birds circling above, my mind racing. There was so much I wanted to say, so many pieces of my life that needed to be explained, but the words tangled up inside me, stubborn and unwilling to spill out. Instead, I settled for a simple shrug. "Just needed a break, I suppose."

His brow furrowed slightly, and I could see him searching my face, the easy charm momentarily fading. "A break? From what, exactly? You were always the one who thrived on chaos."

"Sometimes chaos gets... too chaotic," I replied, my voice barely above a whisper. It felt like a confession, and I could sense the shift in the air as the weight of my unspoken truths settled between us.

"Lana, if something's bothering you—"

"I'm fine," I interrupted, the words coming out sharper than intended. "Really."

He nodded slowly, skepticism evident in his gaze, but chose not to press further. Instead, he changed the subject, a subtle skill he had perfected over the years. "Well, if you're here for a while, you should join us for the county fair next weekend. It'll be fun. You could use some fun."

I chuckled, the idea both appealing and terrifying. The county fair was a delightful cacophony of laughter, fried food, and the occasional mishap involving an overzealous goat. But it was also a place where memories lingered—fragments of summers spent darting through the crowd, hand-in-hand with him, lost in the magic of youth. The thought of navigating those familiar sights and sounds, especially with him by my side, sent a thrill racing through me. "Oh, the fair. Right. Because nothing says 'fun' like carnival rides that may or may not have been inspected this century."

He grinned, his eyes lighting up with enthusiasm. "Exactly! And who knows, maybe you'll even conquer that fear of the Ferris wheel. I still can't believe you let me talk you into riding it last time."

"I thought I was going to die!" I exclaimed, laughing despite myself. The memory rushed back, vivid and warm—a time when the world had felt so uncomplicated, and our laughter echoed against the backdrop of carefree summer nights. "I nearly kicked you off, remember?"

"Wouldn't have been the first time I've been kicked off a ride," he replied, his smirk deepening as he leaned closer. "I'd rather take that than be left behind while you spin around in circles without me."

The spark in his eyes was infectious, igniting a familiar flutter in my chest. For a moment, it felt like the years of separation dissolved, and we were just two kids again, caught in the thrill of endless possibilities. "Maybe I'll think about it," I replied, feigning nonchalance as my heart raced.

"Just think about it?" he asked, feigning disbelief. "Come on, Lana. You can't deny you want to go. It's practically a rite of passage for anyone who grows up around here."

I shifted my weight, trying to mask my eagerness. "Alright, fine. If I can fit it into my busy schedule of... nothingness, I'll consider it."

"Great! I'll hold you to that. Just don't bail on me at the last minute."

The light banter hung in the air like a promise, but just as the moment swelled with warmth, a loud commotion erupted from the direction of the barn. We turned instinctively, the joyous atmosphere suddenly punctuated by shouts and laughter that sounded far from friendly.

"What on earth—?" I began, but before I could finish, a figure burst through the doors, a disheveled man with a wild look in his eyes, hair askew and shirt half-tucked. He skidded to a halt before us, panting, as if he had sprinted a marathon.

"Tyler! You need to come quick! There's a—" he gasped, struggling to catch his breath.

Tyler's expression hardened, the carefree demeanor evaporating in an instant. "What happened?"

"There's a bull loose in the corral! It broke through the fence! We need everyone to help get it back before it gets into town!"

The tension snapped back into focus as the weight of the situation settled over us like a heavy fog. The playful moments we had just shared felt worlds away as urgency took hold.

"Let's go," Tyler said, his voice low and commanding, as he turned on his heel, determination etched into every line of his face.

I felt a swell of panic rise in my chest, but I forced my legs to move, following him as he dashed toward the barn, a rush of adrenaline coursing through my veins. Would the day end with us wrangling a rogue bull? Or would it spiral into something I couldn't predict? I glanced over my shoulder at the picturesque ranch, my heart pounding as the familiar sense of chaos enveloped us once more.

"Hold on tight," I murmured to myself, bracing for whatever awaited on the other side of the barn doors.

Chapter 3: Threads of the Past

The aroma of rosemary and garlic filled the air, swirling around us like a comforting embrace as I watched my grandmother set the table. The antique oak dining table gleamed under the soft glow of the pendant lights, each piece of cutlery polished to a mirror finish that reflected the warmth of our cozy kitchen. Grandma hummed an old tune as she worked, the sound mixing with the gentle clinking of plates, creating a familiar symphony that tugged at the corners of my heart.

Clayton leaned against the doorframe, hands tucked into the pockets of his jeans, a casual yet striking presence in the warm light. I tried to suppress the rush of nostalgia that washed over me, but it seeped through like the scent of fresh-baked bread from the oven. He looked as if he had stepped straight out of my childhood memories—still tall and broad-shouldered, with that familiar tousle of dark hair that framed his face just so. The only difference was the deep lines that etched his forehead, hints of a maturity that life had carved into him. The boyish charm remained, but there was something else now, something heavier, lurking beneath the surface of his easy smile.

Dinner unfolded with the same rhythmic cadence it always had when Clayton was around. Grandma chatted animatedly, her laughter bubbling over as she recounted stories of her garden, her voice a soothing balm that eased the tension swirling between us. I joined in, sharing bits about my life in the city, sprinkling in humor like confetti, but my eyes kept darting to Clayton. He was a study in contrasts, responding with laughter and nods, yet his gaze would sometimes drift to the window, as if he were looking for something far beyond the horizon.

After the last of Grandma's famous apple pie had been served, I found myself lost in thought, my fork tracing patterns on the tablecloth. There was a moment of silence that felt heavy and charged, a pause where the air was thick with things left unsaid. I caught Clayton's eye and felt a jolt of recognition. He was still the boy I had known, the one who had encouraged me to ride bareback, the one who had whispered wild plans for our future under a blanket of stars. And yet, here we were, strangers wrapped in the familiarity of the past.

As the evening wore on, the conversation began to wane. The clatter of dishes and the soft rustle of napkins filled the silence, punctuated by the occasional chirp of crickets outside. It was then that I noticed the way his jaw tightened, the fleeting shadows that passed over his features. There was a story there, buried beneath layers of unspoken words, and I felt an irresistible urge to dig deeper.

"Clayton," I ventured, my voice tentative, "you never told me why you came back." The question hung in the air, heavy with implications. Grandma had excused herself to clear the table, leaving us alone, the silence expanding like an unwelcome guest.

His gaze flickered to the floor, and for a moment, I thought I saw a flicker of vulnerability. "I had some things to sort out," he replied slowly, his voice low and measured. "You know how it is—life gets complicated." There was a sharpness in his tone, a hint of defensiveness that made me wonder just how complicated things had become for him.

I nodded, wishing I could reach across the table and pull him closer, back to the easy camaraderie we once shared. "I get that. But you don't have to do it alone, you know."

He looked up, surprise etched in his features, and for a fleeting second, the walls he had built seemed to waver. "It's not that simple, Jenna," he said, his voice thick with unshed emotions. "Some things you just can't share."

My heart raced at his admission. The intrigue was undeniable. I had spent countless nights imagining the path our lives might have taken had we remained close. Would we have taken those reckless chances together? Would he have been the one I turned to when life got too heavy? The questions whirled in my mind like leaves caught in a windstorm, each one brushing against the walls of my heart.

The moment lingered, stretching between us like a taut string ready to snap. I wanted to pull him back into my orbit, to remind him of the carefree days when laughter came easily and dreams were woven together like threads in a tapestry. But just as quickly as the connection sparked, it flickered out, leaving us standing in the dim light of the kitchen, shadows gathering around us.

Clayton shifted, breaking the silence, and I caught the briefest glimpse of regret in his eyes. "I should go," he said, his voice resolute, yet it felt like a retreat, a withdrawal into the unknown.

The door creaked open, and the evening chill rushed in, a sudden reminder of the world outside our bubble. I swallowed hard, fighting against the sense of loss that settled heavily on my chest. "Are you coming back?" I asked, my voice barely above a whisper, vulnerability cracking through the façade I tried to maintain.

He hesitated, his silhouette framed against the fading light, and for a heartbeat, I dared to hope. "I don't know, Jenna," he replied, and in that uncertainty, I felt the weight of a thousand unspoken possibilities.

With a final nod, he stepped outside, leaving me standing in the doorway, heart pounding against the confines of my chest. The soft sound of his footsteps receded into the night, and I felt the world shift around me, the air thick with unfulfilled potential. I returned to the kitchen, the warmth of the evening still clinging to my skin, but the absence of his presence echoed loudly in the silence that enveloped me.

I glanced around, taking in the remnants of our dinner—the half-eaten pie, the lingering scent of rosemary, the quiet hum of my grandmother's movements as she worked in the other room. This was home, a place steeped in memories and warmth, yet the space felt suddenly vast and hollow without him. A knot twisted in my stomach as I contemplated the threads of our past, weaving them with the uncertainties of our present.

The next morning dawned crisp and bright, the kind of day that promised possibilities wrapped in golden sunlight. I slipped out of bed, my mind still buzzing with fragments of yesterday—Clayton's lingering gaze, the way his smile had flickered, a candle threatened by a gust of wind. The air in my grandmother's home held a comforting warmth, a blend of fresh linen and the faint trace of woodsmoke from the fireplace, but today it felt charged, alive with the tension of our last encounter.

I padded down the hallway, drawn by the promise of breakfast. Grandma had already claimed her usual spot at the kitchen table, her hair a halo of silver curls that danced around her face as she moved. She was deep in concentration, stirring a pot of something savory on the stove, the aroma of sautéed onions wafting through the air like a siren's call. "Good morning, sweetheart! Just in time for my famous vegetable frittata," she beamed, as if the world had not changed overnight.

I took a seat and watched her, captivated by her effortless ability to turn the mundane into magic. Each ingredient she tossed in felt deliberate, measured with love. "You know, Grandma, if the whole gardening thing doesn't work out, you could always open a restaurant," I joked, trying to infuse some levity into my own swirling thoughts.

"Oh, please, my dear," she laughed, her eyes twinkling. "The only customers I'd get are the neighbors, and even they would probably get tired of my cooking after a week." She poured a generous helping of frittata onto my plate, and I dug in, savoring the blend of flavors and the warmth that spread through me like sunshine.

As we ate, the conversation flowed easily, weaving between light-hearted topics and Grandma's latest gardening triumphs. But my mind drifted, caught in a loop of unspoken words. It wasn't until she leaned across the table, her eyes sharp and perceptive, that I realized she had sensed the undercurrents swirling beneath my facade.

"What's on your mind, Jenna?" she asked gently, her voice a soothing balm. "You're not eating enough for someone who just came home."

I hesitated, my fork hovering above the plate. "It's just... Clayton." The name hung in the air, and I felt a weight shift in the room.

Her expression softened. "Ah, Clayton. I always thought you two had something special."

I couldn't help but laugh, a slightly hollow sound. "Special? More like a collection of missed connections and unspoken feelings."

"Missed connections can be quite the blessing in disguise," she replied, a knowing smile playing at the corners of her lips. "Sometimes, it's what lies beneath the surface that truly matters. Have you talked to him since he left last night?"

I shook my head, frustration bubbling beneath my calm exterior. "He didn't ask to see me again, Grandma. He didn't even say when he'd be back. It's like he's trying to keep me at arm's length, and I don't know why."

"Perhaps he's sorting out his own threads, as you say," she suggested, her tone filled with gentle wisdom. "You know, sometimes the past doesn't let go as easily as we'd like. It can cling to us like a shadow."

The image of Clayton's shadowed expression lingered in my mind. What was he hiding? What ghosts danced behind those hazel eyes that had once held such warmth? I pushed the thought away, refusing to let it take root. "I suppose," I replied, my voice trailing off.

The day unfolded like a long-forgotten book, and I found myself outside, wandering through Grandma's garden. It was a riot of color, the flowers vying for attention in a delightful chaos. Bees buzzed lazily, flitting from blossom to blossom, while butterflies danced overhead in a careless ballet. I knelt to inspect a cluster of daisies, their cheerful faces nodding in the gentle breeze, when I heard a familiar voice echoing from the driveway.

"Hey, Jenna!"

I looked up to see Clayton leaning against his truck, a hint of hesitation in his posture. My heart skipped, a rebellious beat that reminded me of the summer days spent stealing kisses behind the barn. He looked good, rugged and real, the kind of handsome that felt both familiar and foreign.

"Hey!" I replied, trying to sound casual, but the word tumbled out like a startled bird.

He pushed himself away from the truck, the sun casting shadows across his face. "I thought I'd swing by. You know, see how you're settling in."

"Very well, thanks," I said, standing up and brushing the dirt from my knees, suddenly aware of how messy the garden could make me look. "What about you? Are you working on anything interesting?"

"Same old, same old. Just trying to get my bearings." He shifted from foot to foot, his eyes flitting around the garden as if searching for something hidden among the petals.

There was a moment of silence, heavy with the weight of our unaddressed feelings. "I, um, wanted to apologize for last night," he finally said, his voice low and earnest. "I didn't mean to just... leave like that."

"Apology accepted," I replied, though the words felt inadequate, like trying to fill a gaping hole with sand. "But it's okay. We both have a lot to unpack, I guess."

He chuckled softly, the sound warm yet tinged with uncertainty. "Yeah, it seems like we've got a lot of baggage to sort through."

Just then, a sudden gust of wind swept through the garden, sending petals scattering like confetti. It felt like the universe was conspiring to push us closer together, yet we stood apart, surrounded by a flurry of blossoms. "Maybe we should talk about it," I ventured, my heart racing.

"Are you sure?" he asked, his expression shifting, a mixture of hope and apprehension. "I don't want to make things more complicated for you."

"Complicated seems to be our default setting," I replied, my voice laced with wry humor, hoping to ease the tension. "What's the worst that could happen? We dig up the past and see what grows?"

A smile crept onto his lips, a hint of relief breaking through the cloud of uncertainty. "Okay, let's do it. But fair warning: I might have to bring out my old horse-riding stories. Those could get embarrassing."

"Bring it on," I teased, feeling a flicker of excitement in the air, the weight of unsaid words now tantalizingly close to being spoken.

With that, we began to walk, the path lined with colorful blooms, our footsteps echoing softly in the quiet of the garden. The tension slowly began to unravel, replaced by the promise of revelations and laughter, as we ventured deeper into the tangled threads of our shared past.

We walked in a comfortable silence, the world around us alive with the gentle hum of nature. The garden unfolded like a canvas of colors, each flower vying for attention, reminding me of the chaotic beauty of our past. I stole glances at Clayton, who walked beside me, his hands shoved into his pockets, shoulders slightly hunched as if bracing for a storm. I felt a strange mixture of nostalgia and apprehension; the old familiarity of him tugged at my heart, but the distance between us felt like an uncharted gulf.

"So," I started, trying to break the tension with my signature charm. "Tell me the story of how you fell off that horse when you thought you could jump a fence. I need a good laugh."

His head jerked up, surprise flickering across his features before morphing into a reluctant smile. "Oh, you remember that, do you? I thought I was invincible. I was riding Thunder, and, well, I learned the hard way that pride comes before a fall."

I laughed, the sound echoing softly among the flowers. "You were so dramatic! I remember you laying there, acting like you'd lost a limb while the horse stood patiently, munching on grass like it was all part of the plan."

"Yeah, well, I was young and full of bravado. Didn't realize that 'fence-jumping' wasn't a skill I possessed." He chuckled, shaking his head, and I felt the warmth of our shared laughter fill the air, soothing the remnants of tension.

"But that's the thing about you, Clayton," I pressed, pushing my luck a bit. "You always took risks, and I admired that. I always wanted to be brave like you."

His smile faltered, a shadow crossing his face. "I don't know if brave is the right word for it. Sometimes, it was just blind stupidity."

"Blind stupidity has its perks," I shot back playfully. "Like not overthinking every little decision until it paralyzes you."

He stopped walking, turning to face me fully, the sun casting a golden glow around us. "Jenna, you're right. But some things—some choices—they have lasting consequences. Maybe that's why I haven't been around. I'm not sure I'm ready to face those yet."

The weight of his words hung in the air, wrapping around us like a fog. I could feel my heart thump in my chest, caught in the crossfire of curiosity and caution. "You don't have to face them alone, you know. I'm here." The sincerity in my voice startled even me, but it felt true, a simple truth among all the complexities swirling around us.

He shifted his gaze, looking past me as if searching for something in the distance. "Maybe that's part of the problem. I've been alone for so long, it's hard to know how to let anyone back in."

"Is that really what you want?" I pressed gently. "To keep everyone at arm's length?"

Clayton looked at me, his eyes a storm of emotions—fear, longing, uncertainty. "No. But I've made mistakes, Jenna. Huge mistakes."

"Everyone makes mistakes. It's what you do after that counts," I said, my voice steady, though my heart raced. I felt as if we were standing at the edge of a cliff, ready to leap into the unknown.

He stepped closer, the air thick with unspoken words. "There's something I need to tell you, something I should have said a long time ago."

Before I could respond, his phone buzzed insistently in his pocket. He cursed under his breath, a flicker of frustration passing over his features. "I'm sorry. I should take this."

As he pulled out his phone, I felt the moment slip away like sand through my fingers. I took a step back, trying to breathe through the sudden tension that had settled around us. Clayton answered the call, his expression shifting to one of concern. I couldn't hear the words, but I watched his body tense, shoulders rigid as he listened intently.

"I'll be right there," he said, voice clipped, and just like that, the moment was over. He hung up, the softness that had wrapped around us shattered into fragments.

"Clayton?" I asked, a knot tightening in my stomach. "What's wrong?"

He looked at me, his gaze intense, filled with a mixture of regret and urgency. "I have to go. Something happened at the ranch. I'll explain everything later."

"Wait, don't just leave me hanging like this! You can't drop a bombshell and then vanish!" I felt the frustration bubble up, the abrupt shift in energy leaving me reeling.

"I promise I'll be back," he said, but the weight of his words felt flimsy against the backdrop of the unresolved tension between us. "I'll explain everything. I swear."

With that, he turned and jogged towards his truck, the gravel crunching beneath his feet, a sound that felt like the echo of our conversation drifting away. I stood there, frozen, watching as he climbed into the vehicle, the engine roaring to life and cutting through the silence.

"Clayton!" I shouted, but the words felt inadequate, swallowed by the distance between us. He glanced back, a flash of something—an emotion I couldn't quite place—passing over his face before he sped away, leaving nothing but dust swirling in his wake.

I returned to the garden, feeling more lost than ever, each step heavy as if the flowers themselves mourned his departure. The sun beat down, a relentless reminder of the day that had started with such promise but had spiraled into chaos. My heart raced, questions spiraling in my mind like leaves caught in a tempest. What had he meant? What was happening at the ranch?

As the sun dipped lower in the sky, shadows began to stretch across the garden, creeping into the corners where light once reigned. I needed answers, but for now, all I had were echoes of laughter, promises lingering like whispers on the wind, and the gut-wrenching fear that I might not see him again.

I turned back to the house, my heart pounding with a mix of determination and dread. Whatever secrets Clayton held, I was resolved to uncover them, to untangle the threads of our past before they slipped away entirely. But as I reached the porch, my phone buzzed in my pocket. Glancing down, my heart plummeted.

An unknown number flashed on the screen, and without thinking, I answered. "Hello?"

"Jenna, it's urgent. You need to listen to me."

The voice on the other end sent a chill down my spine, a sense of foreboding washing over me. "Who is this?"

"You need to be careful. Clayton's not the only one with secrets, and they're coming for him."

The line went dead, and the world around me tilted, a fraying thread about to snap.

Chapter 4: Hidden Hearts

The scent of fresh basil and ripe strawberries hung in the air, a fragrant invitation as I maneuvered through the bustling stalls of the farmer's market. Vendors shouted their wares, their voices blending into a lively symphony that danced around me like a warm breeze. I had come to pick up some local honey—my favorite indulgence—but the moment I saw Clayton, I felt the earth beneath me shift, as if the very ground conspired to remind me of what I was trying to escape.

He was standing there, golden sunlight catching in his hair, that ridiculous wide-brimmed hat of his tipped just so, giving him the air of a cowboy stepping off the set of a romantic comedy. It was infuriatingly charming. I could almost hear the banjos strumming a sweet tune as he flashed his easy smile at Mrs. Reeves, who blushed like a teenager despite being well into her sixties. There was an undeniable magnetism about him, one that drew people in like moths to a flame. And there I was, standing at the edge of the market, half-hidden behind a display of heirloom tomatoes, feeling like a statue carved from the very stone of indecision.

"Mornin', Lana," he called, tipping his hat with a flourish that seemed to defy the gravity of our situation. His voice was smooth, almost melodic, and it sent an unwelcome shiver down my spine. I forced a smile, one that felt more like a grimace as I stepped closer.

"Morning, Clayton," I replied, my voice steadier than my heart. We fell into a rhythm of small talk that felt as strained as a rubber band pulled too tight. I asked him about the market, about the tomatoes he was buying, and he replied with enthusiastic detail, as if discussing the intricacies of ripeness and flavor was the most captivating topic on earth. I had to remind myself not to get lost in the sound of his voice; it was like honey dripping from a spoon—sweet, but it could also stick if you weren't careful.

"I'm hoping to make a caprese salad for dinner tonight," he said, the corners of his mouth curving up in a way that was both endearing and dangerous. "You know, with fresh mozzarella and basil. Can't beat it in the summer." He looked at me expectantly, and for a moment, I could almost picture us in a sunlit kitchen, chopping and laughing, our fingers brushing against each other as we reached for the same ingredient. I quickly shoved the thought away, trying to focus instead on the earthy aroma of the tomatoes and the distant sound of laughter coming from a group of children running past.

"Sounds great," I said, forcing my voice to remain light, though I could feel the weight of unspoken words between us. The past hung there, an unwelcome guest at the party, and neither of us dared to acknowledge it. But I could see it in the way his gaze lingered just a second too long on my lips or the way he shifted slightly closer, drawn by a force neither of us could name.

Suddenly, a commotion broke through the bubble of our conversation. A vendor's cart tipped over, spilling zucchinis and squash onto the cobbled ground, and chaos erupted as people rushed to help. I instinctively moved toward the scene, not because I wanted to, but because I needed an escape from the intensity that crackled in the air between Clayton and me. As I bent down to pick up a fallen squash, I heard Clayton's voice behind me.

"Lana, wait!"

I froze, my heart pounding. What did he want to say? Would he bring up that night—the one I had tried so hard to bury? I turned slowly, preparing myself for whatever was to come, but his expression was a blend of concern and amusement as he caught up to me, a squash in each hand.

"I believe these belong to you," he said, his tone playful as he handed them over. "I didn't want to let you get away with stealing produce."

I rolled my eyes, grateful for the levity. "Oh, please. I would never steal a zucchini—too much pressure to actually cook it." I laughed lightly, and it was then I noticed the way his gaze softened, the tension shifting as we shared a moment of genuine connection, however fleeting.

"You'd be surprised," he replied, his voice dipping low, the laughter fading. "There are worse crimes than stealing vegetables."

The words hung in the air, heavy with meaning. For a heartbeat, it felt like the market faded away, leaving just the two of us standing there, lost in a world of our own making. I searched his eyes, hoping to find clarity, a hint at what he was really thinking. Instead, I found a depth that made my heart race, and I was struck with the realization that I was still drawn to him in ways I couldn't fully comprehend.

Before I could respond, a sudden burst of laughter caught our attention. A little girl in a sunhat danced around, a face painted like a butterfly, and the infectious joy pulled me back to reality. Clayton glanced toward the laughter, and I saw the shadow of regret cross his features.

"We should probably get back to our vegetables," he said, a hint of disappointment lacing his voice. I nodded, feeling the moment slip away like sand through my fingers.

As we resumed our casual banter about recipes and summer dishes, the playful edge returned, yet beneath it all, the unresolved tension simmered, waiting for the right moment to erupt. I couldn't shake the feeling that this was just the beginning of something deeper, something that would either tether us together or tear us apart in the small-town whirlwind of Whispering Hills.

The sun hung low in the sky, casting a golden hue over Whispering Hills as I made my way home from the farmer's market. The weight of the squash in my bag seemed to grow heavier with each step, mirroring the knot of emotions tightening in my chest. Clayton's smile lingered in my mind, the way it faded and flickered, teasing at the boundaries of what we had left unspoken. I tried to shake off the feeling, focusing instead on the hustle and bustle of the small town. A group of children raced past, their laughter spilling into the air, bright and carefree like confetti.

But as I entered my little cottage, its walls adorned with sunflowers and mismatched trinkets that told stories of my past, I couldn't escape the shadow of Clayton. I set the bag down on the kitchen counter and peeled back the layers of my thoughts. He was like a persistent summer storm, one that could burst forth unexpectedly, drenching me in memories I wasn't ready to confront.

"Lana?" My neighbor, Mrs. Whitaker, called through the open window, her voice rich with warmth. She was the embodiment of a well-loved cookbook, full of flavors and stories from decades spent in Whispering Hills. "Are you coming to the book club meeting tonight? We're discussing that new romance novel, and I could use your opinion. You always have the best insights!"

I took a deep breath, ready to change the subject of my spiraling thoughts. "Of course, I wouldn't miss it! I'll be there." I wiped my hands on a dish towel, the simple act grounding me. Perhaps a little literary distraction would do me good.

A few hours later, as the evening crept in, I found myself sitting in Mrs. Whitaker's sunroom, the air filled with the scent of freshly baked cookies and the chatter of familiar voices. The sun was sinking, painting the walls in warm hues, and I settled into my usual spot, surrounded by an eclectic group of women who had become my makeshift family. They shared stories, gossip, and laughter, weaving a tapestry of community that made me feel at home.

"Lana, darling," Mrs. Whitaker said, her gaze penetrating. "You look a bit pensive tonight. Something on your mind?"

"Just contemplating the complexity of love," I replied, attempting a lighthearted tone as I took a sip of my herbal tea. "You know how it is."

"Oh, do tell!" Margaret, with her ever-curious nature, leaned forward, her eyes twinkling like stars. "Are we talking forbidden romances? Star-crossed lovers? Or perhaps a love triangle?"

I laughed, appreciating her flair for the dramatic. "Maybe a little of everything? You know, Whispering Hills is practically a soap opera waiting to happen."

As the evening unfolded, we dove into spirited discussions about character motivations and plot twists, the pages of our chosen novel sparking a warmth that enveloped us. Yet beneath the surface of my laughter lay the unsettling truth that Clayton's name was never mentioned, even though the uninvited thought hung like a ghost in the room, waiting to be acknowledged.

Once the meeting wrapped up, I lingered behind to help Mrs. Whitaker clean up, the rhythm of our movements familiar and comforting. "You know, dear," she began, her voice gentle but laced with curiosity, "I can't help but feel there's something brewing beneath the surface for you. That man, Clayton—he hasn't left your mind, has he?"

I sighed, placing the last of the teacups into the sink. "He's just a part of the town, Mrs. Whitaker. It's impossible to avoid him."

"Or maybe you don't want to avoid him," she mused, her knowing smile illuminating her features. "Life is too short to play it safe, you know. Sometimes, you just have to dive in headfirst, even if you're terrified of what lies beneath."

Her words lingered long after I left her house, hanging in the air like the sweet scent of her cookies. Maybe she was right. Maybe it was time to confront what I felt instead of dancing around it like a hesitant butterfly.

The following day, I found myself wandering back to the market, my heart a mix of hope and anxiety. The stalls bustled with energy, the vibrant colors of fruits and vegetables almost dizzying under the bright sun. I caught sight of Clayton near the honey vendor, his laughter ringing through the air like music. My stomach flipped, a mix of excitement and dread as I approached.

"Lana!" he called out, his voice drawing me closer as if I were a moth, inexplicably drawn to the flame of his charm.

"Hey, Clayton," I managed, my heart racing. We stood close, the familiar tension wrapping around us like a thick fog. The market noise faded into the background, and in that moment, it felt like we were the only two people in the world.

"Did you try that honey yet?" he asked, his eyes sparkling with mischief. "I hear it's a game changer for baking. We should totally make a batch of cookies—"

"Together?" I interrupted, half-joking, half-hopeful. The suggestion tumbled from my lips, and I immediately regretted the boldness of it, the way it opened a door I wasn't sure I was ready to step through.

"Why not?" he said, his grin widening, as if my words had delighted him. "I mean, it's about time we collaborated on something, right?"

"Right," I replied, my heart pounding in rhythm with the possibility hanging between us. "Let's do it."

We exchanged numbers, the simple act igniting a spark of excitement that warmed my chest. As I walked away, I couldn't shake the feeling that something significant was brewing, a storm of emotions threatening to break free, and I was right in its path. With each step, I felt a strange mixture of exhilaration and fear, knowing that the path ahead was anything but predictable. But perhaps that was the beauty of it all—every twist and turn a reminder that love, with all its complexities, was worth pursuing, no matter the risk.

A few days slipped by like whispers, each one carrying the thrill of unspoken promises. Clayton and I had arranged to bake cookies together, and though it was just a casual plan, it felt monumental. I spent the days leading up to it fantasizing about what our time together might look like, envisioning laughter mixing with the warm, inviting smell of cookies wafting through my little cottage. Each time my phone pinged with a message from him, my heart fluttered, reminding me how deeply I'd buried my feelings, only for them to rise like stubborn weeds in a garden.

On the day of our baking adventure, I paced around my kitchen, tidying up nervously. The counters gleamed with an assortment of baking supplies: flour, sugar, chocolate chips—everything to create something delicious and, hopefully, a little magical. I could hardly believe I was about to spend an entire afternoon with Clayton, my stomach in knots like a twisted pretzel.

When the doorbell rang, I nearly dropped the mixing bowl. It felt like the moment before a storm, charged with energy, and I took a moment to compose myself. I opened the door to find Clayton standing there, his smile bright enough to outshine the sun. He held a basket brimming with ingredients, and in his other hand, a bottle of homemade vanilla extract that he had procured from a local artisan.

"Surprise!" he exclaimed, the excitement in his voice contagious. "Thought we could elevate our cookie game."

I couldn't help but laugh at his enthusiasm. "You know, some might say that's a bit overzealous for cookies, but I appreciate the effort."

"Hey, cookies are serious business," he said, feigning indignation. "Especially when it comes to flavor."

We moved into the kitchen, and as we began measuring flour and sugar, the air buzzed with our easy banter. It felt natural, the way we fell into conversation, as if we'd been doing this for years rather than just a few days. He was animated, gesturing as he spoke, and each time our hands brushed, sparks flew between us, igniting something that simmered just beneath the surface.

"I read that the secret to great cookies is all in the technique," he said, leaning in closer as I stirred the mixture. "You have to fold in the chocolate chips just right. Otherwise, you risk ending up with cookie mush."

"Cookie mush?" I echoed, fighting a grin. "Sounds like a catastrophe I'm not prepared to deal with."

"I've made my share of mushy disasters. You'd be surprised," he said, a playful smirk dancing across his lips. "But with you as my partner, I think we'll create a masterpiece."

I couldn't help but feel a thrill at the compliment, our playful competition turning into a gentle camaraderie. As we laughed and baked, the cookies turned golden brown, filling the kitchen with a sweet aroma that was almost intoxicating. It was a blissful chaos, flour dusting our hair and chocolate chips occasionally flying as we tried to outdo one another in a baking duel that felt absurdly competitive.

As the cookies cooled on the counter, I poured us each a glass of milk, and we sat at the small kitchen table, our laughter echoing against the walls. The cookies, I had to admit, were surprisingly good—golden and chewy, with just the right amount of gooey chocolate.

"Not too shabby for a couple of amateurs," I said, taking a big bite. "I'd say we're on the brink of a baking revolution."

Clayton leaned back, savoring his cookie. "I think we should open our own bakery. Call it 'Whimsical Whisk.'"

I burst into laughter, almost choking on my cookie. "And what would we sell? Cookie mush?"

"Only the finest," he quipped, his eyes sparkling with mirth. "I can see it now—an award-winning, Michelin-starred establishment specializing in all things cookie. What more could anyone want?"

"Not a bad dream," I said, the lightheartedness of our conversation settling a comfortable warmth around us.

But then, as the laughter began to fade, the atmosphere shifted subtly. Clayton's gaze turned serious, and he leaned forward, resting his arms on the table. "Lana, can I ask you something?"

My heart quickened. "Sure, what's on your mind?"

"Why have you been avoiding me?" His question hung in the air, heavy and unyielding, as if daring me to respond.

I faltered, caught off guard. "Avoiding you? I—"

"You know what I mean," he pressed, the warmth in his eyes replaced with something more earnest. "There's a connection here, and it's clear you feel it too. But it's like you're dancing around it, and I want to know why."

I took a breath, feeling exposed under his scrutiny. "It's complicated," I said finally, my voice a whisper. "We've had... history. And it's not easy to just jump back in like nothing happened."

Clayton remained silent for a moment, his gaze piercing as he seemed to weigh my words. "Lana, I know what happened was messy. But I don't want to dance around it. I want to know you, all of you, the past and the present."

His sincerity hung in the air like the smell of freshly baked cookies, inviting yet daunting. I could feel the walls I had built around my heart beginning to crack.

"What if I'm not the person you remember?" I said, my voice shaking slightly. "What if I've changed?"

"That's the point," he replied, his tone gentle yet firm. "I'm not looking for who you were; I'm interested in who you are now."

The intensity of his words wrapped around me, making it hard to breathe. I could feel the years of hurt and hesitation bubbling to the surface, the fears I had kept hidden threatening to spill over. I stared into his eyes, searching for a glimpse of the boy I once knew, and finding the man he had become—a man who was unafraid to face the storm that had once torn us apart.

Just then, the doorbell rang again, interrupting the charged moment. I jumped, startled. "Who could that be?"

Clayton looked at me, his brow furrowing in confusion. "You expecting someone?"

"No," I replied, feeling a pang of unease. "I'm not."

The sound of the doorbell echoed in my mind, a sharp contrast to the warmth we had just shared. As I walked toward the door, a sense of foreboding filled the air. What if this was the moment everything changed?

I hesitated for a moment, glancing back at Clayton, who was watching me with a mix of curiosity and concern. With a deep breath, I opened the door, only to find a figure shrouded in shadow, their face obscured.

"Lana," the voice said, sending a chill down my spine. "We need to talk."

My heart raced as I took in the sight before me, the person standing there cloaked in mystery, and I felt the ground shift beneath my feet. In that instant, I knew my world was about to spiral into chaos, and whatever path I had chosen with Clayton would forever be altered.

Chapter 5: The Storm Within

The wind howled, whipping the raindrops into a frenzied dance as I perched on the rickety porch swing, the wood creaking beneath me like an old man's sigh. It felt familiar, the way the storm thrashed against the earth, as if the sky itself were waging war on the very ground beneath my feet. I wrapped my arms around my knees, pulling them close to my chest, trying to contain the tempest that churned within me. Boston had promised adventure, a life far removed from the heartache and tangled memories of this place, yet here I was, back in the town that had cradled both my dreams and my demons.

Clayton. Just the thought of his name sent shivers skimming down my spine, tinged with a warmth I couldn't quite shake. He had this way of bringing the past rushing back, and the moment our eyes locked today, it felt like stepping back into a vivid dream where I could recall every stolen glance, every lingering touch. His tousled hair and that devil-may-care grin were forever etched in my mind, yet today, they were tinged with the weight of unresolved feelings. I cursed under my breath, frustrated that the universe had chosen this moment to pull the strings of fate, dragging me back into the tangled web we'd woven years ago.

The rain poured in sheets, a relentless symphony that echoed my own chaotic thoughts. Each droplet hit the ground with a thud, much like the way my heart thumped in my chest when I remembered the last time we had spoken. It had been a flurry of harsh words and teary goodbyes, a summer storm of emotions that had left me gasping for air. And now? Now he was back, brighter and bolder than before, like a thundercloud bursting with light and life. The nerve of him.

"Just breathe," I muttered to myself, wishing the storm outside could drown out the one brewing within me. I could hear the distant rumble of thunder, a warning to those foolish enough to be outside. The way I felt, I could almost hear my own heart echoing the ominous tones, warning me not to fall back into his orbit. But how could I resist? He had a gravitational pull that was impossible to ignore, a magnetic energy that drew me in like a moth to a flame.

The memories flooded in unbidden—dancing in the rain during our last summer together, his laughter mingling with the raindrops as we stumbled back home, soaked and breathless. I remembered how his eyes had sparkled with mischief, how he'd dared me to jump into the lake despite the chill in the air. I had laughed and accepted, the thrill of the moment overshadowing my fears. And now, standing at the precipice of those memories, I felt the fear creeping back in, heavy and suffocating.

"Regan, are you out there?" a voice called, breaking through my reverie. I turned to see my mother at the doorway, her figure silhouetted against the warm light spilling from inside. She looked worried, her brow furrowed, and for a moment, I wanted to scream at her to leave me be. But she was my anchor, whether I liked it or not.

"Yeah, Mom. Just enjoying the storm," I replied, my voice barely rising above the drumming rain.

"Come inside before you catch your death! You'll regret it when you're all sniffly and sneezing." She waved her hands, a gesture I had seen countless times growing up.

I couldn't help but smile a little, the corners of my lips lifting despite the storm raging in my mind. "I'm fine! Just thinking," I called back, turning my gaze back to the rain-soaked hills.

"Thinking, or overthinking?" she retorted, a teasing lilt to her voice that made me roll my eyes.

"Same difference," I muttered under my breath, but the truth was, I was overwhelmed by the whirlwind of emotions. The last thing

I needed was my mother's insight into my tangled feelings about Clayton. "I'll be in soon!"

As I watched the rain streak down, I caught a glimpse of movement in the corner of my eye. A figure emerged from the sheets of water, silhouetted against the gray sky. My heart stopped, my breath catching in my throat. It couldn't be. But there he was—Clayton, standing at the edge of my driveway, rain soaking his clothes, his expression a mix of determination and uncertainty.

What was he doing here? Hadn't we left things unsaid, unresolved? The storm outside seemed to pale in comparison to the one brewing in my heart, a fierce mix of excitement and dread. I wanted to turn away, to retreat into the safety of the house, but my feet felt rooted to the ground, like the trees swaying helplessly in the wind.

He lifted his hand, as if to wave, but the rain blurred the lines of our unspoken tension, shrouding the moment in a haze of nostalgia and regret. The world around us faded, and for a heartbeat, time stood still, holding its breath as we stared at each other across the distance, two souls caught in a tempest neither of us could control.

"Regan!" he shouted, his voice barely carrying over the roar of the storm. I felt a shiver run down my spine, a mix of fear and exhilaration.

I stood there, caught between the past and the present, knowing that whatever came next would alter the course of my life once again.

The dance floor, dimly lit and crowded, swirled with laughter and the clinking of glasses. I caught fleeting glimpses of other couples, their movements effortless and uninhibited, as if the years had melted away in this little pocket of time. I had once felt that same sense of freedom, but now, with Clayton so close, I couldn't shake the weight of memories that clung to me like a second skin. Our bodies swayed in sync, an age-old rhythm resurfacing with every beat, and in that moment, the world around us faded.

"Do you remember the last time we danced like this?" Clayton murmured, his breath warm against my ear. I wanted to laugh at the absurdity of it all—here we were, two grown adults tangled in a shared past, fumbling through the remnants of our younger selves. Yet, there was a sincerity in his tone that stirred something deep within me. The memory tugged at my mind: a summer evening, just after graduation, when we had danced in the parking lot under a sky speckled with stars, the promise of endless possibilities hanging in the air like fireflies.

"Not exactly," I replied, trying to sound nonchalant while my heart raced. "But I imagine it involved less flannel and more freedom."

He chuckled, the sound rich and familiar. "Ah, the flannel phase. I like to think it was my way of rebelling against the preppy look everyone was sporting." His teasing tone softened the edges of the moment, wrapping us in a bubble of nostalgia.

"Is that what you call it? I thought you were just channeling your inner lumberjack." I felt the heat of his gaze, and it stirred something inside me, something both thrilling and terrifying.

Clayton's eyes sparkled with mischief. "You weren't complaining back then. Besides, I needed something to distract from my less-than-stellar dancing skills."

"True," I admitted, allowing a small smile to escape. "You did have a way of making even the most mundane moves look... interesting." The playful banter flowed effortlessly, yet beneath it, I could sense the underlying tension, a mix of unresolved feelings and hesitant hope.

The music shifted, a slower ballad washing over us, and I found myself leaning closer, resting my head against his shoulder, inhaling the scent of his cologne mixed with the stale beer and popcorn in the bar. I closed my eyes for just a moment, allowing the familiar sensation to wash over me. Yet, in that fleeting bliss, a knot of apprehension tightened in my stomach. Did I really want to open this door?

As if sensing my internal struggle, Clayton pulled back slightly to meet my gaze. "What are you thinking about?" he asked, his voice low and earnest.

"Just... how strange it is to be here with you," I confessed, the words spilling out before I could stop them. "I didn't expect this tonight."

"Neither did I," he admitted, the hint of a smile tugging at his lips. "But here we are. Maybe it's fate, or just really bad planning on our parts."

"Fate and bad planning—quite the combination," I replied, my voice laced with sarcasm, but my heart raced with a thrill of uncertainty.

He took a step back, breaking our connection momentarily. "What if we were meant to be here? Together? Maybe we owe it to ourselves to find out what this is."

"What, like a grand experiment?" I asked, arching an eyebrow. "You want to mix old memories with new realities? That sounds like a recipe for disaster."

"Or a bestseller," he countered, leaning in with that confident smile that always made my stomach flutter. "Imagine the plot twist. 'Two ex-lovers reunite at a bar and discover—'"

"—they hate each other's guts," I finished for him, rolling my eyes but unable to suppress my grin.

His laughter rang out, brightening the dim bar. "That's a good one! But how about this? 'They uncover buried feelings and rekindle an old flame.'"

"Much more romantic, but let's not get carried away," I teased, even as a flicker of hope ignited within me. The idea was absurd, yet exhilarating. What if we could rewrite our story?

The moment lingered, the tension between us a living thing, almost palpable. I shifted my weight, biting my lip as the music faded into a slow hum. The reality of the night pressed upon me, making me acutely aware of the risks involved. If we crossed this line, there would be no turning back.

"I can see the wheels turning in your head," he said, tilting his head as if reading my thoughts. "What if we just... took it one day at a time? No pressure, no expectations."

"Easier said than done," I replied, my voice quieter, the weight of his suggestion settling in. "What if we end up just like before, hurt and confused?"

"Then we'll deal with it," he said simply, a trace of sincerity in his eyes that made my heart skip. "Life's too short to not take risks. What's the worst that could happen?"

"Famous last words," I murmured, half teasing, half serious. Yet beneath the layers of skepticism, I felt a flicker of excitement at the prospect of exploring whatever 'this' was.

Chapter 6: Unexpected Break

Just as I was about to respond, my phone buzzed in my pocket, a sudden interruption that snapped me back to reality. I fished it out, glancing at the screen, my heart sinking at the name flashing across it. My sister, always good at timing, her calls often filled with the chaos of her life that I couldn't quite escape.

"Hey, I have to take this," I said, stepping away, reluctant to break the moment but unable to ignore the tug of family obligations.

Clayton nodded, his expression unreadable, but I sensed the shift in the air as I moved away. I felt torn, caught between the safety of the past and the thrill of an uncertain future.

"Of course," he replied, a hint of disappointment lacing his voice. "I'll be right here."

As I answered the call, my heart raced—not just from the unexpected joy of reconnecting with Clayton but from the realization that perhaps, just perhaps, I was ready to explore whatever lay ahead, even if it meant facing the echoes of love that refused to fade.

The phone call was a familiar interruption, like a pebble thrown into a still pond, sending ripples through my moment with Clayton. I stepped aside, attempting to absorb the chatter from my sister while my eyes stayed fixed on him across the bar. He leaned against the wall, casual yet attentive, watching me with a curiosity that made my stomach flip.

"Lila! I'm so glad I caught you!" My sister's voice was bright, but I could hear the undercurrent of urgency. "You won't believe what just happened!"

I forced myself to focus, bracing for whatever chaos she was about to unleash. "Is everything okay?"

"Of course! I mean, not everything. But I just ran into Greg! You know, my ex? The one who ghosted me right before our anniversary?"

I nodded, even though she couldn't see me. "And you're talking to him now? Did you throw your drink in his face, or was it the standard 'let's pretend it didn't happen' pleasantries?"

"Neither! I did something better. I told him off! I mean, really, Lila, I told him he was an idiot for treating me like I was nothing. I even reminded him of all the terrible things he did." Her voice was a mix of pride and disbelief.

"Good for you! That's the spirit! Did he look shocked?"

"More like embarrassed. But that's not the point. I was feeling bold and—"

"Boldness sounds dangerous, sis. Should I be worried?"

She laughed lightly, the sound almost infectious, making me want to smile even though I was still keenly aware of Clayton's gaze on me. "Not about me. I'm fine! But it got me thinking... you know, maybe I should take a leaf out of your book. You've been doing some serious soul-searching, haven't you?"

"I'm not sure about that," I replied, my voice tinged with doubt. "It's complicated. I'm just trying to figure things out with—"

Before I could finish, I saw Clayton push off from the wall, his expression shifting as he moved toward me, determination etched on his face. The sight of him made my heart race again, this time with a twinge of apprehension.

"I gotta go," I told my sister hastily, ending the call before she could respond. Clayton was nearly upon me, and I could sense the weight of the moment hanging between us like an electric current.

"Everything okay?" he asked, concern flickering across his features.

"Just sisterly chaos," I said, trying to downplay it. "You know how it is."

"Sounds about right," he replied, tilting his head as if gauging my mood. "But I thought we agreed to take things slow?"

A spark of challenge ignited in me. "We did, didn't we? But here you are, coming in hot like a summer storm."

He laughed, a rich sound that warmed the corners of the bar. "Can't help it if you're distracting me with all this—" he gestured to the empty space between us "—potential."

"Oh, so I'm just a distraction now?" I teased, raising an eyebrow.

"More like an intriguing puzzle I can't resist solving," he replied, his voice dropping to a whisper as he leaned in closer. I could see the glimmer of mischief in his eyes, and it sent a shiver down my spine.

"Good luck with that," I shot back, matching his playful energy. "I'm a bit of a Rubik's cube. You might just end up frustrated."

"Frustration can be motivating," he countered, his eyes sparkling with challenge.

Just as I was about to retort, the band struck up a lively tune, an upbeat melody that echoed with energy. "Dance?" Clayton suggested, his hand reaching out to me once more.

I hesitated, feeling a pulse of nervous excitement as I considered the implications of accepting his offer. But the music swirled around us, filling the air with an irresistible call. "Why not?" I replied, placing my hand in his.

As we moved to the center of the floor, the crowd parted slightly, allowing us space to breathe. The beat thumped through my chest, each note resonating with the raw tension lingering between us. Clayton spun me around, his laughter mingling with the music as I struggled to keep up.

"I'm going to step on your toes," I warned, breathless.

"Only if you try too hard," he shot back, his grin infectious. "Just feel the rhythm!"

And just like that, I did. I let go of my apprehensions and surrendered to the moment. We danced, losing ourselves in the energy around us, the laughter, the shared glances. It felt like we were the only two people in the universe, a world filled with warmth and connection.

But as the song reached its crescendo, a sudden commotion erupted at the back of the bar. A loud crash followed by a shout sliced through our bubble, pulling my attention away. I turned to see a couple arguing near the pool table, the atmosphere shifting from light-hearted to tense.

"Hey, let's check that out," Clayton suggested, his eyes bright with curiosity.

"Or we could pretend we didn't see anything," I replied, not entirely sure I wanted to dive into whatever chaos was unfolding.

"Where's the fun in that?" he challenged, tugging me along with him as we navigated through the crowd.

As we drew closer, the situation escalated. The woman, red-faced and gesturing wildly, accused the man of cheating during the game. It was messy and uncomfortable to witness, and I felt my heart sink for her.

"Let's get out of here," I murmured to Clayton, feeling the weight of the tension settle in my bones.

"Not yet," he urged, his gaze fixed on the scene. "It's almost like a train wreck. You can't help but watch."

Just then, the man shoved the pool table, and the sound of wood creaking and falling glasses drew a collective gasp from the onlookers.

"Okay, now I'm worried," I said, feeling the anxiety in the air like a live wire.

"Let's just back away slowly," he suggested, but before we could retreat, the man turned, locking eyes with us, a look of rage flashing across his face.

"What are you staring at?" he barked, taking a step toward us.

I felt my heart race, adrenaline flooding my veins. "Maybe we should really get out of here," I whispered, grabbing Clayton's arm.

"Yeah, I think that's wise," he said, but before we could make a quick exit, the man charged forward, fists clenched and fury etched in his features.

"Get out of my way!"

The air crackled with tension as I realized the night was about to take an unexpected turn, one that could change everything in an instant.

Chapter 7: A Shattered Dream

The soft hum of the coffee shop enveloped me, a familiar cocoon of warmth and caffeine-laced anticipation. I nestled deeper into the corner booth, my favorite refuge, cradling a chipped mug that promised comfort in its weathered embrace. The scent of roasted beans wafted through the air, mingling with the faint undertones of cinnamon and nutmeg, a blend that had always drawn me back to this haven. My fingers drummed lightly on the table, betraying the disquiet brewing beneath my otherwise calm facade. I knew I shouldn't be surprised when the phone rang. Even the tiniest twist of fate had a way of slinking back into my life like a stray cat, uninvited yet strangely familiar.

"Emily," my old boss's voice crackled through the receiver, sharp and businesslike, cutting through my reverie. "We need you back. The project is critical. Can you start next week?" The words fell like stones, heavy and inevitable. A tightness gripped my chest, and I forced myself to breathe, each inhale a conscious effort against the rising tide of panic.

"Next week?" I echoed, my voice lighter than I felt, as if putting on a mask of nonchalance would somehow shift the reality looming over me. "I'll need to check a few things first."

He didn't even wait for my reply. "I know you'll make it work, Em. You always do." The line went dead, leaving a silence that felt like a gaping chasm in my chest.

I set the phone down and gazed out the window, where a light rain began to patter against the glass, a rhythmic reminder of the turmoil inside me. The streets of Asheville were a collage of color and life, vibrant even under the gray canopy. The quaint shops lining the street were decorated for autumn, their windows showcasing pumpkins and leaves that blazed with the fiery hues of a sunset. In a few days, the town would be brimming with tourists, eager to sip cider and roam the pumpkin patches. I had once thrived in that bustling energy, but now it felt like an impending storm, one I wasn't sure I could weather.

"Hey, you okay?" asked a voice, slicing through my thoughts. It was Mia, my best friend, her dark curls bouncing as she slid into the seat across from me. "You look like you've seen a ghost."

I forced a smile, though I knew it didn't quite reach my eyes. "Just a call from the past, that's all."

She raised an eyebrow, her intuition sharper than a chef's knife. "Clayton again?"

The mere mention of his name sent a tremor through me. Clayton had been my anchor, the person I thought I'd build my life with. But leaving him had felt like cutting away a part of my soul, an act of self-preservation that now threatened to unravel me further. "Not exactly," I replied, trying to keep the tremor from my voice. "It's work. They want me back in Boston."

Her expression morphed into a blend of sympathy and encouragement. "Boston? That's huge, Em! You've been working for that firm for years. This could be your big break."

"Yes, but—"

"But you'd have to leave all this behind," she finished for me, her gaze softening. "You've built something beautiful here, Em. A life."

"I know," I whispered, glancing out the window again. The rain had intensified, each droplet a reminder of the storm gathering within. "But that life feels fragile. And with Clayton still around, it's complicated."

Mia leaned forward, her voice dropping to a conspiratorial whisper. "Look, if you're feeling this much anxiety, maybe it's not the right time to leap back into the arms of your old job. You don't owe them anything."

"Maybe," I mused, but doubt clawed at me. What if this was the opportunity I'd been waiting for, the one I needed to reclaim my former self? A knock at the door drew my attention, and I watched as a figure stepped inside, shaking off the rain like a dog returning home. My heart stuttered as recognition hit—Clayton.

He looked just as I remembered: tousled hair, that infuriatingly charming smile, and eyes that seemed to see right through me. Time had painted him with a touch of sophistication, the casual grace of a man who had grown into himself. He spotted me immediately, his gaze locking onto mine with an intensity that sent a bolt of electricity through the air.

"Emily," he said, striding over as if we were the only two people in the world. "Fancy seeing you here."

"Hi, Clayton," I managed, my heart racing despite my best efforts to appear unfazed. "What brings you to this side of town?"

He shrugged, his casual demeanor belying the tension crackling between us. "Just picking up a coffee. Didn't expect to run into you."

I couldn't tell if his words were a casual observation or a hint of something deeper. My mind raced, recalling the moments we had shared, the laughter, the arguments, the quiet understandings. But beneath it all was the ache of what we had lost, and the fracture that had formed when I walked away.

"Yeah, just catching up on some work," I said, gesturing to the laptop in front of me, though I doubted he noticed.

He leaned closer, the scent of his cologne—a blend of cedar and citrus—enveloping me. "You always did work too hard. Remember when we used to just sit and talk for hours?"

I swallowed hard, nostalgia washing over me like a bittersweet tide. "Things change," I replied, my voice steadier than I felt.

"Do they?" he mused, his expression contemplative. "Sometimes I wonder if we change or just adapt."

The air thickened with unspoken words, a tempest brewing in the fragile space between us. As the rain beat against the window, I felt the weight of decisions pressing down like a storm cloud ready to burst. Would I choose the familiar embrace of the past, or the uncertain promise of a future yet to unfold? In that moment, everything hung in the balance, suspended between the ghosts of yesterday and the promise of tomorrow.

The rain continued to drum against the window, a rhythmic insistence that mirrored the chaos in my mind. Clayton lingered at the edge of my world, a magnet pulling me toward memories I had carefully tucked away. His presence, while familiar, was also a jarring reminder of the choices I had made. I forced myself to meet his gaze, studying the way his lips quirked into that lopsided smile that had once made my heart race.

"Still working too hard, I see," he teased, glancing at my laptop. "You know, it's a coffee shop, not a conference room."

"Excuse me for trying to make a living," I shot back, the playful banter rolling off my tongue with surprising ease. "Some of us have deadlines that don't magically disappear just because it's Friday."

"Touché," he conceded, raising his hands in mock surrender. "I guess I should have brought my own work. Or better yet, a board game. You're just too much of a distraction."

There was something oddly comforting in our exchange, a familiar rhythm that felt like slipping on a favorite old sweater, albeit one frayed at the edges. The tension between us crackled, charged with the electricity of unresolved feelings. I caught a glimpse of his hands, long fingers that had once danced over mine, now casually resting on the table.

"So," he said, leaning in slightly, his expression growing serious. "What's the real reason for all this?" He gestured vaguely, encompassing my laptop, the coffee shop, and, perhaps, even us. "You've been avoiding me since you got back."

I swallowed hard, the lump in my throat rising with every word I fought to articulate. "I've been busy, Clayton. You know how it is. Life doesn't stop just because I'm home."

"Right. The never-ending whirlwind of tasks and projects," he replied, a hint of sarcasm lacing his tone. "But I know you better than that. You don't just dodge someone like me without a reason."

His gaze bore into me, deep and searching, and I felt my carefully constructed barriers begin to crack. "Maybe I'm just trying to figure things out," I admitted, my voice barely above a whisper.

"What's there to figure out?" he asked, his brow furrowing. "You've got this amazing opportunity waiting for you. You're brilliant, Em. Go back to Boston, and show them what you're made of."

"Brilliant or not, I'm not sure I want to go back," I said, the words spilling out before I could stop them. "I thought I wanted to leave, but being here feels... different. It's complicated."

His expression softened, and I could see the hint of vulnerability beneath his bravado. "Complicated is what life is made of, isn't it? You could have everything you ever wanted in Boston, but it seems like you're hesitating. Why?"

Because of you, I wanted to scream, but instead, I settled for silence, letting the unspoken truth hang heavy between us. He didn't push; instead, he waited, and that patience only served to draw me further into his orbit.

"I don't know, Clayton. Maybe I'm afraid of what I'll find back there. Or who I'll become," I confessed. "When I left, I thought I was breaking free, but now... now it feels like I'm on the edge of a precipice, and I don't know if I should jump or turn back."

"Why do you think it has to be a jump?" he asked, tilting his head thoughtfully. "What if it's more like a leap? Something exhilarating, with the wind in your hair, and a chance to soar?"

"Or fall flat on my face," I countered, but the way he looked at me made me feel reckless, alive in a way I hadn't experienced in far too long.

"Em, we can't predict the future. You can only decide what's best for you, even if it means taking risks. I know what you're capable of."

The way he spoke, filled with confidence and belief, sent a shiver of hope through me. Yet, lurking beneath that hope was the familiar grip of fear. "What if I fail? What if going back means I have to face all the things I've tried to forget?"

He leaned in closer, his voice dropping to a conspiratorial whisper. "What if facing those things leads you to something even better? Sometimes, we need to confront our past to understand our future."

Just then, a gust of wind rattled the door, and a burst of chilly air swept through the shop, mingling with the warm aromas of coffee and baked goods. It sent a shiver down my spine, a sudden realization that time was slipping away. I couldn't sit here, tangled in old memories, forever. I had a choice to make, and I could either remain trapped in this moment or step into the unknown.

"What about you?" I asked, the question tumbling from my lips before I could rein it in. "What are you doing here? Still hanging around Asheville, I see."

His expression shifted slightly, a flicker of something that looked almost like regret crossed his features. "Life happens, I guess. I've been working at a local firm, trying to find my footing after..." He trailed off, his gaze dropping to the table, the weight of unspoken words lingering in the air between us.

"After what?" I pressed gently, desperate to understand the man sitting before me—the man I once thought I knew so well.

"After everything," he finally said, the vulnerability in his voice palpable. "I thought I could forget what we had, but it just... it doesn't work like that."

"I know," I replied, feeling a kinship in our shared pain. "It's hard to let go of things that mattered so much."

His gaze snapped back to mine, fierce and unyielding. "But maybe that's not what we should do. Maybe we should stop trying to let go and start figuring out what it means to carry those memories with us instead."

I felt my heart quicken at his words, a jolt of realization sparking in my chest. He was right; confronting my past didn't mean running away from it. It meant integrating it into the fabric of who I was becoming. Perhaps returning to Boston didn't have to be about erasing who I had been, but rather embracing the next chapter of my life with all its complexities and challenges.

The rain lightened outside, transforming into a gentle drizzle, and I took a deep breath, feeling the tension in my shoulders ease just slightly. "You really think I can do this?"

"I know you can," he said, a smile breaking across his face, a flicker of that old Clayton lighting up the room. "Just think of it as your own little adventure. And remember, you don't have to do it alone."

His words lingered in the air, a sweet promise woven with unspoken possibilities. It felt like a lifeline, something to hold onto as the path ahead twisted and turned, uncertain yet promising. Perhaps the ghosts of my past were not meant to haunt me but to guide me, nudging me toward a future that could be bright and full of life.

The moment stretched like taffy between us, a sweet, sticky tension that neither of us wanted to break. Clayton's gaze flickered to the door, where a gust of wind rattled the entrance, sending another chill through the café. He caught my eye again, and I could see the resolve forming in his features. "So, what do we do now?" he asked, leaning forward, his elbows resting on the table, as if anchoring himself to this conversation, to me.

"I suppose that depends on what we want," I replied, my heart racing in a way I hadn't felt in ages. The air was thick with possibility, a delicious tension that felt both terrifying and exhilarating. "You're here. I'm here. Maybe we should stop dancing around this."

His brow arched playfully, the corners of his mouth tugging upward. "Dancing? I thought we were more of a tango kind of duo—passionate, intense, and slightly out of sync."

"More like a clumsy waltz, if you ask me," I quipped, unable to suppress a smile. "Two steps forward, one step back."

He laughed, the sound warm and inviting, reminiscent of countless evenings spent wrapped up in deep conversation and easy laughter. "Well, clumsy or not, at least we're still dancing."

The moment was punctuated by the jingle of the café door swinging open, letting in a burst of fresh air. I watched as a couple entered, dripping umbrellas in hand, laughing as they shook off the rain. They looked impossibly happy, the kind of joy that felt like a warm blanket on a chilly day. I couldn't help but wonder if that was how Clayton and I had once appeared—two souls blissfully entangled, unaware of the world around us.

"Remember the night we got caught in that storm at the lake?" he said, and his voice pulled me back to a time when everything felt simpler. "We thought we'd never make it back, soaked to the bone and laughing like idiots."

"I remember," I replied, my cheeks warming at the memory. "You kept insisting we could outrun the rain, and I nearly broke my ankle trying to keep up with you."

His eyes sparkled with mirth. "And you still hold that against me? I thought it made for a great story."

"A story that involved me nearly losing my favorite shoes," I shot back, though I couldn't help but grin. "They never recovered."

"Ah, but you did. You always do." He leaned back, his expression shifting slightly, turning serious. "And now? What's the story you want to write next?"

A weight settled on my chest as I considered his question. The choice before me was monumental, an intersection of paths that could lead to joy or regret. "I want to embrace whatever comes next," I said, my voice steadier than I felt. "Even if it scares the hell out of me."

He nodded, the intensity in his gaze never wavering. "That's the spirit. And if you decide to head back to Boston, I'll be cheering you on from the sidelines."

I opened my mouth to respond, but before I could speak, my phone buzzed on the table. A notification. I glanced at the screen and froze. It was a message from my old firm, a group chat filled with familiar names, each one a reminder of the life I had temporarily set aside. My heart raced as I read the words, each one a jolt of electricity.

"Urgent meeting on Monday. New project details to discuss. Your presence is mandatory."

The ground felt like it was shifting beneath my feet. "They need me back... right away."

Clayton frowned, concern etching lines across his brow. "What does that mean for you?"

I swallowed hard, the lump in my throat swelling with uncertainty. "It means I have a choice to make, and I don't know if I'm ready."

"Emily, listen." He reached across the table, his hand brushing mine, and a spark ignited between us, warm and grounding. "You're not alone in this. No matter where you go, I'm here, and I'm not going anywhere."

The sincerity in his voice was a balm against my swirling thoughts, but the weight of his words was daunting. "But what if I go back and things don't work out? What if I fall apart again?"

"You won't," he assured me, his thumb stroking my knuckles gently. "You're stronger than you think. You always have been. And if you do stumble, I'll be there to help you back on your feet."

His words wrapped around me like a lifeline, but they also raised the stakes. Did I dare let him back into my life, knowing full well the complications that came with it? Just then, the café door swung open again, and the bright chatter of new customers flooded the space. I tore my gaze from Clayton, taking a moment to collect my racing thoughts.

Before I could respond, a figure slipped into my peripheral vision, and I turned, my heart sinking. There, standing just inside the door, was Lisa, my former colleague, her eyes scanning the café until they locked onto mine. She looked out of place, with her tailored blazer and perfectly styled hair, a stark contrast to the cozy, relaxed atmosphere.

"Emily!" she called, her voice cutting through the warm murmur of conversation. "There you are! I thought I'd find you here."

My stomach twisted into knots, a flash of anxiety coursing through me. "What are you doing here?" I managed to ask, attempting to keep my tone light even as my heart raced.

"Just catching up on some work, like you," she said, brushing past a table, completely oblivious to the tension in the air. "I didn't realize you were back in town. Heard you were leaving us again. I assume that's why you didn't respond to the group chat?"

Clayton's hand slipped away from mine, and I felt the loss keenly. "I was just—"

"Just what?" she pressed, her gaze sharp, an unyielding glint in her eyes. "Trying to figure out if you want to be part of the team again? Because they really need you, you know."

I felt the weight of her words like a boulder on my chest. "I'm... still deciding."

"Deciding?" She leaned in, her tone dripping with disbelief. "You don't get to decide. They want you back, and you owe it to yourself to take this opportunity."

As the air thickened with unspoken words, I sensed Clayton's presence shift beside me, his tension palpable. "She's not obligated to anything," he said quietly, but his voice was firm, an unexpected support that made me glance at him.

Lisa's gaze flicked between us, her brow arching. "Oh, I see. The old flame returns to rekindle the fire? How quaint."

A knot of anger twisted in my stomach, and I shot Clayton a look that screamed for support. "This isn't just about the job, Lisa," I said, my voice sharper than I intended. "It's about what I want, too."

"Right, because what you want matters more than the team that's been holding its breath for you," she shot back, her impatience bubbling over. "You think they care about your personal life? They don't. They just want results."

My cheeks flushed, a mix of humiliation and indignation boiling beneath the surface. "You know what? I'm not a cog in your machine. I'm a person with choices."

The heat in the café seemed to rise as the tension escalated, drawing the attention of nearby patrons. Clayton shifted closer, the warmth of his body grounding me as I faced Lisa. "I think you should leave," he said, his voice steady but low, a quiet storm threatening to break.

"Excuse me?" she said, taken aback, her eyes narrowing. "Who do you think you are, stepping in like this?"

"I'm someone who cares about Emily's choices," he replied, unwavering.

The standoff was electric, an undeniable current pulsing between us. Just as the air thickened, my phone buzzed again, another message. With my heart pounding, I glanced at the screen. My heart stopped.

"Emily, we really need to talk. There are things you need to know."

The sender's name made my blood run cold: Ruth.

I exchanged a glance with Clayton, my thoughts racing. The weight of the world pressed down, and I could feel the moment teetering on the edge. Something was shifting, a storm brewing on the horizon, and I could either face it or run. In that breathless instant, the café faded away, and all that remained was the urgent need to decide who I wanted to be in this unpredictable tapestry of life.

Chapter 8: Crossroads

I stood at a crossroads, the kind where the universe seems to hold its breath, waiting for me to choose. The air was thick with the scent of pine and the distant murmur of the creek, a melody that tugged at memories I thought I had neatly packed away. Whispering Hills, with its rolling hills and quirky charm, felt like a siren's call, wrapping around me like the gentle breeze that rustled the leaves overhead. Here, everything was familiar yet tinged with a bittersweet ache—an ache that beckoned me to linger just a moment longer.

In Boston, I had carved out a life—a polished, ambitious existence filled with meetings and deadlines, where I had once thrived amid the chaos of the city. The skyline, a jagged silhouette against the sun, felt like a cage I had designed myself, each glass office a reflection of my painstaking efforts to climb the corporate ladder. My apartment was a testament to my success, a chic studio with stainless steel appliances and floor-to-ceiling windows that overlooked the cacophony below. But as I stood in that sun-dappled clearing, surrounded by the tall pines and the soft hum of nature, the city felt like a distant echo, its vibrancy overshadowed by the warmth of the sun on my skin and the promise of simpler pleasures.

And then there was Clayton. Each time our paths crossed, it was as if we were two magnets, drawn together despite the barriers of time and hurt. Our encounters had started with awkward small talk—him trying to coax a smile from my lips, me deflecting with sarcasm honed by years of city living. The first time I saw him again at the diner, I had almost dropped my coffee. His presence was as solid as the wooden table beneath my hands, and I couldn't help but notice how the years had sculpted him into something undeniably handsome, with a ruggedness that sent my heart racing. I wanted to turn back the clock and rewrite our history, but the weight of our shared past sat heavily between us like a wall of granite.

I'd caught him staring more than once, his gaze a mixture of regret and longing. Each look sent a jolt through me, igniting memories I had tried to bury—those lazy afternoons spent in the shade of the old oak tree, sharing dreams of the future as the sunlight danced through the leaves. Now, as adults, we had become strangers wearing the same skin, both of us haunted by the choices that had led us to this moment. The tension was palpable, thick enough to slice through with a knife, and each accidental brush of our hands sent shivers coursing through me, awakening a part of myself that I thought had been extinguished.

As I wandered deeper into the woods, the tranquility enveloped me, and the chirping of birds became a soothing soundtrack. It was here that I could contemplate my dilemma, away from the prying eyes of the town and the burdens of my career. But every decision felt weighted. I could return to Boston, where I was a respected marketing executive, a woman of influence in an industry that thrived on competition. Yet the thought of sitting in a conference room, discussing quarterly reports, left me cold. How could I walk away from this new-found connection with the land and the people who had shaped my youth?

My thoughts drifted back to Clayton, who had become an anchor amidst the tumult of my emotions. We had shared late-night conversations, our voices mingling with the crickets' symphony, each word weaving us closer. One evening, while sitting on his porch, he had finally confessed that he regretted how things had ended between us. "You never gave me a chance, you know," he said, his voice low and steady, as if he were unveiling a secret he had guarded for too long. I could see the sincerity etched in his features, the way his eyes sparkled in the dim light. "I was young, I was stupid, but I would have fought for you."

And there it was, the seed of a possibility—could I let go of the past? Could I trust him again? A part of me wanted to shake my head, to remind him of the hurt, the way it had felt when he walked away without looking back. But the other part of me, the one that craved connection, longed for the warmth of his laughter and the way his hands felt steady and strong as they brushed against mine.

I took a deep breath, feeling the cool air fill my lungs, grounding me. The crossroads I faced was not just about choosing a place but deciding who I wanted to be. Could I leave behind the comforts of Boston, the career I had built, for the uncertainty of a life intertwined with someone who had once broken my heart? The sunlight broke through the branches, bathing the path in a golden hue, a reminder that clarity often comes in moments of quiet reflection.

As I turned to head back toward town, I caught a glimpse of Clayton walking along the creek, his silhouette framed by the flickering sunlight. My heart raced at the sight, a mixture of dread and excitement knotting in my stomach. Each step felt heavier than the last, the weight of my decision pressing down on me like a gathering storm. What if I chose wrong? What if the past truly couldn't be rewritten? The questions buzzed in my mind, an insistent drone that mirrored the sound of the cicadas in the trees.

Yet beneath that uncertainty lay a thread of hope, whispering of new beginnings and the chance to rewrite my story. If I could face the fear that had haunted me for so long, maybe I could carve out a path that led to something beautiful, something worth fighting for. With a deep breath, I took a step forward, ready to face whatever lay ahead.

The sun dipped lower in the sky as I made my way back to town, casting long shadows across the familiar dirt road. Each step echoed in my mind, a rhythmic reminder of the weight of choice that pressed against my chest. I could almost hear the whispers of the trees urging me to stay, to embrace the enchantment of Whispering Hills and its tapestry of memories. But the thought of returning to the corporate grind filled me with a conflicting mix of dread and anticipation. It was hard to ignore the allure of the bustling city life I had built, the tantalizing prospect of success and stability, juxtaposed against the magnetic pull of home, where every corner cradled a cherished moment.

As I approached the heart of the town, the warm glow of the evening sun illuminated the quaint storefronts, each one a slice of history. The Corner Café, with its cheerful yellow awning and the intoxicating aroma of fresh coffee wafting through the open door, beckoned me. It was here that I had spent countless hours with friends, their laughter mingling with the soft jazz that played in the background. Stepping inside felt like a return to the embrace of old friends, even if they weren't all physically present.

"Look who decided to grace us with her presence!" Amy, the café owner, called out from behind the counter, her voice rich with warmth and mischief. She wiped her hands on her apron and grinned at me, her dark curls bouncing as she leaned over the counter. "Thought you'd forgotten we existed out here."

"Forget you? Never," I replied, a smile breaking through the tumult of my thoughts. "I just needed a moment to clear my head."

"Or to avoid Clayton," she teased, raising an eyebrow. "You two are practically starring in your own rom-com with all the tension in the air."

The comment hit home, and I could feel my cheeks warm. "It's not a movie, Amy. It's more like a poorly scripted soap opera."

"Please," she scoffed, pouring me a cup of coffee. "If you don't want the leading man, I'll take him. He's been in here enough lately, and I'm starting to think he's going to ask for a loyalty card."

I rolled my eyes playfully, accepting the steaming mug from her hands. "Very funny. But he's not the issue. It's me. I'm the one who can't figure out if I'm coming or going."

"You're not a lost cause, you know," Amy said softly, leaning closer. "You just need to decide what makes your heart sing. Is it the thrill of the city or the comfort of home?"

Taking a sip of the rich brew, I contemplated her words. The warmth spread through me, anchoring my thoughts. "What if it's both? What if I'm meant to find a balance?"

"Then that's what you should fight for. Life isn't always black and white, you know. Sometimes, it's about blending the colors to create something new."

I pondered that as I stepped back outside, the cool evening air wrapping around me like a soft shawl. The sun painted the sky in hues of orange and pink, and I felt a spark of determination ignite within me. Perhaps my story didn't have to end with a clear-cut choice. Maybe it was more like a tapestry woven from the threads of my past and the possibilities of my future.

As I walked down the street, the laughter of children echoed from the nearby park, reminding me of the carefree days of my youth. The sight of the old swing set, slightly rusty but still standing, brought a smile to my lips. It was a reminder of innocence, a time when the biggest decisions were whether to play tag or climb the tallest tree.

"Are you going to let nostalgia get the best of you?" a voice interrupted my reverie.

Turning, I found Clayton leaning against the fence that bordered the park, his hands stuffed casually in his pockets, the soft glow of the fading sunlight illuminating the angles of his face. The casual air he projected belied the intensity that swirled beneath the surface, a stark reminder of the storm brewing between us.

"Maybe I just enjoy reliving my glory days," I replied, my tone teasing. "You know, the time I could swing without worrying about adult responsibilities."

"Glory days? More like the days of splattered ice cream and scraped knees," he shot back with a grin, his eyes sparkling with mischief.

I laughed, the tension between us lightening for a moment. "At least those scraped knees meant we were living life, not just spectating."

Clayton moved closer, the space between us shrinking. "So, are you going to keep running from your past? Or do you think you might actually face it?"

His question hit like a bolt of lightning, a reminder of everything I had been trying to avoid. "Isn't that what we're all trying to do?" I shot back, raising an eyebrow. "Face our pasts? Yours just happens to be more handsome."

He chuckled, and the sound sent a flutter through me. "Well, I wouldn't say I'm handsome. Maybe ruggedly charming?"

"Right, because 'ruggedly charming' is the bar we're all aiming for," I replied, rolling my eyes dramatically. "What's next? You're going to tell me you're the town's most eligible bachelor?"

"Only if you promise to return," he countered, his tone shifting, sincerity spilling into the playful banter. "I mean it, Jess. You can't keep avoiding what's here. We both know there's something between us."

The air thickened with unspoken words, the tension swirling like a summer storm. I could feel the pull of the past, the way our shared history weighed heavily upon us, yet the spark ignited a hope I had long buried. "And what exactly do you want from me?" I asked, heart racing, both exhilarated and terrified by the vulnerability that seeped into my voice.

"Honestly? I want to see you here, in this town, with me. I want to show you that what we had back then doesn't have to be the end. It can be a new beginning," he admitted, his gaze steady, unwavering.

The earnestness in his eyes drew me in, a beacon in the fog of uncertainty. The world around us faded into a blur as I wrestled with the implications of his words. Could I allow myself to be vulnerable again? Could I risk it all for a chance at something beautiful, something real?

"Clayton," I began, my voice shaky, caught between desire and fear. "I've spent so long building a life that feels secure, and the thought of risking it all—it terrifies me."

"Sometimes, what scares us the most is exactly what we need," he replied, taking a step closer, his presence grounding me. "What if we took it slow? Just let things unfold without the pressure of what happens next?"

The idea stirred something deep within me, a tantalizing possibility that whispered of hope. "So, what's your plan? Picnics by the creek? Late-night stargazing?" I asked, trying to inject humor into the gravity of the moment.

"Absolutely," he said, his smile wide. "And maybe a little of this ruggedly charming aspect you seem to enjoy so much."

"Let's not get ahead of ourselves," I quipped, but the smile on my face was genuine, the laughter lightening the weight I had been carrying.

As the sun slipped below the horizon, painting the sky in shades of indigo, I took a deep breath, feeling the tension slowly unravel. Maybe this crossroads wasn't about choosing one path over another but finding a way to merge them into something entirely new.

The evening air turned cooler as the last rays of sunlight slipped behind the horizon, draping Whispering Hills in a deep indigo blanket. I leaned against the fence, aware of the charged silence that hung between Clayton and me. My heart raced, caught in the current of his presence, as if we were suspended in time, both waiting for something to break the spell.

"You know," I started, breaking the stillness, "it feels like we're two characters in a really cliché romance novel. The brooding hero and the woman torn between two worlds." I couldn't help but smirk at the absurdity of it all, even as the truth of my words echoed in my chest.

Clayton laughed, the sound deep and genuine, a warmth that seeped into the chill of the evening. "Well, if this is a cliché, I'll gladly take the role of the hero. But I'd like to think there's a twist waiting to be revealed, something that sets us apart from the rest of the plot."

I tilted my head, a teasing glint in my eye. "So you think you're the plot twist? I'd need some convincing, because right now, it feels more like I'm the one standing on the precipice of disaster."

He stepped closer, his gaze intense, a storm brewing in those deep brown eyes. "You're not in danger, Jess. You're at the edge of an adventure. This isn't just about your past; it's about what you want moving forward. You can't keep running from it, or from me."

I felt a flutter of something—was it excitement or fear? Perhaps both. "I'm not running, Clayton. I'm simply... contemplating my options," I replied, trying to maintain a casual tone while my pulse quickened at his proximity.

"Contemplating how many coffee cups it takes to make a life decision?" he shot back, a playful smirk tugging at his lips. "You know, I don't think I'd need more than one if that decision involves us."

His confident banter was both charming and disarming, the perfect blend of humor and sincerity. But beneath the lighthearted façade lay an undercurrent of truth that left me breathless. "What if I don't know what 'us' even means?" I asked, my voice barely above a whisper. "What if this is just a moment, a flash in the pan?"

Clayton stepped even closer, and I could feel the warmth radiating from him, a comfort amidst the uncertainty. "Then let's take it one moment at a time. No pressure, no expectations. Just two people trying to figure out if they fit together in this crazy world."

His words wrapped around me like a soft embrace, coaxing out a smile despite the whirlwind in my chest. "Alright, Mr. Hero. Let's pretend this is a rom-com and see where it leads us. But if you start narrating my thoughts like a cheesy voiceover, I'm out."

"Deal," he chuckled, a mischievous glint in his eyes. "I promise not to narrate. Just be prepared for some spontaneous adventure."

As we stood there, the weight of the world seemed to lift, replaced by a lightness I hadn't felt in ages. Maybe this was the twist I needed, a chance to explore what lay beyond the well-trodden paths of my life.

A sudden rustle in the bushes nearby interrupted our moment, and my heart skipped a beat. "Did you hear that?" I asked, peering into the shadows.

"Probably just a raccoon looking for dinner," Clayton said, though his tone had shifted, a hint of alertness creeping in. "Or a very confused deer."

Before I could respond, a figure emerged from the trees—a tall man, dressed in dark clothing, his face partially obscured by a hood. My breath caught in my throat as I instinctively stepped closer to Clayton, who immediately positioned himself protectively in front of me.

"Who are you?" Clayton called out, his voice steady, though tension laced every word.

The stranger paused, his posture tense as if weighing his next move. "I'm looking for someone," he said, his voice low and gravelly, sending a shiver down my spine.

"Looking for who?" I asked, stepping out from behind Clayton, my curiosity getting the better of my instinct to flee. "You're not exactly in the right part of town for a friendly visit."

"I need to speak to Jessica," he replied, locking eyes with me. There was an intensity in his gaze that felt unsettling, like he held secrets I was not ready to confront.

I exchanged a quick glance with Clayton, who appeared torn between protecting me and demanding answers. "And why would you be looking for me?" I asked, trying to keep my voice steady despite the unease bubbling within.

The man took a cautious step forward. "It's about your father."

My heart raced at the mention of him. "My father? What do you know about my father?" I demanded, every protective instinct igniting within me.

"He's in trouble," the stranger said, and the gravity of his words hung in the air like a dense fog. "And you're the only one who can help."

"Help how?" I shot back, fear and anger coursing through me. I hadn't seen my father in years, and the thought of his involvement in something troubling filled me with dread.

The man hesitated, glancing back toward the trees, as if afraid of being overheard. "I can't discuss it here. Too many eyes. But trust me, you need to come with me. This isn't just about him; it's about you, too."

Clayton stepped forward, his expression shifting from protective to a mix of concern and determination. "She's not going anywhere with you until we know exactly who you are and what you're talking about."

"I'm a friend," the stranger replied, a flash of impatience crossing his face. "But time is running out. We don't have the luxury of discussing this in public."

I felt my heart hammering in my chest, torn between the safety of the known and the unsettling pull of the unknown. This was not the adventure I had envisioned with Clayton, and yet here it was—an unexpected twist in a story that was already filled with uncertainty.

"Jessica, we should get out of here," Clayton urged, his voice low but firm. "This doesn't feel right."

I hesitated, caught between the two men—one representing my past, the other my uncertain future. "Wait," I said, raising my hand. "If there's something going on with my father, I can't just ignore it. I need to know the truth."

The stranger's eyes flickered with a hint of relief, but Clayton's expression darkened, a protective instinct surging to the forefront. "You don't know what you're getting into," he warned, his voice laced with concern.

But I had already made my decision. I could feel the weight of the moment settle around me, thick with tension and uncertainty. "I need to hear him out. I can't turn my back on my father again."

Before I could second-guess myself, I stepped toward the stranger, the night air charged with an unsettling electricity. Clayton's hand shot out, gripping my wrist, his touch both grounding and infuriating. "Jess, think about this!"

"I am thinking," I shot back, determination flooding my veins. "If there's a chance to help him, I can't walk away."

As I prepared to follow the stranger deeper into the shadows, I caught a glimpse of Clayton's face, a mixture of fear and anger. But just as I turned away, the distant sound of sirens pierced the air, growing closer, and everything shifted once again.

"Run!" Clayton shouted, pulling me back just as the stranger took off into the trees, vanishing into the night like a ghost. The sirens wailed louder, echoing through the quiet streets, and a chill raced down my spine.

"What just happened?" I gasped, adrenaline coursing through me as we sprinted away from the encroaching chaos, unsure of what lay ahead or if I would ever be able to return to the quiet life I had so recently embraced.

Chapter 9: A Spark Between Us

The leaves crunched underfoot as we walked, a familiar sound that brought back memories of lazy afternoons spent wandering those very trails. The air was thick with the scent of pine and wildflowers, a heady perfume that evoked the kind of nostalgia that tugs at the heart. Each step felt like a delicate negotiation, a dance of avoidance and attraction that had become our new norm. Clayton and I hadn't shared this space in years, yet the contours of our old haunts felt like an extension of the bond we had once forged.

He walked beside me, his presence as palpable as the heat radiating from the sun. Every so often, I caught a glimpse of him from the corner of my eye, the way his dark hair fell across his forehead, the easy way he carried himself as if he belonged to the earth beneath our feet. I could see the boy I used to know, the one who made me laugh until my stomach hurt, but beneath that familiar façade, there was something more—a man who was determined to unravel me.

"Remember when we tried to climb that stupid rock?" he finally said, breaking the silence that hung between us like a fragile web.

"How could I forget?" I chuckled, the memory rushing back in vivid colors. "You insisted we could do it, and I ended up with mud in my hair for a week."

Clayton grinned, the kind of smile that could light up the gloomiest of days. "You were so determined to show off that you could keep up with me. I thought you might take my head off with your flailing."

"Flailing?" I gasped, pretending to be affronted. "I was merely trying to preserve my dignity! It's not my fault you have the grace of a mountain goat."

He laughed, the sound rich and warm, wrapping around us like a soft blanket. "Maybe I do. But you've grown. You have this whole... confidence about you now. I like it."

That compliment hung between us, thick and sweet, and my cheeks flushed, betraying the nervous flutter in my stomach. "Thanks, I guess. Boston's been good for me," I replied, choosing to divert the conversation. "I've had to get used to the whole city thing. You know, the skyline, the coffee shops that sell overpriced lattes..."

"And yet you're back here, in our little corner of the world," he interjected, a knowing look in his eyes. "What's pulling you back?"

It was as if he had peeled back a layer of my carefully constructed facade, exposing a truth I hadn't yet acknowledged myself. "Sometimes," I started, the words tumbling out with unexpected ease, "you realize how much you miss the simplicity of home. The rhythm of life here is... different. Calmer."

"Calm," he repeated, a hint of disbelief dancing in his voice. "That's one way to put it. It's more like it's in a constant state of hibernation."

"True, but at least the air is clean, and I can hear myself think."

He stepped a little closer, our shoulders brushing ever so slightly. "Is that what you want? To think?"

The challenge in his tone sent my heart racing. "It's not all I want," I said, daring to meet his gaze. "But it's definitely part of the equation."

The conversation was a precarious balance, like walking a tightrope stretched between two cliffs—one side, the safety of my life in Boston; the other, the alluring danger of what might lie ahead if I let myself be swept away by the current of my feelings.

We continued down the trail, the sun casting dappled shadows on the ground as the trees whispered secrets to one another. I could feel the warmth radiating from him, an intoxicating force that beckoned me closer. Just as I thought we might slip into comfortable banter once more, he halted, turning to face me fully.

"Can I ask you something?"

"Sure," I replied, bracing myself for the question that hung in the air like a heavy storm cloud.

"Why did you really come back?"

The sincerity in his voice made me hesitate. Here was a man who had known me inside and out, yet I felt like a puzzle missing too many pieces to ever be complete. "I came back to sort things out," I finally admitted. "To reconnect with who I used to be."

His brow furrowed slightly. "And who is that? The girl who climbed rocks and got muddy? Or the woman who's too busy for hometown drama?"

I opened my mouth to respond, but the truth was complex, winding through memories and emotions like a tangled vine. "Both, I suppose. But it's easier to keep the past buried than to face it."

"Is that what you're trying to do? Bury what's between us?"

The challenge in his eyes caught me off guard, and I took a step back, the distance feeling like a lifeline. "That's not fair, Clayton. I didn't ask for this."

"No one ever does," he said, his voice softening. "But here we are. The question is, what are we going to do about it?"

His words lingered in the air, thick with possibility and tension. I could feel my heart thudding against my ribcage, each beat a reminder that I was still very much alive, teetering on the edge of something dangerous and exhilarating. I opened my mouth to speak, to push back against the torrent of emotions threatening to overwhelm me, but the truth was, I didn't know what I wanted anymore.

The wind rustled the leaves above us, and for a moment, the world narrowed down to just the two of us. In that silence, I felt the weight of choices yet to be made and the dizzying allure of a path that could lead to both heartache and healing. My gaze locked onto his, and it was as if we were suspended in time, caught between past and future, between safety and the unknown.

The world around us faded, leaving only the palpable tension crackling between our gazes. I could see the questions swirling in Clayton's eyes, the same ones that had haunted me since I returned. Why had I come back? What was I hoping to find? Just as I opened my mouth to form a response, a sharp rustle in the underbrush startled us both, pulling us out of our standoff.

"Did you hear that?" I asked, instinctively taking a step closer to him.

"Probably just a squirrel," he replied, but his voice held an edge of amusement. "Or maybe it's the infamous 'Tennessee monster' looking for dinner."

I laughed, a sound that felt bright and freeing, cutting through the tension like a beam of sunlight. "Oh yes, because that's definitely what I want—a close encounter with a mythological creature while I'm trying to figure out my life."

"Hey, it's more interesting than the coffee shop scene in Boston," he teased, leaning slightly toward me as if to emphasize his point. "At least here, you can claim you faced danger. 'I once stood toe to toe with a wild beast!'"

I rolled my eyes, but the warmth blooming in my chest made it hard to feign annoyance. "You're ridiculous. I can already see the headlines: 'Girl Faces Fearsome Squirrel, Comes Out Victorious!'"

"Now that's a story worth telling," he shot back, his grin infectious. For a fleeting moment, the heaviness of our earlier conversation dissipated, and laughter danced between us, a thread of connection woven through our banter.

But as the laughter faded, the underlying questions loomed larger. I shifted, the gravel crunching beneath my feet, suddenly acutely aware of the sun's heat and the sweat trickling down my spine.

"What if I don't want to fight off squirrels, Clayton? What if I just want to escape all of this?" I gestured vaguely, hoping he understood that I was referring to more than just the trees and the winding path.

"You're running away, then?" His voice softened, the playfulness giving way to something more serious.

"I'm trying to figure out what I want. And the truth is, being back here… it's complicated."

His eyes narrowed slightly, as if he were attempting to read between the lines. "Complicated can be good or bad, you know. You can't avoid it forever."

"Wow, you sound like my therapist." I couldn't help but smirk, but the truth was, I had been grappling with my feelings since I arrived. "Are you here to analyze me, or is that just a side gig you've picked up?"

"Hey, I'm a lawyer, not a psychologist," he retorted, his tone light but his gaze steady. "Though I'm more than willing to take a stab at it if you want."

"Don't tempt me. I might just take you up on that," I replied, my heart racing at the thought.

"Good luck. I'm not exactly trained for emotional analysis." He chuckled, shaking his head. "But I'm pretty good at listening. So, spill it."

The challenge hung in the air, and I hesitated, caught between the urge to confide and the instinct to protect my heart. "I don't know where to start," I finally admitted, my voice barely above a whisper.

"Start with what's bothering you. You can't just shrug it off as 'complicated' forever."

The sincerity in his voice coaxed me to push past the barriers I'd built. "Alright, here goes nothing. I thought coming back would help me feel… settled. But it's just reminded me of everything I left behind."

"Like what?" he asked, his gaze never wavering.

"Like the person I used to be—the carefree girl who didn't worry about the future or what everyone thought of her. I've traded that in for a life filled with expectations."

"You can be both, you know," he said gently. "You don't have to choose."

The kindness in his tone threatened to unravel me further. "And what if I don't know how to balance them? What if I end up disappointing everyone?"

"Then you find a way to redefine what those expectations are," he replied, his voice steady. "You're not meant to be boxed in, Chloe."

"Redefine, huh?" I couldn't help but smile at his conviction. "You make it sound so easy."

"Nothing worthwhile is easy. Just look at us."

His expression shifted, an intensity returning to his gaze that made my heart race anew. "Us? What exactly does that mean?"

"Exactly what it sounds like. We're standing here, two people tangled in the past, trying to figure out the future."

I pondered that for a moment, feeling the weight of his words settle in my chest. "Is that what we are? Tangled?"

"Seems fitting, don't you think? We're stuck in this dance, like we never quite left the floor."

With a playful flick of my hair over my shoulder, I quipped, "Just don't step on my toes."

His laughter rang out, a melodic sound that wrapped around us like the warm Tennessee breeze. "Deal. But it's only fair if you promise not to trip me."

"Tripping you would be the highlight of my day," I said, the words slipping out before I could catch them.

The air shifted again, the levity falling away as we regarded each other, the silence stretching like the horizon. I could feel the tension building again, and it felt thrilling and terrifying all at once. "You know, I never thought I'd see you again like this," he admitted, his voice low. "Not after... everything."

"Everything," I echoed, my heart pounding at the unspoken memories that lingered just beneath the surface. "What happened between us is still a lot to unpack."

"We could start now."

His challenge hung in the air, and as I searched his face, I realized that our past was a tapestry of both joy and heartache. It was a woven pattern I was desperate to explore, even as it made me vulnerable. "What if I don't like what I find?"

"Then we figure it out together."

In that moment, everything felt infinitely possible, and for the first time since returning, I felt the edges of my uncertainty begin to soften. Perhaps it was the promise of understanding—or maybe it was just the undeniable spark between us—but suddenly, I could see a path ahead, illuminated by the potential of what could be. I took a breath, ready to step into the unknown, ready to embrace whatever twists and turns awaited us in this tangled dance of ours.

As the weight of his words hung between us, I found myself at a crossroads, teetering on the brink of something beautifully terrifying. Clayton's eyes, dark and deep, seemed to beckon me to leap, to abandon my reservations and plunge headfirst into the murky waters of our shared history. Yet, every fiber of my being whispered caution, reminding me of the life I had built so far—a life where the echoes of a past I couldn't quite escape kept rattling around in my mind like loose change in a pocket.

"What if I just want to walk away?" I ventured, surprising myself with the audacity of my own question.

"Then I guess you'll miss out on the best adventure of your life," he replied, a teasing smile playing at the corners of his lips. But beneath that lighthearted tone was a layer of sincerity that made my heart skip a beat.

"Adventure?" I scoffed, my brows arching in disbelief. "This feels more like an emotional minefield."

"True, but isn't that what life is? A series of choices between safety and risk? If you're only ever safe, you miss out on the incredible parts."

I chewed on his words, feeling the prick of truth laced within. He was right, of course. Life in Boston had been predictably safe but devoid of any real thrill. The routine had settled around me like a thick fog, blurring the edges of my dreams. But here, surrounded by the towering trees and the promise of adventure, I felt that fog beginning to lift, revealing the vibrant colors of possibility.

"What if I decide to take that risk?" I asked, my voice wavering slightly as I sought clarity in my swirling thoughts.

"Then we'll make a plan," he said, his expression suddenly serious. "We can't force anything, but we can explore what this—whatever this is—means for both of us."

The sincerity in his gaze felt like a balm to my racing heart. "Explore," I repeated, allowing the word to settle in. "That sounds dangerously vague."

"Isn't that what makes it exciting?" he countered, his tone lightening again. "Besides, if things get too wild, I'll carry the emotional weight while you throw things at me."

I couldn't help but laugh, the tension in my shoulders easing ever so slightly. "Now there's a tempting offer. Just so you know, I've got a mean aim."

"Good to know. I'll take my chances," he replied, the playful twinkle in his eye igniting a spark of hope within me.

We resumed our walk, the trail winding ahead like a ribbon, offering glimpses of the landscape beyond—rolling hills that cradled the sky, dotted with bursts of wildflowers swaying lazily in the breeze. It was a landscape that felt like a memory, yet vibrant enough to tease new beginnings.

"Tell me about Boston," he prompted, glancing sideways at me. "What's it like?"

"It's... bustling," I started, gathering my thoughts. "Everyone's always in a rush. You can walk down the street and feel like a stranger in your own skin. It's lonely, even in a crowd."

He nodded, a look of understanding washing over his features. "That sounds exhausting."

"It is. It's like I'm always trying to keep up with a version of myself that doesn't really exist. Sometimes I wish I could just hit pause."

"And what would you do with that pause?"

I hesitated, considering the question deeply. "I'd probably go back to places like this, to moments that remind me of who I am beneath all the expectations."

"Then why not stay here?" he suggested, the intensity in his gaze returning. "Why not take that leap?"

"Because I don't know what I'd find. Maybe I'd find someone who used to be me but doesn't fit anymore."

"Or maybe you'd find a version of yourself that you forgot existed," he replied, his voice a gentle caress that wrapped around my heart.

Just then, the path opened up to a clearing, revealing a stunning view of the valley below, bathed in the golden hues of the setting sun. I felt the breath catch in my throat as the beauty enveloped us like a warm embrace. "Wow," I whispered, taking a moment to drink it all in.

Clayton stepped closer, his presence a steady anchor as I gazed out at the breathtaking scene. "It's incredible, isn't it?"

I nodded, speechless, as the vibrant colors danced across the sky. "I had forgotten what beauty felt like," I finally murmured, the emotion swelling within me.

"And that's just the beginning," he said softly, his eyes locked onto mine, deep and earnest.

In that moment, the gravity of our connection surged like an electric current, sending shivers down my spine. But before I could respond, a rustle in the underbrush shattered the tranquil atmosphere. My heart raced as a figure emerged from the shadows—a stranger, tall and broad-shouldered, with an expression I couldn't quite decipher.

"Hey! What are you two doing up here?" he called, his voice gruff yet curious, shattering the intimate moment we had created.

I glanced at Clayton, whose expression shifted to one of guarded curiosity. "Just enjoying the view," he replied, maintaining a relaxed demeanor.

The stranger approached us, his eyes darting between us with an unsettling intensity. "You two shouldn't be out here alone. It's not safe."

My pulse quickened, tension coiling in the air as I exchanged a worried glance with Clayton. "Safe? What do you mean?"

"Just that things have been... strange in these woods lately," the man said, crossing his arms over his chest, his gaze shifting toward the tree line behind him. "You'd be surprised what can happen when the sun goes down."

"What are you talking about?" I pressed, the unease creeping up my spine.

He leaned in closer, lowering his voice. "There are stories, rumors. Some say people have gone missing."

Clayton stepped forward, his protective instincts kicking in. "We appreciate your concern, but we can handle ourselves."

The stranger smirked, the expression unsettling. "You'd think that, wouldn't you? Just remember, sometimes the most dangerous things hide in plain sight."

As his words lingered in the air, a shiver ran down my spine, and I turned to Clayton, who wore a grim expression that spoke volumes. This was no longer just a simple hike or a chance to rekindle old flames. There was a weight to the atmosphere that hinted at unseen dangers lurking just beyond the trees.

"Maybe we should head back," I suggested, my voice trembling slightly as I tried to gauge the stranger's intentions.

Clayton's hand found mine, the warmth grounding me amidst the uncertainty. "Yeah, let's not push our luck," he said, giving the stranger one last wary glance.

But just as we turned to retrace our steps, the sound of snapping twigs echoed behind us, sending my heart racing. The trees trembled slightly, and before I could process what was happening, a low growl reverberated through the air, chilling me to the bone.

"Run!" Clayton shouted, pulling me along as adrenaline surged through my veins.

The laughter of a distant memory was drowned out by the sound of something lurking just beyond the trees, and as we sprinted down the path, I realized that the adventure we had contemplated had just taken a dark turn—one that promised no easy answers and far more danger than I had ever imagined.

Chapter 10: Falling into the Past

The sun dipped low, casting long shadows that stretched across the dusty road as I slid into the saddle. The familiar creak of the leather against my legs felt like an embrace from a past I had tried to outrun. Clayton was next to me, his presence a mix of nostalgia and an unsettling warmth that sent shivers down my spine. He mounted his horse with a fluid grace that belied the years since I'd last seen him. His blue eyes sparkled with mischief, reminding me of summer days filled with laughter and secrets shared under the sprawling oaks.

As we set off down the winding path, the air thick with the sweet scent of wildflowers, I couldn't help but steal glances at him. His hair, darker now, framed his face in a way that made my heart race as if we were teenagers again, full of reckless dreams and whispered promises. "You still ride like a pro," he said, a teasing lilt in his voice that made me smile, even as my insides twisted in uncertainty.

"You think I could forget how to ride in a few years?" I shot back, matching his playful tone. But I felt the weight of my reality creeping in, the questions that had gnawed at me since I returned home. Did I truly belong in this life again, or was I just a visitor in my own memories?

We rode along the banks of the creek, the water glinting like diamonds in the fading light. I could hear the distant chatter of cicadas, their song a rhythmic reminder of the summer that seemed endless, filled with late-night bonfires and starlit confessions. It was a lullaby of the past, but it also hinted at something more—a sense of belonging I hadn't realized I craved until now.

"Do you ever think about those nights by the fire?" Clayton asked suddenly, pulling me from my reverie. His gaze was intense, holding a sincerity that caught me off guard.

"All the time," I replied, my voice barely above a whisper. "But I thought they were just... memories." I shifted uncomfortably, the heat rising in my cheeks as I recalled the secrets we had shared—the dreams we had painted together, the futures we had imagined. "And what about you? Do you still dream?"

He smiled, a slow, genuine curve of his lips that sent a thrill through me. "You mean the ones where I'm saving the world? Yeah, those haven't changed." He laughed, a rich sound that echoed in the quiet of the evening. But there was an undertone to his humor, a flicker of something deeper. "Honestly, though, I've been thinking a lot about the future. It's hard not to, especially with you back in town."

I felt the weight of his words, heavy with the implications I dared not voice. What did that future look like for him? For us? The memories tugged at me—our laughter, our shared dreams, but also the reasons I had left. I had promised myself I wouldn't get lost in the past again. Yet, every moment with him felt like stepping into a dance I hadn't known I missed.

We paused on a rise, overlooking the vast expanse of the ranch. The sun painted the sky in hues of orange and pink, a breathtaking canvas that seemed to celebrate our reunion. Clayton's presence beside me felt so right, yet so wrong. "You know," he said, his voice thoughtful, "this place holds a lot of memories for me too. I never thought I'd see it with you again. It's... different now."

"Different good or different bad?" I asked, turning to him, my heart pounding.

"Complicated," he replied, running a hand through his hair, the gesture so familiar and yet laden with new meanings. "But I think we can figure it out."

His words lingered in the air between us, a fragile promise that held the weight of our shared history. The honesty in his gaze sent warmth flooding through me, igniting sparks of hope I had long buried. I wanted to reach out, to bridge the distance that felt like a chasm opening up between us. "What if we don't have to figure it out right away?" I suggested, trying to keep my voice light even as the tension crackled like static in the air. "What if we just... enjoy being here now?"

He grinned, a genuine, boyish smile that made my heart skip. "Now you're talking my language, Lana."

As we continued our ride, the air between us thickened with unspoken words. The landscape shifted, revealing the rugged beauty of the countryside that had framed our youth—fields of golden wheat swaying in the gentle breeze, their rustling a familiar symphony of the past. But underneath the comfort of the scenery lay the complexity of the present, of the choices we faced.

It was only when we reached the old oak tree, the one where we had carved our initials years ago, that the weight of our silence became palpable. The tree stood tall, its gnarled branches a testament to the passage of time, just as we were. I dismounted, feeling an inexplicable pull toward it, and ran my fingers over the bark, tracing the initials we had etched in a moment of innocent defiance.

"Do you remember this?" I asked, glancing up at him.

"How could I forget?" he replied, stepping closer. "You insisted we should carve it high enough that nobody could see."

I laughed, the sound bright and free, a stark contrast to the swirling thoughts in my head. "And you almost dropped the knife in the process!"

His eyes sparkled with mischief, a reflection of our shared memories, but there was something deeper brewing. "We were so young and fearless."

"Or foolish," I countered lightly, but the truth of it hung heavy between us. Those carefree days felt like a different lifetime, and yet here we stood, like echoes of that past, standing on the precipice of a future that felt both terrifying and exhilarating.

Clayton took a step closer, his voice dropping to a near whisper. "Do you ever think about what could have been if things were different?"

The question hung in the air, laden with the weight of choices and what-ifs, and I felt the ground shift beneath me. I wanted to scream my answer, to fling open the door to a world where our paths had never diverged. But instead, I simply nodded, feeling the pulse of time echoing in my chest.

The sun dipped beneath the horizon, painting the sky in hues of purple and gold as we lingered beneath the oak tree, caught in the gravity of our shared past. Clayton's gaze held mine, the weight of unsaid words pressing down like the humidity in the air. The laughter of our youth seemed to drift around us, an echo that felt both comforting and bittersweet. I wondered if he could sense my hesitation, the internal battle I waged between what was familiar and what felt utterly foreign now.

"What if I told you I've got a surprise?" he said, breaking the thick silence that had settled like dust. The glint in his eye was playful, mischievous, and it tugged at something deep within me.

"A surprise?" I arched an eyebrow, a smile teasing my lips. "Are you taking me to a secret hideout? An abandoned amusement park where we can relive our glory days?"

His laugh rang out, a rich sound that danced across the twilight. "Close, but no. You'll have to follow me to find out. I promise you won't regret it."

Curiosity flared, igniting a spark of adventure in me. I was drawn to the idea of reclaiming those lost moments, however fleeting. "All right, lead the way, Mr. Mysterious."

He mounted his horse, and with a swift motion, gestured for me to do the same. I climbed back into the saddle, feeling the familiar rhythm of the horse beneath me as we trotted along the path that twisted through the fields. The world seemed to blur around us, the evening air thick with the scent of earth and grass, the sky stretching endlessly above.

As we rode, Clayton regaled me with stories of the ranch and the quirky characters that had come and gone, his voice weaving a tapestry of laughter and nostalgia. I felt the walls I had built around my heart begin to crumble, each tale a gentle reminder of the bond we had once shared. The cadence of his words wrapped around me, warming me against the chill of doubt that lurked at the edges of my mind.

Finally, we arrived at a clearing, a hidden nook that I had all but forgotten. In the center stood a weathered wooden shed, its paint peeling and worn, but still charming in a way that made me smile. "This is it," he announced, dismounting with a flourish. "Welcome to my secret fortress."

I laughed, shaking my head. "A fortress? More like a glorified tool shed."

"Exactly!" he replied, grinning as he pushed open the creaky door, revealing a treasure trove of memories. Inside, old farming equipment mingled with forgotten toys—rusty bicycles, a deflated soccer ball, and even a dusty old radio that looked as if it had once held the power to bring us joy on long summer nights. "It's a bit of a mess, but it's ours."

I stepped inside, overwhelmed by a flood of emotions. "I can't believe you kept all this."

"Of course! I was hoping we could fix it up together one day," he said, his tone shifting, a hint of seriousness creeping in. "I thought it might be nice to have a place to hang out, to reminisce. Maybe even make some new memories?"

The air thickened with the weight of his implication, and I felt my heart race. This place was a relic of our youth, a canvas waiting for the strokes of our renewed friendship—or something more. "You really want to do this?" I asked, searching his face for clarity.

"Why not?" He stepped closer, his presence a comforting warmth that enveloped me. "We both know there's something here worth exploring. Something that never quite finished."

I swallowed hard, the weight of his words sinking in. The truth hung between us, suspended in the air, and I felt both exhilarated and terrified. "But what if we open that door and find it's too late?"

"Then we deal with it together," he replied, his voice steady, laced with a confidence I found grounding. "I've missed you, Lana. The real you. Not the one who ran away but the one who dared to dream big."

That statement struck a chord, reverberating through the confines of my heart. I had been running, fleeing not just the memories but also the person I once was. The girl who believed in fairytales and happy endings. "What if those dreams are no longer possible?"

"Then we create new ones," he said simply, his gaze unwavering. "Together."

His words hung in the air, charged with a promise that both thrilled and terrified me. I took a step back, momentarily overwhelmed. "You make it sound so easy."

"Life isn't easy, Lana," he countered, his voice dropping to a whisper, as if he were revealing a secret meant only for us. "But it's worth the risk if you're with the right person."

With a deep breath, I glanced around the shed, taking in the remnants of our past. Memories flickered in the shadows like fireflies, and I felt the walls I had constructed around my heart begin to crumble, brick by brick. "Fine. Let's see what we can do with this fortress of yours."

His eyes lit up, a spark of excitement igniting between us as he clapped his hands together. "That's the spirit! First things first, we need some paint and tools. And a little elbow grease."

"And a plan," I added, finding my own enthusiasm bubbling up. "We can't just dive in without some semblance of order."

"Is that the engineer in you talking?" he teased, nudging my shoulder.

"Possibly," I shot back, feeling a warmth spreading through me. "And just so you know, I'm the reigning champion of fort construction."

"Oh really?" He raised an eyebrow, amusement dancing in his eyes. "I'm going to hold you to that."

We spent the rest of the evening brainstorming ideas, tossing around suggestions, and laughing until our sides hurt. The atmosphere crackled with energy, the past melding seamlessly with the present, and I felt the foundations of my apprehension starting to give way. In that little shed, surrounded by the echoes of our childhood, I realized that I wasn't just reclaiming memories; I was building a bridge back to the person I had once been—and perhaps even something more.

As night descended, we stepped outside, the stars twinkling above like a million tiny promises. The moon cast a silver glow over the fields, illuminating the path ahead, and for the first time in what felt like an eternity, I dared to hope.

We spent the next few days diving into the old shed like two kids on a summer break, fueled by nostalgia and an undeniable chemistry that sparked with every shared smile. Each evening, we returned, armed with paintbrushes and laughter, transforming the dusty space into a vibrant reflection of our youthful imaginations. I found joy in the small things—a splash of color here, a light fixture there—and Clayton's playful banter kept me anchored, reminding me that this was no mere project; it was a revival of everything we had once cherished.

One afternoon, I sat cross-legged on the floor, trying to untangle a string of fairy lights. "These look like they survived the Great

Collapse of '08," I remarked, wrestling with the stubborn cords. "I think the last time we used them, we were trying to outshine the stars."

Clayton leaned against the wall, arms crossed, a smirk playing on his lips. "We definitely failed at that. But if I remember correctly, we had fun trying."

"Fun? I'd say we were more like cosmic disasters," I shot back, finally managing to free the lights. "But there was a certain charm in our chaotic genius."

"Chaotic genius? Is that what we're calling it now?" His eyes twinkled with amusement, and I could feel the warm pull between us growing stronger with each passing day.

As we worked, the conversation flowed easily, the comfortable rhythm between us replacing the tension that had once filled the air. Yet beneath the surface, I felt the weight of the unspoken—the questions I hadn't dared to voice, lingering like shadows in the corners of my mind.

"Do you think people can change?" I asked suddenly, breaking the easy banter. The question hung there, heavy and unexpected, and I held my breath, waiting for his response.

He pushed off the wall, striding over to sit beside me. "Absolutely. People can grow, adapt, and redefine who they are. It's one of the few constants in life." He met my gaze, his expression earnest. "But it's not easy. And sometimes it takes a catalyst to make it happen."

"And what about the past?" I pressed, feeling my heart race. "Does it ever really go away?"

Clayton paused, considering his words carefully. "The past is like a tattoo—it might fade, but it never truly disappears. It shapes us, for better or worse. The key is how you choose to carry it."

"Such wisdom for a guy who spent most of his youth covered in dirt and grease," I teased, trying to lighten the mood.

"Don't underestimate the wisdom that comes from working with your hands," he retorted, a smile dancing in his eyes. "That's how you learn to build something new."

His words resonated within me, stirring a part I had buried for far too long. Perhaps I could learn to build something new, with him. The idea was intoxicating, but so was the fear of losing everything again. Just as I was about to voice my uncertainty, the door creaked open, interrupting our moment.

"Hey, you two!" My grandmother's voice cut through the air like a playful knife, and she stepped into the shed, her eyes sparkling with mischief. "I brought lemonade! Thought you could use a break."

"Perfect timing, Grandma," I said, grateful for the distraction. I shot Clayton a knowing look, and he chuckled softly, the tension easing for the moment.

As we sipped our lemonade, my grandmother's presence filled the space with warmth. She was the kind of person who made every gathering feel special, and the comfort of her company eased my earlier worries. "I was just telling Lana that the two of you should consider organizing a community event," she suggested, her eyes sparkling with excitement. "Something to bring everyone together. A good old-fashioned barn dance, perhaps?"

Clayton's face lit up at the idea. "That could be fun! We could use the old barn at my family's place. It's been ages since there's been a good party around here."

I hesitated, picturing the daunting task of wrangling the community together. "But what if no one shows up?"

"Then we'll just have to make it the best darn party for ourselves," Clayton said, his enthusiasm contagious. "Think of the stories we could create."

I found myself smiling despite the lingering apprehension. "Alright, let's do it. But only if we can make it as chaotic as our childhood parties."

With laughter ringing in the air, we began planning. My grandmother made her way back to the house, leaving us to brainstorm ideas. "What if we set up games and a bonfire?" Clayton suggested, his excitement palpable. "And maybe some live music?"

"Sure, if you can convince anyone to play," I replied, fighting to keep my own enthusiasm in check. "This isn't exactly Nashville."

"Challenge accepted," he grinned, determination shining in his eyes. "We'll make this happen, Lana. I can feel it."

The next few days flew by as we worked together to prepare for the event. With each passing moment, the lines between friendship and something deeper began to blur. There were stolen glances, lingering touches, and shared laughter that echoed with unspoken promises. Yet, the shadows of my past loomed large, whispering doubts that threatened to undermine everything we were building.

On the evening before the dance, I found myself standing in front of the mirror, contemplating the woman staring back at me. My heart raced, and I felt a twinge of insecurity twist in my gut. What if Clayton's interest was merely a passing whim, a response to the thrill of rekindling a childhood bond?

Just as I was about to drown in my swirling thoughts, there was a knock at the door. I opened it to find Clayton, his expression serious but soft. "Hey, can I come in?"

"Sure," I replied, stepping aside to let him enter. He seemed different, an energy crackling around him that made the air feel electric.

"I wanted to talk," he said, his voice steady. "About tomorrow. And us."

The simple statement sent my heart into overdrive. "Us?" I echoed, my voice barely above a whisper.

He took a step closer, the weight of his gaze making my breath hitch. "Yeah. I know we're having fun with the dance and everything, but I don't want to pretend that this isn't something more."

My heart raced as I searched his expression, desperately hoping for reassurance. "But what if this is just nostalgia?"

"Or maybe it's something new," he replied, stepping even closer, the tension between us crackling like static electricity. "I've missed you, Lana. More than I realized."

I opened my mouth to respond, but the words caught in my throat. Just then, a loud crash echoed from outside, a sound so jarring it shattered the moment.

"What was that?" I asked, my heart racing as I rushed to the window. Outside, I saw a figure darting through the trees, a shadow slipping away like a ghost into the night.

"Lana, wait!" Clayton called, but I was already moving, driven by an instinct that pulled me toward the unknown.

"What was that?" I whispered, feeling an unsettling chill race down my spine.

"I don't know, but we should check it out," he said, urgency lacing his voice.

Together, we stepped into the night, the stars above dimmed by an uneasy sense of foreboding. The air felt thick with tension, and as we moved cautiously toward the edge of the trees, I couldn't shake the feeling that something was lurking just beyond our reach—something that would force us to confront the past, and maybe even change everything we had begun to rebuild.

Chapter 11: Beneath the Stars

Riding with Clayton felt like slipping into a memory, but it wasn't the same. We weren't the same people we'd been years ago, and the unspoken tension between us only grew as we navigated the undulating landscape of open fields. The air was crisp, whispering secrets of autumn as we moved beneath a sky sprinkled with stars so bright they seemed to pulse with life. The vast expanse overhead reminded me of a canvas splattered with diamonds, a backdrop for a story yet to be told. We stopped at the old oak tree where we'd spent so many summers, its gnarled branches reaching out like the arms of a long-lost friend, welcoming us back to a time of laughter and innocence.

For the first time, the silence between us felt full—charged with everything we weren't saying. The familiar scent of earth and grass surrounded us, mingling with the sweet, fading perfume of wildflowers. It was intoxicating, both a comfort and a reminder of all that had come between us. Clayton shifted in his saddle, his presence an anchor in the swirling sea of my thoughts. He turned to me, his eyes dark and serious, carrying the weight of unspoken history. "Why did you leave, Lana?" he asked, his voice low and careful, as if the question could shatter the fragile moment.

I swallowed hard, feeling the rawness of the past tightening around my throat like a noose. The truth was there, waiting to spill out, but I hesitated, torn between the desire to explain and the fear of reopening old wounds. The memories flooded my mind—each one a ripple in the still water of my heart, a reminder of the choices we made. I looked into his eyes, searching for the boy I once knew, the one who had shared secrets beneath this very tree, but all I saw was a man shaped by time and experience, just as I had been.

"I left because..." I began, but the words faltered on my lips. What could I say? That the world felt too small for the dreams I had? That the weight of expectations had driven me away like a bird needing to stretch its wings? I glanced around, as if the trees might offer a reprieve, a way out of this conversation. But the truth was relentless, gnawing at my insides, demanding to be spoken. "I needed to find myself. To see what else was out there."

His brow furrowed, and for a moment, the light of the stars dimmed, shadowed by the reality of our lives. "But did you ever find what you were looking for?" His question hung heavy in the air, laden with a bitterness that made my heart ache. It was as if the universe had conspired to keep us apart, to build walls of regret and unfulfilled promises between us.

"Some days, yes. Other days, it feels like I'm still wandering." I met his gaze, and in that instant, we were no longer two separate souls but a shared history, a tapestry of moments woven together by laughter, tears, and unspoken love. "I thought it was what I needed. To escape, to discover. But the truth is, leaving also meant leaving behind the people I cared about."

A silence settled between us, thick and palpable, as we both leaned into the gravity of that truth. The world felt distant, the sounds of the night fading into a soft hum as if nature itself was holding its breath. I couldn't shake the feeling that this moment was both a beginning and an end—an intersection where our paths could either collide or diverge forever.

"I had no idea you felt that way." His voice broke the stillness, laced with a hint of vulnerability. "I thought you were just...gone. Like a candle snuffed out."

"I didn't want to hurt you," I replied, the sincerity in my voice almost surprising me. "It felt like the only way to figure things out, to stop being who everyone expected me to be." I took a breath, feeling the air thicken with the weight of my confession. "But I never stopped thinking about you, about us."

He shifted closer, the warmth of his body igniting a spark of courage within me. "You were always my North Star, Lana. I could never forget that." There was a vulnerability in his words, a rawness that sent a thrill coursing through my veins. It felt like standing on the edge of a cliff, the world spread out beneath us, waiting to see if we would take that leap together.

"What do we do now?" I asked, my voice barely above a whisper. The question hung between us like the promise of dawn, full of potential and yet shrouded in uncertainty. The night sky felt infinite, a reminder that the universe held more possibilities than we could fathom.

"I guess we figure it out," he said, a slow smile creeping onto his face. The corners of his mouth turned up in a way that felt like the sun breaking through clouds after a long storm. "One step at a time."

And just like that, the weight of the past began to lift, replaced by the tentative hope of what could be. The night enveloped us in its embrace, a promise of new beginnings mingling with the remnants of old memories. As we stood beneath the stars, I realized that maybe, just maybe, the path ahead didn't have to be paved with regrets. Perhaps it could be forged anew, with the same passion and desire that once had brought us together, and a chance to rediscover the love that had never truly faded.

The air crackled with unspoken emotions, and I could feel the pull of his gaze like a magnet, urging me to reveal the secrets buried deep within my heart. The old oak, with its sprawling limbs and thick trunk, had borne witness to our youthful promises and the whispered dreams that had seemed so vital back then. I could almost hear the echoes of laughter mingling with the rustling leaves, a gentle reminder of what once was.

"Why did you leave, Lana?" Clayton's voice lingered in the air, echoing with a weight that settled heavily on my shoulders. There was a tenderness to his tone, yet it cut through the evening like a knife, sharp and precise. I felt the familiar knot tighten in my stomach, a reminder of the hurt that had driven us apart. The crickets chirped softly, punctuating the stillness, their rhythm a soothing backdrop to our quiet desperation.

"I left because I was afraid," I admitted, the words spilling out before I could rein them in. "Afraid of what was expected of me, of being trapped in a life I hadn't chosen. I thought I could escape it all." My voice wavered, the admission feeling both freeing and painfully raw. I watched as a flicker of understanding crossed his face, the corners of his mouth turning down in an expression I couldn't quite place.

"But running away doesn't change who you are, does it?" he countered gently, his eyes holding mine with an intensity that made my heart race. "You can't outrun yourself."

"Believe me, I tried," I replied, a hint of bitterness creeping into my tone. The honesty in our exchange felt exhilarating and terrifying all at once. "Every city, every new job—it was like trying to patch a hole in a dam with bubblegum. No matter where I went, the water still rushed in."

He chuckled softly, the sound rich and warm, breaking the tension between us. "So, you're saying you're a bubblegum engineer now?" The smile on his face, combined with that playful glimmer in his eyes, pulled me in. There was the Clayton I remembered, the one who could lighten the heaviest of moments with a single quip.

"Bubblegum engineer extraordinaire, actually. I've perfected the art of distraction," I replied, meeting his gaze with a smirk. "But it never lasted. I'd sit in cafes in cities where no one knew my name, and it always felt...empty. Like I was going through the motions without ever really living."

"Why didn't you tell me?" He leaned closer, his voice dropping to a conspiratorial whisper. "We could have figured it out together."

The sincerity of his question struck a chord deep within me, and the lump in my throat grew larger. "You were so sure of yourself back then, Clayton. You had dreams and ambitions, and I was just...lost." The weight of those words hung between us, a reminder of how deeply I had underestimated my own worth. "I thought I'd be dragging you down."

"Lana, you could never drag me down," he said, his expression softening. "You were my anchor. Without you, I was adrift."

His admission washed over me like a balm, soothing the old wounds that still throbbed beneath the surface. We stood there in the warm glow of the stars, two lost souls rediscovering the paths we had once walked together, yet unsure of where those paths might lead now. I could feel the electricity of the moment wrapping around us like a cocoon, pulling me closer to him.

"Look at us," I said, a note of disbelief creeping into my voice. "Standing beneath the stars, digging up old graves of regrets. I half-expect a ghost to pop out and join the conversation."

"Maybe it's the ghosts of our past trying to remind us we're still alive," he joked, but there was a depth to his words that resonated in my chest. "Or maybe it's just a bad horror movie waiting to happen."

Laughter bubbled up between us, a delightful distraction from the gravity of our conversation. It felt good, almost freeing, as if the barriers we had built around ourselves were starting to crumble. But beneath the humor, the tension lingered like an uninvited guest. I could sense the invisible line between us, drawn by the scars of our shared history, each one a testament to the complexity of love and loss.

"So, what now?" I asked, my voice suddenly serious, the laughter fading like the last remnants of daylight. "Do we pretend this moment doesn't exist and go back to our lives, or do we dare to explore what's left between us?"

He paused, the moonlight illuminating his features, casting shadows across his face in a way that made him look both thoughtful and impossibly handsome. "I don't want to pretend anymore, Lana. I want to know if there's still a spark. If we can rebuild what we had."

My heart raced at his words, a flicker of hope igniting within me. "Rebuild?" I repeated, the concept feeling as daunting as it was exhilarating. "That sounds a bit like giving a tornado a new address."

He chuckled, the sound rich and familiar, easing some of the tension that had settled in my chest. "Maybe, but sometimes tornadoes bring change. Maybe this is our chance to create something new."

I bit my lip, the idea swirling around in my mind like a thousand fireflies dancing in the darkness. "What if it's not as simple as that? What if we try and it just...falls apart again?"

"Then we'll be right back where we started," he said with a shrug, a playful glimmer in his eyes. "But at least we'll know we tried. We owe it to ourselves to find out."

The sincerity in his voice resonated within me, nudging me toward a decision. Maybe the universe had brought us back to this place for a reason, a chance to rewrite the script we'd once lived by. I could almost feel the weight of the stars above us, shimmering with the promise of new beginnings, and for the first time in a long while, I dared to believe in possibilities.

"Okay," I said, my heart pounding with a mix of excitement and trepidation. "Let's see what happens. Let's explore this tornado of ours."

Clayton's smile widened, and as he reached for my hand, the warmth of his touch ignited something within me—something I thought I had lost forever. It felt like stepping back into a dream, a leap of faith into the unknown, and the thrill of that uncertainty sent shivers down my spine. Beneath the vast canopy of stars, we stood on the precipice of a new adventure, ready to discover the twists and turns that awaited us on the journey ahead.

The moment hung between us, thick with the unsaid, a delicate balance of vulnerability and tension. I could feel the warmth radiating from Clayton, a comfort amidst the swirling confusion in my mind. His presence was both familiar and new, like wearing an old favorite sweater that suddenly feels too tight. The stars twinkled above us, a backdrop to our unspooling dialogue, their light a reminder of the paths we once traversed and the ones we had yet to explore.

"I left because I thought it was the right thing to do," I finally admitted, my voice barely above a whisper. "It felt like I was standing at the edge of a cliff, and I had to jump. But the ground I landed on? It was shaky." I glanced away, my heart aching at the honesty that had surfaced. "I thought I'd find something better out there. Instead, I found only echoes of what I'd lost."

"Maybe what you lost wasn't meant to be found," he countered, a softness in his tone that made the ache in my chest deepen. "But that doesn't mean it isn't worth pursuing again."

The gravity of his words resonated with me, tugging at the strings of hope that had been carefully tucked away. "And what if we're just repeating mistakes?" I shot back, half in jest and half in fear. "What if we dig up all those old skeletons and find out they still have teeth?"

His laughter rang out, bright and unguarded. "Well, I've always had a thing for archaeology. Besides, it's better to have skeletons than ghosts, right?" He leaned closer, mischief dancing in his eyes. "At least we can poke fun at the skeletons."

I couldn't help but chuckle, feeling the tension dissipate like morning mist. "You make it sound so appealing, but I'm not sure I want to host a bone party."

"Just think of it as a reunion. With a few more laughs and a lot less drama," he said, a twinkle in his eye that suggested he wasn't quite serious.

"But what if the reunion doesn't go as planned? What if the past turns into a drama fest of epic proportions?" I asked, my heart racing with both excitement and trepidation. The idea of unearthing old memories felt exhilarating, but what if those memories were tangled in pain and regret?

He considered my question, his expression shifting to one of genuine thoughtfulness. "Life is messy, Lana. We can't keep running from the past just because we fear what we might find. Sometimes we have to dive into the chaos to uncover what's worth holding onto."

His words hung in the air, stirring something deep within me. "Diving into chaos sounds a lot like a recipe for disaster," I teased, but there was a glimmer of truth beneath my playful jibe. "I mean, have you seen my luck?"

"Your luck is about to change," he replied confidently, his eyes sparkling with determination. "You've got me now. And I'm pretty good at defying odds."

"Is that so?" I raised an eyebrow, intrigued. "What's your track record? Winning lottery tickets? Discovering lost treasures?"

"More like rescuing wayward souls from their own spirals," he said, the grin on his face widening. "You'd be surprised how often I've had to bail myself out of trouble, too."

"That's quite the talent," I teased back, feeling the warmth of camaraderie wrap around us like a cozy blanket. "But are you sure you're ready for this kind of adventure? We're talking about resurrecting a vintage chaos that's been buried for years."

"Bring it on," he said, the confidence in his voice infectious. "Let's go full-on Indiana Jones with this thing. I'll be your trusty sidekick. You handle the skeletons; I'll handle the boulders."

"Boulders?" I laughed, shaking my head at the absurdity. "Now you've gone too far. I'm not signing up for a sequel to a disaster movie."

"Ah, but that's where the fun is!" His enthusiasm was infectious, and I felt a spark of excitement ignite within me. "You and I—together, we can rewrite our story, one laugh at a time."

For a moment, the weight of our past faded beneath the lightness of our banter. There was an exhilarating freedom in allowing ourselves to entertain the idea of moving forward, the possibility of rediscovering what we once had. The oak tree loomed above us, a sentinel to our shared history, a reminder that we had roots deeper than we had ever acknowledged.

The laughter subsided, and a comfortable silence enveloped us again, the stars twinkling like distant watchers. "So," I ventured, my heart pounding with a mix of trepidation and thrill, "what's the first step?"

Clayton looked thoughtful, his brow furrowing as he surveyed the landscape. "How about we start with the most difficult part? Let's face the people we left behind."

I felt a flicker of unease at his suggestion. "You mean, face your mother?"

"Yes. And my dad, too. They need to know that we're not the kids they think we are anymore." He paused, his expression shifting to one of determination. "It's time to stop hiding and show them who we've become."

"Okay, but we're not diving in headfirst like some kind of crazed divers," I said, my voice steady but my pulse quickening at the thought of confrontation. "We need a plan."

"Absolutely," he said, a playful smirk on his lips. "I'll bring the snacks, and you bring the courage."

"Snacks?" I laughed, the lightness returning. "You think a cheese platter will soften the blow?"

"Why not? Everyone loves cheese. And if they don't, we'll use it as a bargaining chip."

"Classic Clayton," I said, shaking my head with a grin. "Always ready to negotiate with brie."

As we shared a laugh, a chill wind swept through the trees, rustling the leaves as if nature itself was conspiring with us. But beneath the lightness of our banter, an undercurrent of tension persisted, a reminder that the past was not easily buried.

"Let's go," he said suddenly, his eyes gleaming with determination. "Let's make that call, face the music. We can't let fear dictate our lives anymore."

With a newfound sense of purpose, we mounted our horses, the familiar rhythm of hooves against the earth grounding us as we set off. The world around us transformed with each stride, the night alive with the symphony of crickets and the soft rustle of wind through the grass.

But just as the anticipation built, a sound pierced the stillness—a crack, sharp and jarring, echoing through the night. I turned, my heart leaping into my throat, as a shadow emerged from the tree line. A figure stepped forward, silhouetted against the moonlight, an unmistakable presence that sent a jolt of recognition racing through me.

"Clayton!" The voice was familiar yet cold, slicing through the warmth of our moment. "I've been looking for you."

The air thickened with tension, and I felt my heart drop into my stomach as I realized who had come to disrupt our fragile connection. The night, once promising and filled with hope, suddenly felt like the edge of a precipice, and I could sense that whatever came next would change everything.

Chapter 12: The First Kiss

The kiss enveloped us in a cocoon of warmth, erasing the distance of years spent apart. Time, usually a relentless march forward, paused as I surrendered to the moment. The taste of him, a blend of fresh mint and something indefinably Clayton, ignited a fire within me that I thought had long since faded. It was as if all our shared laughter, late-night conversations, and the fleeting glances across crowded rooms had culminated in this singular, electrifying connection.

Clayton's hands found their way to my waist, grounding me as though he feared I might float away into the constellation-studded sky. The world around us faded into a blur—no cars honking, no distant laughter from partygoers spilling into the street, just us. I lost myself in the warmth of his body, in the faint scent of cedar and citrus that clung to him like a comforting embrace. The stars twinkled above, twirling their silent dance, and I felt as though we were suspended in a moment that could last forever.

I broke away first, gasping for air, the reality of what had just happened crashing back over me like a rogue wave. His eyes, deep pools of mystery and mischief, searched mine for a reaction, a clue to what this all meant. What was I supposed to say? "I've missed you?" would be too simple, too mundane for the tempest of emotions swirling inside me. Instead, I found myself smiling, an uncontrollable expression of pure joy, as if we were the only two people in the universe.

"What was that for?" Clayton asked, his tone teasing, yet his gaze was earnest, hopeful. He brushed a stray hair behind my ear, the touch both tender and electric, sending ripples of awareness coursing through me. I wanted to play coy, to laugh it off as a moment of whimsy, but the truth was etched in every beat of my heart. I wanted more. More than just a kiss, more than just a memory; I wanted him back in my life.

"Isn't it obvious?" I replied, arching an eyebrow as I tried to summon the bravado I usually carried like armor. "You're quite a good kisser, Clayton. I thought it was worth repeating."

He chuckled, the sound rich and deep, reverberating through me like a favorite song. "Well, you know, practice makes perfect." He paused, his expression shifting slightly, the air around us thickening with something deeper, something unspoken. "But seriously, where does this leave us?"

The question hung between us, laden with implications I wasn't ready to confront. How could we even begin to navigate the choppy waters of our shared past? Memories flooded my mind—of summer nights spent whispering secrets under the stars, of fights that felt monumental at the time, of the hurtful words we had thrown at each other when we'd decided it was over. Yet here we stood, after all that time, and the pull between us was undeniable.

"I don't know," I confessed, the weight of uncertainty hanging heavily on my shoulders. "I just got here, and everything feels so... complicated. My life back in Boston is... well, it's waiting. It's all laid out for me. I have a job, a place to stay, and yet..." I let the words fade, the truth barely a whisper on my lips. Yet here I was, wanting to stay, wanting to explore the possibilities we once dreamed of.

Clayton stepped closer, his warmth radiating against the cool night air. "What if you gave yourself a little time? Just a few days. No plans, no pressure. Just us. Would that be so bad?" His eyes held a flicker of hope, like a candle fighting against the encroaching darkness.

Could I? My mind raced with the practicality of it all. My life in Boston was a tangled web of commitments and responsibilities. Yet, my heart, that traitorous organ, thudded insistently, urging me to take a leap, to cast caution aside for just a little while. "Time," I echoed softly, letting the word hang in the air, rich with possibility.

"I promise," he said, his voice a soothing balm against my spiraling thoughts, "no pressure. Just us figuring things out. I've missed you too, you know."

His admission struck a chord deep within me, resonating with unspoken feelings I had buried over the years. The thought of rekindling the flame we once had felt both exhilarating and terrifying. I had built walls to protect myself, walls that now seemed so fragile, so easily toppled by a mere kiss.

"I can't pretend this doesn't matter," I said finally, my voice firm yet vulnerable, laying bare the confusion in my heart. "What if it complicates everything? What if I fall back into old patterns?"

Clayton's expression turned serious, the lightness evaporating into the night. "What if it doesn't? What if we're both different now? What if this time, it's everything we dreamed it could be?"

His words hung in the air, a challenge and an invitation all at once. The weight of the decision bore down on me, but in that moment, I felt a shift, as if a door had creaked open, allowing a rush of fresh air to sweep through the shadows. Maybe we could write a new chapter together, one filled with laughter, adventure, and the uncharted territory of second chances.

I hesitated, a thousand scenarios playing out in my mind. But then I looked up at him, and the familiar spark ignited once more, pulling me closer. "Alright," I said, my voice steadier than I felt. "Let's see where this takes us."

A grin broke across Clayton's face, bright and infectious. "You won't regret it," he promised, and in that moment, with the stars as our witnesses, I believed him.

The warmth of the moment lingered, swirling around us like the scent of summer blossoms carried on a gentle breeze. Clayton's presence was magnetic, his smile a beacon in the midnight blue that stretched above us. I could see the subtle constellations reflecting in his eyes, as if the universe itself had conspired to bring us back to this juncture. He leaned in closer, the space between us shrinking until it felt like we could share the same breath.

"Tell me something," he said, breaking the spell with his teasing tone. "If I were to play the role of the charming rogue, would you be my damsel in distress, or is that a cliché too far?" His grin was lopsided, a rogueish tilt that made my heart flutter in defiance of reason.

I rolled my eyes, refusing to let him sway me with his charm. "Charming rogues are so last season, Clayton. I think I'd prefer to be the hero who saves herself, thank you very much." I crossed my arms, feigning defiance, but the truth was I was anything but unaffected. A part of me wanted to indulge in the fantasy he painted—a world where every kiss was an adventure and every laugh an echo of joy.

He chuckled, the sound rich and warm, his eyes dancing with mischief. "So, what does that make me then? The noble steed? A sidekick?" He arched an eyebrow, and I could almost see the gears turning in his mind, constructing a narrative around us that I wasn't sure I was ready to embrace.

"More like a reluctant wizard," I shot back, unable to hide my smile. "Full of magic tricks, but who can't quite conjure up a spell without causing a little chaos along the way."

His laughter rang out, bright and unguarded, filling the night air with its sincerity. "Chaos? Me? Never." The feigned innocence in his voice was laced with just enough sarcasm to hint at the misadventures we had experienced together in our younger days.

As we stood there, the chemistry between us crackled with an electric tension, reminding me of all the times we had laughed until our sides hurt, only to be caught up in the mischief we created. This, however, was different. There was an undercurrent of something deeper—a yearning that pulsed beneath the light-hearted banter, ready to burst forth if we allowed it.

"What are we doing here?" I finally asked, my tone shifting as I felt the gravity of the moment sink in. "We can't just pretend the past doesn't exist. What if we end up hurting each other again?" The vulnerability in my voice was a stark contrast to the playful exchange, laying bare the very real fear that accompanied my budding hope.

Clayton's expression turned serious, his smile fading as he considered my words. "I won't let that happen," he said firmly, stepping closer, his voice low and steady. "I'm not the same person I was back then. I've learned a few things—mostly that life is too short to avoid the things that matter."

His honesty disarmed me, stirring a whirlwind of emotions I had thought safely tucked away. I wanted to believe him, to trust that we could navigate whatever complexities awaited us, but the ghosts of our past loomed large, casting long shadows across my heart.

"Okay," I replied softly, feeling a tremor of uncertainty. "But let's take it slow. No grand declarations or pressure. Just... us figuring things out."

His grin returned, the warmth flooding back into his eyes. "Deal. Slow and steady wins the race, right?"

"Only if the race has snacks," I quipped, letting a teasing smile slip through. "And preferably some shade because I'm not fond of getting sunburned."

We both laughed, and it felt like a reset, as if we were crafting our own narrative, one that didn't hinge on the mistakes of the past. A few moments passed, charged with promise and tentative hope.

Then, the serenity was shattered by the abrupt approach of a small group of our old friends, spilling out of a nearby bar, laughter ringing through the air like chimes. They were blissfully unaware of the charged atmosphere that had enveloped us moments before. I could hardly blame them; it was a typical Friday night in this town, filled with revelry and carefree spirits.

"Hey, look who it is!" one of them called, a playful glint in their eye. "The lovebirds finally got together! What's the plan? A midnight picnic under the stars?"

Clayton glanced at me, his expression half-amused, half-slightly mortified. "We were just discussing the merits of... well, snacks," he replied, feigning innocence while shooting me a sideways glance that danced with mischief.

"Snacks, huh? Is that code for making out?" another friend chimed in, and I could feel my cheeks flush as laughter erupted around us. The light-hearted teasing sent a jolt of embarrassment through me, but it was also a welcome distraction from the weight of our conversation.

"Let's just say we're working on our culinary skills," I quipped, straightening my posture as I played along. "If you want to join, you might need to bring your own gourmet items. No hot dogs or chips allowed."

"Hot dogs? Pfft! That's so pedestrian!" one of them replied, putting on an exaggeratedly haughty expression. "What about artisanal cheese? A lovely charcuterie board?"

I exchanged a glance with Clayton, both of us sharing a silent laugh at the absurdity of it all. The group continued to banter back and forth, and for a moment, I felt as if I was basking in the warmth of a familiar, carefree camaraderie.

But underneath the laughter and playful jabs, I sensed Clayton's gaze on me, probing, wondering if this sudden influx of friends had derailed our fragile moment. I leaned closer, our shoulders brushing, a silent reminder that while the past might have its shadows, we had the chance to create something new amidst the light.

"So, what's next?" I asked, diverting the conversation back to us as the laughter faded slightly. "Are we still going to brave the beach bonfire this weekend, or has that plan been scrapped in favor of more 'refined' dining?"

Clayton grinned, a spark of adventure igniting in his eyes. "The beach is calling, and I'll bring the snacks—artisanally, of course."

I laughed, unable to resist the playful challenge in his tone. "Just make sure you don't set anything on fire. I don't think the beach patrol would appreciate a bonfire gone rogue."

"I can promise nothing," he shot back, mock-seriousness on his face. "But I can assure you that no hot dogs will be harmed in the making of this weekend's festivities."

As the laughter erupted again, I felt a rush of gratitude wash over me. Perhaps this was the beginning of something extraordinary—a chance to rediscover who we were, both individually and together. As the night unfolded, the uncertainty that once weighed heavily upon my heart began to lift, revealing a path paved with unexpected delights, old friends, and the tantalizing possibility of love rekindled.

The laughter of our friends faded into the background, a comforting murmur against the vibrant pulse of the night. As Clayton and I shared sidelong glances, it felt like we were coconspirators in a delightful game, the world around us shrinking to just the two of us, surrounded by the teasing warmth of camaraderie and the heady thrill of rediscovery.

"So, bonfire this weekend," I said, breaking the momentary silence that enveloped us. "What are we planning? A grand feast of s'mores and questionable marshmallow roasting techniques?"

Clayton's grin widened, his eyes sparkling with mischief. "Absolutely. I'm going to create the finest s'mores this side of the Mississippi. Trust me, they'll be so gourmet you'll have to give them a five-star review."

"Five stars? You're really setting the bar high there," I teased, nudging him playfully. "What if they're just average, you know, like your cooking skills back in high school?"

"Hey! Those cooking classes were a trial by fire—literally!" He held a hand to his chest in mock offense. "And anyway, I've improved. I once sautéed vegetables without setting off the smoke alarm. It's a real achievement."

"Truly remarkable," I replied, feigning astonishment. "Perhaps you should consider a career change. Celebrity chef, perhaps? Or at least a Pinterest account showcasing your culinary disasters?"

"Don't underestimate my potential, Amelia," he said, winking at me. "One day, I'll have my own cooking show: 'Chaos in the Kitchen with Clayton.' It'll be a hit!"

I couldn't help but laugh, the sound ringing out like a bell, clearing away the tension that had snuck in after our kiss. It felt effortless, a reminder of how easily we slid back into our familiar rhythm. But deep down, a nagging thought reminded me of the complexities looming on the horizon.

As the night wore on, the crowd began to dissipate, our friends moving on to new adventures, their laughter trailing off into the distance. Clayton and I lingered, the atmosphere now quieter, the air heavy with unspoken words.

"Are you ready for the bonfire, or are you still hung up on your illustrious chef dreams?" I asked, nudging him lightly, trying to gauge the shift in our dynamic.

"Honestly? I can't wait," he said, a glint of sincerity in his eyes that made my heart leap. "It's not just about the s'mores, you know. It's about... us."

The way he said "us" sent a shiver down my spine, tinged with both excitement and fear. I wanted to embrace this renewed connection, to throw caution to the wind and dive headfirst into whatever awaited us. Yet, uncertainty lurked in the shadows, ready to pounce.

"Are you sure about this?" I asked, my voice softer now, almost a whisper. "What if it all goes wrong? What if we end up hurting each other again?"

He took a step closer, closing the space between us, and I could see the earnestness etched on his face. "I'm willing to take that risk if you are. I want to make things right between us. We can't change the past, but we can shape our future."

The intensity of his gaze held me captive, and for a heartbeat, the world faded away. But the creeping doubts in my mind refused to stay silent. "And what if we don't?" I asked, my heart racing. "What if we fail?"

"Then at least we tried," he replied, his voice steady. "Isn't that worth something?"

There it was—the challenge that flickered like a flame between us. I felt myself leaning in, inching closer to the promise that lay ahead. "Alright," I finally said, daring to believe in the possibility of something beautiful. "Let's do it. Let's see where this takes us."

Just then, a commotion erupted from the group of friends, laughter followed by shouts that pulled us back into the reality of the night. They were huddled around a small fire pit, their faces illuminated by the glow, and suddenly I felt a swell of excitement wash over me.

"Come on!" Clayton urged, grabbing my hand and tugging me toward the gathering. "Let's see what chaos they've conjured up!"

We joined the crowd, and I quickly found myself swept up in the infectious energy. The fire crackled, casting shadows that danced across the faces of our friends, their laughter punctuating the air like fireworks.

"Amelia!" one of them called, waving me over. "We need your expert marshmallow roasting skills!"

"Expert? Have you seen my technique? It's more like a strategic disaster!" I shot back, eliciting a chorus of laughter.

As I settled next to the fire, the warmth radiated against my skin, mingling with the cool night air. I watched as Clayton moved effortlessly within the group, cracking jokes and tossing marshmallows into the flames like confetti. He was in his element, and the sight of him sent a thrill through me.

A short while later, the group began to build their s'mores, laughter erupting as someone inevitably dropped a marshmallow into the flames, sending a plume of smoke into the air.

"See? This is the chaos I'm talking about!" Clayton exclaimed, grinning as he expertly skewered a marshmallow, holding it over the fire with the finesse of a seasoned pro. "Watch and learn, my friends!"

"More like watch and laugh!" I chimed in, unable to resist the urge to tease him.

The evening wore on, laughter mingling with the sound of crackling wood, but as I watched the camaraderie unfold, a sense of unease gnawed at my insides. My heart was light, but my mind was a tumult of thoughts. Could we truly rebuild what we had lost? Would the past allow us to create something beautiful, or was it destined to repeat itself?

"Hey," Clayton said, leaning closer, his voice barely above a whisper as he caught my gaze across the flames. "You alright? You seem a little... distant."

"Just thinking," I replied, forcing a smile to cover the uncertainty swirling within me. "About how this all feels a bit surreal. I didn't expect any of this."

He nodded, his expression softening. "Yeah, me neither. But sometimes the best things come when you least expect them."

Just as I opened my mouth to respond, a loud pop from the fire sent embers spiraling into the air. It was a moment of distraction, but then it happened—my phone buzzed insistently in my pocket, cutting through the laughter like a knife. I fished it out, glancing at the screen.

My heart dropped.

It was a message from my boss, a reminder of the life I had left behind in Boston, a life that suddenly felt all too real and insistent.

"We need to talk. Urgent."

The weight of the words settled heavily on my shoulders, and suddenly the warmth of the fire felt colder. My gaze darted to Clayton, who was still basking in the glow of the bonfire, laughter ringing out around him. How could I possibly explain this? How could I allow the chaos of my life to disrupt this fragile moment?

I swallowed hard, my heart racing as I contemplated the decision ahead. The warmth of the night faded, replaced by an icy grip of dread. Would I have to choose between my past and this beautiful, unexpected connection we were building?

"Amelia?" Clayton's voice cut through my thoughts, concern threading through his tone.

I glanced up, meeting his gaze, and in that moment, everything felt suspended—time, laughter, warmth—caught in the space between us. I opened my mouth to answer, to share the whirlwind of emotions churning inside me, but as I did, a sudden commotion erupted from across the beach, snapping my attention away.

A figure emerged from the shadows, illuminated by the flickering flames. My heart raced as recognition dawned, a surge of adrenaline flooding my veins. I hadn't seen him in years. The past, it seemed, was not done with me yet.

"Amelia!" he called, his voice cutting through the night air, and I felt my world tilt on its axis.

Clayton's gaze shifted to me, confusion mingling with concern. I opened my mouth to speak, but the words caught in my throat, the implications of his arrival crashing down like a wave. I was standing at the precipice of two worlds, and I had no idea which way I was about to fall.

Chapter 13: The Aftermath

The kiss lingered on my lips, a sweet but bitter echo of everything I had tried to leave behind. I had thought I was strong enough to resist, but as I drove away from Clayton, the night stretched before me like a shadowy abyss. The farmhouse loomed in the distance, its outline blurred by the mist that hung like a shroud over the land. My heart hammered in my chest, each beat a reminder of the chaotic dance of emotions swirling inside me.

I pulled into the gravel driveway, the crunch of stones beneath my tires punctuating the heavy silence. The old oak tree stood sentinel at the edge of the property, its gnarled branches swaying slightly in the cool breeze, as if trying to whisper some sense into my tangled thoughts. I could almost hear it, a murmured warning. But warnings had never deterred me before; I was drawn to the reckless thrill of the unknown, a moth to a flame that always left me scorched.

Stepping inside, the familiar scent of aged wood and lavender greeted me, wrapping around me like an embrace from an old friend. I flicked on the lamp in the living room, its soft glow illuminating the walls adorned with photos of my past. Each snapshot was a reminder of who I was, the laughter and the love, but also of the pain that came with them. My gaze fell on a picture of me and Clayton, our smiles frozen in time, and I felt a stab of nostalgia mixed with regret.

He was my first love, the boy who had once made me feel like the only person in the world. But that was before everything fell apart. I took a deep breath, shoving those memories deep down where they wouldn't rear their ugly heads. I had spent years building walls to protect myself from the hurt, and this moment of weakness felt like a betrayal of everything I had worked for. I wouldn't let one moment unravel the threads of my carefully woven life.

As I made my way to the kitchen, my heart still racing, I busied myself with making tea. The kettle hissed and sputtered, the steam curling up like wisps of thoughts I couldn't grasp. I poured the boiling water over the teabag, watching as the liquid transformed from clear to a deep amber, much like my mood—infused with warmth yet tinged with bitterness. The rhythmic clinking of the spoon against the cup was a brief distraction, but the silence of the house was a suffocating reminder of the choices I had made.

Just as I settled into the comforting embrace of my thoughts, my phone buzzed against the countertop, breaking the tension like a clap of thunder. I hesitated before picking it up, my heart sinking as I saw Clayton's name flash across the screen. I knew I should ignore it, but something compelled me to open the message.

I'm sorry. Can we talk?

It was simple, yet it felt monumental, like a rock thrown into still waters, sending ripples that reached every corner of my heart. I leaned against the counter, my fingers trembling slightly as I read and reread his words. In that moment, the last remnants of resolve began to slip away, like sand through my fingers.

Just then, the door swung open, and my brother, Nate, stomped in, shaking off the dampness of the evening. He was a whirlwind of energy, his messy hair and scruffy beard a testament to his perpetual state of chaos. "Hey, sis! You won't believe the wild storm that's rolling in! It's like the sky is having a meltdown," he said, his eyes twinkling with excitement.

"Great," I replied, forcing a smile that didn't quite reach my eyes. "Just what I need—more drama."

Nate plopped down at the kitchen table, his gaze piercing through my facade. "What's going on? You look like you've seen a ghost. Or kissed one." His playful jab caught me off guard, and I couldn't help but chuckle despite the weight on my chest.

"Very funny," I shot back, leaning against the counter, pretending to examine the kettle as if it held the answers to my woes. "Just... you know. Life."

He raised an eyebrow, his expression shifting to something more serious. "Come on, Claire. You know you can't keep running from things forever. If something's bothering you, spill it."

I sighed, the dam of emotions threatening to burst. "It's just... I saw Clayton tonight."

Nate's eyes widened. "The Clayton? The one you haven't mentioned in years?"

I nodded, and the air thickened with the weight of my confession. "We kissed."

"Whoa," he breathed, leaning back as if I had slapped him. "That's a big deal."

"I know! But it was a mistake," I insisted, my voice rising slightly. "I can't go back to that. Not after everything."

"Did you ever think maybe that's exactly why you should?" he countered, his tone teasing but edged with concern. "You've spent so long avoiding him, maybe it's time to confront what happened."

His words hung in the air, heavy with implications. The idea of confronting my past felt as terrifying as standing on the edge of a cliff, looking down into an abyss. What if diving back in meant drowning in old feelings, or worse, old failures?

"Look," Nate said, his voice softening. "You can't let fear dictate your life. If you keep running, you'll end up alone, staring at those old photos, wondering what could have been."

His words pierced through my defenses, and I could feel the cracks beginning to form. "I just... I can't take that risk. I'm not that girl anymore."

"But maybe it's time to let her come back," he suggested gently, pushing back his chair and rising to his feet. "Just think about it, Claire. You deserve to be happy, whatever that looks like."

As he walked away, his footsteps echoing in the silence, I sank back into my thoughts, my heart racing once again. The storm outside began to rage, the wind howling like a pack of wolves, mirroring the turmoil within me. The past I thought I had buried was clawing its way to the surface, and I couldn't help but wonder if I had the strength to face it. The kiss had been a momentary lapse, but it had opened a door I wasn't sure I was ready to walk through again.

The storm outside roared like a beast unleashed, rattling the old windows of the farmhouse as if it were trying to break in. Rain lashed against the roof, a rhythmic reminder of the chaos swirling in my mind. I wrapped my arms around myself, cocooned in the warmth of a blanket that felt less like a shield and more like a thin veil against the cold truth of my predicament. I had kissed Clayton, and now, the echoes of that moment ricocheted through my thoughts, intertwining with memories I thought I had neatly tucked away.

The clock ticked with relentless precision, each second stretching into eternity. Sleep eluded me like a ghost, just out of reach. I tossed and turned, the sheets twisting around me, mirroring the knot in my stomach. I glanced at my phone again, resisting the urge to check for messages. The last thing I needed was to dive deeper into that whirlpool of confusion. But my fingers itched to reach for it, to see if he had sent anything more after that simple apology.

With a frustrated sigh, I swung my legs over the side of the bed and padded into the kitchen, the coolness of the floor a stark contrast to the turmoil simmering beneath my skin. I filled the kettle again, its familiar whistling a small comfort in the storm's cacophony. While waiting for the water to boil, I allowed my thoughts to drift to the first time I met Clayton, that summer when everything felt possible.

The memory flooded back with vibrant clarity. I could see the golden light filtering through the trees, hear the laughter of kids playing by the river. We had been inseparable, two sides of the same coin, tangled in shared secrets and stolen glances. But somewhere along the way, that summer had slipped into autumn, and everything had changed. The laughter faded, replaced by unspoken words and a chasm that grew deeper with every passing day.

Just as the kettle reached its boiling point, a loud crash of thunder shook the farmhouse, jolting me back to the present. I poured the water into a mug, watching the steam curl upwards, trying to ground myself. The warmth seeped through the ceramic, a small balm against the chill in the air. I took a sip, savoring the bitterness of the tea, and tried to clear my head.

Suddenly, the phone vibrated on the counter, its insistent buzz sending a jolt of adrenaline through me. My heart raced as I reached for it, half-expecting to see Clayton's name again. Instead, it was a message from Jess, my best friend since childhood.

Hey! You free tomorrow? I need a distraction.

I smiled at her words, grateful for the lifeline she always threw my way. Jess had an uncanny ability to drag me out of my spirals, her enthusiasm a refreshing counterpoint to my brooding.

Absolutely. Let's do something fun.

Meet me at the diner at noon?

I agreed, the thought of catching up with her nudging me towards a brighter mood. Maybe I could distract myself from the swirling thoughts of Clayton, even if just for a few hours. Jess would know how to make me laugh, how to pull me out of this dark fog, even if just temporarily.

The next morning dawned gray and moody, but I welcomed the rain as it pattered against the windows, a symphony of nature echoing the chaos inside me. I dressed quickly, opting for my favorite oversized sweater and jeans, a cozy outfit that felt like a comforting hug. The drive to the diner was a brief reprieve, the familiar roads winding through the countryside, each curve revealing the beauty of the landscape, even under a slate sky.

As I parked outside the diner, I caught a glimpse of Jess through the window, her bright hair a beacon in the dim light. She waved enthusiastically, her smile wide and infectious. I opened the door, the bell jingling above me, and stepped inside, instantly enveloped by the rich aroma of coffee and the chatter of patrons.

"Claire! There you are!" Jess exclaimed, jumping up to pull me into a tight embrace. "I was starting to think you'd run off to join a convent after last night."

"Not quite," I chuckled, sliding into the booth opposite her. "Just grappling with a kiss that felt like a freight train."

She raised an eyebrow, leaning forward, her interest piqued. "Do tell! Was it a good kiss, at least?"

"An earth-shattering one," I admitted, unable to suppress a smile despite the turmoil still brewing within. "But it came with all the complications of my past. You know how that goes."

Jess rolled her eyes, a playful smirk on her lips. "Complications are my middle name. But seriously, Claire, you can't let one moment define everything. You deserve some fun, some joy! Life's too short to be a hermit."

I nodded, grateful for her relentless optimism. "You're right. I just need to figure out what I want without getting lost in the mess of it all."

"Start with breakfast!" she declared, motioning to the waitress who approached our table. "I'll have the usual, and Claire will have... something decadent. Treat yourself!"

I laughed at her enthusiasm, the weight on my shoulders feeling just a little lighter. "Fine. I'll take the chocolate chip pancakes, but you're covering the bill."

As Jess ordered, I looked around the diner, the walls adorned with vintage photographs and local memorabilia, each piece telling a story of the small town we called home. I felt a surge of warmth—this was my safe haven, a place where memories were forged over meals shared with friends.

When the food arrived, a towering stack of pancakes glistening with syrup, I felt a sense of normalcy wash over me. Jess and I dove into conversation, her animated stories about work and the latest drama among our mutual friends drawing me in. For a moment, I forgot about Clayton, about the kiss that had turned my world upside down.

"Okay, now that you've had a sugar rush, spill the tea on Mr. Clayton," Jess said, her eyes sparkling with curiosity. "What's he like now? Still the charming boy who swept you off your feet?"

"He's... complicated," I replied, the laughter fading slightly as I considered my words. "Still charming, yes. But there's a depth to him now that I didn't expect. It's like he carries a weight I can't quite understand."

"Maybe he's carrying the weight of regret?" she suggested, tilting her head thoughtfully. "People change, Claire. You know that better than anyone."

I sighed, pushing the remnants of my pancakes around on the plate. "It's just hard to reconcile the boy I knew with the man he's become. And the last thing I want is to get hurt again."

"Then maybe it's time to confront that fear," Jess said, leaning in, her voice low and earnest. "You won't know unless you try. Take it slow. You're not the same girl who ran away before."

Her words hung between us, heavy with promise and uncertainty. I nodded, feeling the familiar stirrings of hope alongside my apprehensions. Perhaps it was time to see where this new path might lead, even if it meant stepping into the unknown.

As the rain continued to fall outside, I found myself smiling, buoyed by the warmth of friendship and the tantalizing prospect of what lay ahead. The storm might rage, but in that moment, surrounded by laughter and love, I felt ready to face whatever came next.

The sun peeked through the clouds the next morning, casting a tentative light across the farmhouse as if testing the waters after the storm. I sipped my coffee, the rich aroma mixing with the crisp morning air, and felt the warmth seep into my bones. Jess had left me with a sense of optimism I hadn't realized I was craving. Maybe I could figure this out, or at the very least, learn to navigate the tangled web of emotions that came with seeing Clayton again.

The quiet of the morning wrapped around me like a soft blanket. I decided to take a walk around the property to clear my head. The gravel crunched beneath my boots as I made my way to the edge of the yard, where the land dropped away into a patch of wildflowers that danced in the gentle breeze. I paused, taking in the beauty of it all—the colors vibrant against the backdrop of the blue sky, the way the sun kissed the petals just right. Nature had a way of soothing my restless spirit, reminding me that life went on despite the messiness of human connections.

Just as I was about to turn back, my phone buzzed in my pocket, jolting me from my reverie. I pulled it out, my heart racing as I saw Clayton's name flash across the screen.

Can we meet? I think we need to talk.

My stomach twisted, a mix of anxiety and curiosity washing over me. Did I really want to see him? Was I ready to face the unresolved feelings that had been stirred back to life? I tapped my foot against the ground, contemplating how to respond.

Okay. Where?

His reply came quickly. The old diner? 2 PM?

I stared at the screen, my heart thudding in my chest. The old diner was our place, a cozy little spot where we had shared countless meals and dreams. It felt both familiar and terrifying, the prospect of reopening old wounds mingling with the thrill of possibility.

With a resigned breath, I replied, I'll see you then.

The rest of the morning dragged by in a blur of chores and distracted thoughts. I dusted the shelves, organized the pantry, all the while imagining how the conversation might unfold. Would he apologize for the kiss? Would he try to convince me that he had changed? The questions piled up, each one more daunting than the last.

As noon approached, I donned a light jacket and stood before the mirror, trying to muster a confidence I didn't quite feel. My reflection stared back, a mixture of apprehension and determination etched on my features. "You've got this, Claire," I muttered to myself, though the words felt more like a mantra than a reality.

The drive to the diner was punctuated by a mix of anxiety and anticipation. The familiar neon sign buzzed in the daylight, its retro charm inviting and oddly comforting. As I stepped inside, the familiar sound of sizzling on the griddle greeted me. The diner was nearly empty, save for a few regulars scattered at the counter, their conversations low and cozy.

Clayton was already there, sitting in our favorite booth, the sunlight streaming through the window highlighting the sharp angles of his face. He looked up as I approached, his expression a blend of relief and nervousness. The air felt thick between us, charged with unspoken words.

"Hey," I said softly, sliding into the booth opposite him.

"Hey," he replied, running a hand through his hair, a nervous habit I remembered all too well. "Thanks for coming."

"Of course." My voice was steadier than I felt. "What did you want to talk about?"

He took a deep breath, his gaze flickering to the window as if searching for the right words among the clouds. "I wanted to apologize for last night. I shouldn't have—"

"Clayton," I interrupted, my heart racing. "You don't need to apologize. I kissed you, too. It was just... unexpected."

His eyes met mine, and I could see the emotions swirling in their depths. "It felt right in the moment, but I didn't mean to throw you off balance. I know we have history, and I didn't want to complicate things more."

"Complicating things is kind of my specialty," I said, attempting a lightness I didn't feel. "But I guess the kiss opened up a whole lot of questions."

"Like what?" he asked, leaning in slightly, the intensity of his focus making my heart flutter.

"Like why now? Why after all this time?"

Clayton's gaze dropped for a moment, the vulnerability in his posture striking me. "I've thought about you every day since…" His voice trailed off, but I could feel the weight of his words hanging in the air. "I was an idiot, Claire. I let my fears and insecurities push you away. But seeing you again, it made me realize how much I missed you, and how much I want to try again."

I opened my mouth to respond, but the words caught in my throat. Try again? Did I even want to consider the possibility of reopening that door? The memories flooded back—our laughter, our dreams, but also the heartbreak that had followed.

"Do you remember that summer we spent on the lake?" he continued, his eyes lighting up with the memory. "We built that ridiculous raft, and it sank before we could even paddle out. We ended up soaked but laughing on the shore."

"Yeah, and we got scolded for tracking mud into your parents' car," I replied, a smile creeping onto my face despite the seriousness of the moment.

"Exactly. It was messy and chaotic, but it was also fun. That's what I want, Claire. I want to create more moments like that, messy or not."

His words struck a chord, igniting a spark of hope deep within me. But doubt loomed, like the shadows that clung to the edges of the diner. "But what if it doesn't work? What if we end up right back where we started?"

"We can't know unless we try. But I swear to you, I'll fight for us this time. I've changed. I've learned. I'm not the same guy who ran away."

Before I could respond, the door swung open, and a gust of wind blew through the diner, chilling the air. My heart dropped as I turned to see a figure silhouetted against the sunlight. It was Nate, his expression serious as he scanned the room before locking eyes with me.

"Claire!" he called out, urgency lacing his voice.

Clayton's gaze flickered between us, confusion etched across his features. "What's wrong?"

Nate reached our table, breathless. "It's Mom. She... she's in the hospital."

A wave of ice cascaded through my veins as reality hit hard. The world outside felt muted, as if someone had pressed pause on the chaos swirling around us. "What happened?" I barely managed to ask, my heart pounding in my chest.

"Car accident. She's stable, but..." His voice cracked, the weight of the moment palpable.

The noise of the diner faded, my focus narrowing on Nate's words, each syllable heavy with dread. Clayton's presence felt distant now, the warmth of our conversation evaporating into thin air. All thoughts of rekindling the past vanished in an instant, replaced by a surge of fear and urgency that overshadowed everything else.

Nate's eyes searched mine, and I felt the world shift beneath me, leaving me teetering on the edge of uncertainty. I grasped the edge of the table, the reality of the situation washing over me. "I have to go," I whispered, the words barely escaping my lips.

As I stood up, the weight of Clayton's gaze bore down on me, filled with questions I couldn't answer. But right now, all that mattered was family, and the looming uncertainty that awaited me outside those diner walls.

Chapter 14: Torn in Two

The days blurred together after that night. I threw myself into helping my grandmother around the farm, trying to forget about Clayton and the kiss we'd shared. But it was impossible. Every time I closed my eyes, I saw him—his smile, the way his eyes crinkled at the corners when he laughed, and that indescribable warmth that enveloped me whenever he was near. Every time I walked through town, I half-expected to run into him. And when I didn't, the ache in my chest grew stronger, an insistent reminder that something had shifted within me. I couldn't deny it anymore—I was torn.

Boston had been my escape, my chance to build a life on my own terms, a life filled with ambition and the tantalizing possibility of freedom. But here, in Whispering Hills, with Clayton, everything I thought I wanted started to unravel. The farm buzzed with the sounds of summer—bees humming around the wildflowers, the distant caw of crows, and the low murmur of my grandmother's voice as she hummed a tune from days long past. The scent of freshly turned earth mingled with wild mint, creating a heady aroma that was both comforting and suffocating. The more I tried to fight it, the more it consumed me, like ivy creeping up a weathered wall.

"Are you going to help me pick these tomatoes, or just daydream all afternoon?" my grandmother's voice broke through my reverie, pulling me back to the present. I looked at her, her hands gnarled but strong, moving deftly among the green vines heavy with plump, red fruit. She had a way of grounding me, her presence a constant reminder of the love and stability this place had always offered.

"Sorry, Grandma," I said, forcing a smile as I grabbed a basket and joined her. "Just thinking about... stuff." I couldn't mention Clayton. Not yet. Not when I was still sorting through what it all meant.

"Thinking about that boy from town, I wager," she said, raising an eyebrow at me, a sly grin forming on her lips. I knew she was teasing, but there was a flicker of seriousness in her gaze, as if she could see right through my defenses.

I laughed, though it felt hollow. "Oh, come on. It's not like that. We're just... friends." The lie hung in the air, thin and fragile. We both knew it wasn't true. The kiss had been electric, sending ripples of confusion through me. My heart raced at the memory, a mix of longing and fear churning within me.

"Friends, huh?" she mused, plucking a perfect tomato and tossing it into my basket. "You know, dear, sometimes friends have a way of turning into something more, especially when the summer heat starts to settle in." Her eyes sparkled with mischief, and I couldn't help but chuckle at her feigned innocence. My grandmother had a knack for seeing the truth, even when I tried to mask it behind a veil of nonchalance.

We continued to pick tomatoes in comfortable silence, the sun dipping lower in the sky, casting a golden glow across the fields. As I worked, I couldn't shake the feeling that I was being pulled in two directions—one leading me back to the safety of Boston, with its bustling streets and bright lights, and the other toward Clayton, with his warm laughter and the promise of something deeper. The tension between the two worlds hung like a tightrope stretched above the chasm of my uncertainty.

Later that evening, as the last rays of sunlight melted into the horizon, I stood on the porch, watching fireflies dance in the twilight. The air was thick with the scent of freshly cut hay, and the soft rustle of leaves whispered secrets I longed to hear. Just as I was lost in thought, I heard the familiar sound of tires crunching on gravel. I turned, my heart skipping a beat when I saw Clayton's truck pulling up.

He stepped out, his silhouette framed by the fading light, and for a moment, all the noise around me faded away. It was just him, and the world around us felt impossibly still. My stomach twisted into knots, a swirl of excitement and apprehension.

"Hey there, neighbor," he called, his voice rich and warm, wrapping around me like a favorite blanket. "I hope you don't mind me dropping by."

"Not at all," I replied, attempting to keep my tone casual, though the flutter in my chest betrayed me. I leaned against the porch railing, trying to appear nonchalant while my mind raced with the implications of his visit.

"I brought something," he said, walking towards me with a grin that lit up his face. In his hands was a mason jar, filled to the brim with a golden-yellow liquid. "Homemade lemonade. Thought you might need a refreshing drink after a long day in the sun."

"Is this your secret recipe?" I quipped, accepting the jar with a playful smirk. "Or just a way to get me to give you my grandmother's secret tomato sauce recipe?"

"Maybe a little of both," he winked, leaning against the porch railing next to me. The warmth radiating from him felt intoxicating. "But seriously, I wanted to check on you. I know things got a little... intense the other night."

A rush of heat flooded my cheeks at the memory. "Intense" felt like an understatement. It was as if we had crossed an invisible line, stepping into a territory that was as thrilling as it was terrifying.

"I've been thinking about it too," I admitted, taking a sip of the lemonade, the tartness exploding on my tongue. "About us."

His expression shifted, a mix of surprise and something darker swirling in his gaze. "Yeah? What about us?"

I felt the air thicken, the weight of his question hanging between us like an unspoken promise. In that moment, the world beyond the porch faded, leaving just the two of us and the uncharted territory we were standing on.

The sun dipped lower, casting elongated shadows across the porch, while a summer breeze tousled my hair, sending a shiver down my spine. The jar of lemonade sat like a glowing beacon between us, its cool surface glistening as I nervously swirled it in my hands. Clayton shifted closer, the warmth of his presence drawing me in like a moth to a flame, and the weight of unspoken words hung heavily in the air, a tension that buzzed like the crickets in the distance.

"I've been thinking about it too," I said finally, the words tumbling out before I could stop myself. "About us."

Clayton's expression flickered, his eyebrows knitting together as if he were trying to solve a complex riddle. "Yeah? What about us?" he asked, a hint of wariness threading through his voice.

I took a deep breath, my pulse quickening. "I mean, we kissed. It was... memorable." I added the last word with a wry smile, hoping to lighten the mood. "But what does it mean? I don't want to complicate things."

"Complicate? That's rich coming from someone who's been avoiding me like I'm contagious," he retorted, crossing his arms with a playful huff. There was that familiar banter, a soft cushion against the weight of our reality, and I couldn't help but chuckle.

"Okay, okay, maybe I have been a little distant," I admitted, scrunching my nose. "But you have to understand, Clayton. I'm still trying to figure everything out. I've built this life in Boston, and then you came along and—"

"And what? Broke all your perfectly laid plans?" He leaned in closer, the playful spark in his eyes turning serious. "Look, I didn't mean to complicate anything, but I can't pretend that kiss didn't mean something. At least not to me."

His confession hung between us like a delicate thread, and I could feel my heart racing, caught in a whirlwind of confusion and longing. The soft sound of his voice wrapped around me, comforting yet dangerous, like stepping onto a tightrope stretched over a precipice. I had never been good at balancing, and the thought of falling was both exhilarating and terrifying.

"I didn't plan on falling for you, either," I blurted out, a confession that felt both freeing and risky. "You're... complicated, and I'm... I'm still figuring it all out."

Clayton laughed softly, the sound rolling over me like a warm wave. "Complicated? Honey, you have no idea. I'm just a guy trying to keep my head above water in a small town where everyone knows my business."

"Touché," I replied, crossing my arms defiantly. "But if we're being honest, I'm not exactly a simple girl myself. I'm stuck between two worlds—one that's familiar and safe, and one that's... well, full of surprises."

"Surprises can be good," he said, his gaze steady and earnest. "Sometimes, they lead to the best things in life."

He leaned in closer, our breaths mingling in the summer evening air, and for a moment, the world around us faded, leaving just the two of us suspended in time. I could feel my heart thumping loudly in my chest, echoing the chaos of my thoughts. But before I could respond, the sharp honk of a car horn shattered the moment, pulling me back into reality.

"Ugh, my sister," I groaned, breaking away from the spell he had woven. "She's probably here to drag me off to some family dinner or another." I tried to sound annoyed, but deep down, I knew I was grateful for the interruption, a reprieve from the intensity that hung in the air like an impending storm.

"Don't let her chase me off," Clayton said, a teasing glint in his eyes as he stepped back, raising his hands in mock surrender. "I was just getting to the good part."

I rolled my eyes but couldn't suppress my grin. "Good part, huh? I'll let you know if I'm free later for more of your insights on life and love."

"Count on it," he replied, the promise lingering as he took a step back, reluctantly letting the distance grow between us.

I waved him off with a mixture of reluctance and hope, feeling the heat of his gaze on my back as I turned. Just as I reached the door, I glanced over my shoulder, catching a glimpse of his smile—warm, genuine, and utterly distracting.

The moment I stepped inside, I was bombarded by the familiar cacophony of my family's laughter mingling with the clatter of dishes. My sister, Marissa, was already setting the table, her long hair bouncing as she moved around with the grace of someone entirely too confident for her own good. She turned, her face lighting up when she spotted me.

"There you are! Mom was just saying how she wanted to see you," she called, her voice bright and cheerful. "What were you doing out there? Staring at the stars or daydreaming about your mysterious farm boy?"

"Very funny," I muttered, rolling my eyes as I moved to help her. "And it's not like that. We were just talking."

"Uh-huh," she said, shooting me a sly look. "Talking, or whatever you kids call it these days."

The playful banter continued as we set the table, but my thoughts drifted back to Clayton, the memory of his smile and the tension that simmered beneath our words. I tried to shake it off, reminding myself that I had chosen this life in Whispering Hills for a reason. I was here to support my grandmother, to reconnect with my roots, and to find clarity. Yet, the more I pushed the thoughts of Clayton away, the more they fought to claw their way back into my consciousness.

Dinner passed in a blur of laughter and conversation, but my mind remained half-occupied, flitting between the warmth of my family and the electric connection I had with Clayton. Marissa regaled us with tales of her latest escapades, and my parents chimed in with their own anecdotes, but I felt strangely detached, as if I were watching the scene from behind a glass wall.

"Earth to Mia!" my mother called, pulling me back from my reverie. "What's going on with you tonight? You've been unusually quiet."

"Oh, just... thinking," I replied, forcing a smile as I fiddled with my fork. "About some things."

"Thinking can be dangerous," my dad interjected with a wink. "Especially when it involves boys."

The teasing laughter erupted around the table, and I felt my cheeks flush. "Really, Dad? I'm way past the boy-crazy stage," I said, a bit too defensively.

"Sure you are," Marissa teased, smirking at me. "Just wait until you see him again."

"Who?" my mother asked, a knowing look in her eyes.

"No one," I retorted quickly, heart racing at the thought of spilling everything. "Just... nobody important."

"Is that so?" my dad chuckled, eyes twinkling with mischief. "You know, I'm all for a little romance to shake things up around here."

The conversation continued, but I felt my heart race, a mix of embarrassment and exhilaration at the thought of Clayton, of what might unfold. The rest of the night flew by in a blur, but I couldn't shake the feeling that I was standing at a crossroads. Choices loomed ahead, each one leading me down a different path, and with every passing moment, I felt the pull of Whispering Hills tugging at my heart.

The lingering tension from dinner hovered in the air long after the plates were cleared and the laughter faded into the comfort of evening stillness. I lay in bed, staring at the ceiling, my mind replaying every word Clayton and I had exchanged, every look that sparked like electricity. The moonlight spilled through my window, casting a silvery glow across the room, illuminating the remnants of my childhood scattered about—old books, photographs in mismatched frames, and a collection of trinkets that felt like echoes of a simpler time. Yet, instead of comfort, they stirred a sense of restlessness within me.

I rolled over, glancing at the clock on my bedside table, its ticking amplifying the solitude of the night. Midnight had come and gone, but sleep evaded me like a runaway horse. My heart raced at the thought of Clayton, his laughter and warmth drawing me closer to a world that felt both exhilarating and dangerous. I could almost hear the whispers of the fireflies outside, calling me to venture out into the cool night air, to seek the clarity I craved.

With a soft sigh, I swung my legs over the side of the bed, my bare feet touching the cool wooden floor. I tiptoed past the framed memories of my family, each one telling a story I both cherished and felt the weight of. As I crept down the hall, the creak of the old wooden floorboards felt like a warning, but I was determined to break free of the suffocating confines of my thoughts.

Outside, the night wrapped around me like a comforting shawl, the air fragrant with the scent of blooming jasmine and damp earth. The stars sparkled above, countless pinpricks of light illuminating the vastness of the sky. I took a moment to breathe deeply, letting the fresh air fill my lungs, grounding me. And then I moved, guided by an instinct that pulled me toward the sound of rustling leaves and distant laughter.

The path to Clayton's family's barn wound through fields dotted with wildflowers, their colors muted in the moonlight. As I approached, I heard voices drifting through the air, laughter mixed with the familiar hum of summer. Peering around the corner, I spotted a group gathered around a makeshift fire pit, the flickering flames casting playful shadows against the barn walls. Clayton stood among them, animatedly recounting a story that drew hearty laughter from his friends.

My heart raced at the sight of him, the way the firelight danced in his eyes, illuminating his features in a way that made him look almost mythical. He caught my gaze from across the yard, his smile brightening, sending a jolt of warmth through me. I hesitated, caught between the safety of my solitude and the intoxicating pull of his presence.

"Mia!" he called, waving me over as if sensing my internal struggle. "Come join us! We could use another storyteller."

"Or a referee," someone shouted, and the group erupted in laughter again. I couldn't help but smile, the ease of their camaraderie pulling me in like a tide.

Taking a deep breath, I stepped into the light, my heartbeat steadying with each stride. As I approached, the warmth of the fire enveloped me, and I felt the weight of my worries lift slightly. "What's the story this time?" I asked, feigning nonchalance as I took a seat on the weathered log next to Clayton.

"Oh, just a little adventure involving a runaway goat and a very confused tourist," he replied, a twinkle of mischief in his eye. The others chuckled, and I found myself leaning closer, eager to absorb every word.

As he spoke, I caught snippets of the others' conversations—an easy rhythm of friendship and familiarity that tugged at my heartstrings. I had yearned for this connection in Boston, where ambition often overshadowed genuine relationships. Here, with Clayton and his friends, life felt richer, full of laughter and unguarded moments.

"Your turn, Mia!" Clayton announced suddenly, breaking me from my reverie. The attention of the group turned toward me, and I felt the familiar pang of self-consciousness rise. "You've got to have a good story up your sleeve."

"Me?" I sputtered, feeling the heat rise to my cheeks. "I'm not sure my life is nearly as interesting as a runaway goat."

"C'mon, everyone has a tale," he urged, a grin playing at the corners of his mouth. "Even if it's just how you almost burned down the kitchen trying to impress your family."

Laughter erupted around the fire, and I couldn't help but join in, despite the flurry of nerves dancing in my stomach. "Okay, okay! But you have to promise to keep your judgment to yourselves."

With their eager encouragement, I dove into a story from my childhood, how I had attempted to bake cookies for my grandmother's birthday, only to end up with a gooey disaster that resembled something out of a horror movie. The laughter was infectious, and with each chuckle, I felt the last remnants of my reservations begin to dissolve.

But then, as the laughter faded into soft banter, the mood shifted. A tension emerged, an undercurrent of unspoken words hanging between Clayton and me. He was sitting close, his shoulder brushing against mine, and I could feel the warmth radiating from him, a magnetic pull that made my heart race once more.

"Okay, serious question," he said suddenly, his tone shifting as he leaned closer, his voice low and earnest. "What's your real plan, Mia? I mean, do you see yourself going back to Boston for good, or...?"

His question felt like a spotlight, illuminating the shadows of doubt I had tried to avoid. The weight of my decision pressed down on me, and the laughter of the group faded into the background. "I don't know, Clayton," I admitted, my voice barely above a whisper. "I thought I had everything figured out, but now... now I'm not so sure."

His gaze held mine, the intensity in his eyes igniting a fire of emotions I struggled to contain. "You know, it's okay not to have all the answers. Sometimes the best journeys start with a little uncertainty."

His words lingered, and I felt a flicker of hope rise within me, battling against the weight of fear and doubt. "What if I choose wrong?" I blurted, the vulnerability spilling out before I could rein it in.

"Then we figure it out together," he said firmly, and the sincerity in his voice sent a thrill down my spine. It felt like an invitation, a promise of support and companionship in a world that had suddenly grown complicated.

Before I could respond, a loud crash erupted from behind the barn, followed by shouts that broke the fragile moment. The group turned, startled, and I felt my heart leap into my throat.

"What was that?" one of the girls exclaimed, her eyes wide with surprise.

"I'll check it out," Clayton said, rising to his feet, his demeanor shifting from playful to protective in an instant. "Stay here."

The urgency in his tone sparked a sense of urgency in me. "No, I'm coming with you," I insisted, standing up and brushing off the remnants of my earlier discomfort.

As we moved toward the sound, the atmosphere crackled with tension. I could hear my heart pounding in my ears, the thrill of adrenaline mingling with a newfound resolve. Just as we reached the edge of the barn, another crash reverberated, this one louder and more insistent.

"Clayton!" I called out, but the noise swallowed my words.

He turned to look at me, concern etched across his face, and just as he opened his mouth to respond, the barn door swung open violently, revealing a shadowy figure silhouetted against the dim light inside. My breath caught in my throat as I instinctively reached for Clayton's arm, the weight of dread coiling tight within me.

"Who's there?" Clayton called out, stepping protectively in front of me, his stance resolute.

The figure stepped forward, and a flash of recognition ignited fear in my chest. I felt as if I'd been thrown into a whirlwind, a storm of uncertainty, and everything I thought I knew was about to unravel.

Chapter 15: A Letter from Boston

The letter was neatly folded, the edges crisp, as if it had been meticulously prepared by someone who knew the weight it carried. The embossed logo of the Boston architectural firm glinted in the soft morning light filtering through the window, casting a halo around my indecision. I could practically hear the distant hum of the city, a reminder of the vibrant life that awaited me. But each time I picked it up, something clawed at my insides, a trepidation I couldn't quite shake. I was stuck, hovering between two worlds, one full of promise and the other steeped in the bittersweet familiarity of my life in this sleepy coastal town.

The kitchen was my refuge, with its mismatched dishes and the faint aroma of vanilla lingering in the air from last night's baking escapades. It felt like a sanctuary—at least, it had until that letter arrived. Now, it was a battleground where my dreams clashed with my heart. My fingers traced the edge of the paper, feeling the smooth surface beneath my skin, and with it came a flood of memories: the laughter shared with friends over late-night dinners, the quiet mornings spent sipping coffee while the sun peeked over the horizon, painting everything in golden hues. Could I really walk away from that? From the people who had become my family, who had welcomed me with open arms after my return?

I glanced outside, watching as the leaves danced in the crisp autumn breeze, their colors a riot of orange and crimson. The sight should have brought me joy, but instead, it only deepened my sense of loss. I had spent years cultivating this little corner of the world, nurturing friendships and carving out a niche for myself, and now it felt like I was standing on the precipice of a decision that would change everything. Just then, the door swung open, and Sophie, my closest friend and the one person who could usually read me like an open book, swept into the room.

"Hey, what's the deal? You've been all quiet and broody lately," she said, tossing her bag onto the counter and fixing me with an expectant look. Her blonde hair fell in wild waves around her shoulders, a halo of energy that I admired even when I felt weighed down by my thoughts.

"Just...thinking," I replied, forcing a smile that didn't quite reach my eyes. I didn't want to burden her with the turmoil swirling inside me, but the moment I said it, I could tell she wasn't buying it.

"Thinking about what? Don't tell me you've been pondering the meaning of life again. You know that's my job." She grinned, but her eyes were sharp, scanning my face for clues.

I hesitated, the letter still lying there like an unwelcome guest at a party I didn't want to host. "It's nothing, really. Just a little—"

"A little what? A little life-altering job offer that's making you feel like you're being pulled in two different directions?" She stepped closer, arms crossed, the playful demeanor dropping to reveal the concern etched in her features.

There was no use in pretending any longer. "It's from my old boss in Boston," I admitted, my voice barely above a whisper. "He wants me back, and it's a promotion, Sophie. The job I always dreamed of."

Her eyebrows shot up, and the surprise on her face quickly morphed into an enthusiastic grin. "That's amazing! Why aren't you jumping up and down? This is what you've always wanted!"

And there it was, the crux of it all. "But...what if it's not what I want anymore?" The words escaped me like a sigh, heavy with the weight of uncertainty. "What if I leave all of this behind? My life here, my friends, the way the sun sets over the water every evening? I just... I don't know if I can do it."

Sophie studied me, her expression softening. "You're not just leaving; you're moving forward. Sometimes we have to let go of the things we love to embrace something even better. But you also have to figure out what that means for you. What does your gut say?"

I looked down at the letter again, its presence a palpable pressure against my chest. My gut was a cacophony of conflicting emotions, a frenzied mix of excitement and dread, hope and despair. "It's telling me I might regret it if I don't go. But it's also telling me I might regret it if I do."

She stepped closer, a warm hand resting on my shoulder. "Then why not find a way to take both? You're not making this decision in a vacuum. You can take the leap and still cherish what you have here. You can make it work."

Her words wrapped around me, a gentle reminder that life didn't have to be a series of black-and-white choices. But as I stood there, feeling the weight of her support, I couldn't shake the feeling that there was something lurking beneath the surface, an unseen force pulling me away from my familiar life. I glanced out the window again, where the wind played with the leaves, and a sudden thought struck me. What if there was a way to merge the two lives I loved? What if this wasn't just a farewell but an evolution, a chance to weave together the threads of my past with the tapestry of my future?

As I looked back at Sophie, something shifted inside me—a flicker of possibility ignited by her encouragement. "Maybe you're right. Maybe it's not just about making a choice but about crafting something new."

Her smile widened, and for the first time in days, I felt the stirrings of excitement flutter in my chest. The letter wasn't just a burden; it was an invitation, a chance to redefine my life in a way I had never considered before. I took a deep breath, the air tinged with the sweetness of baked goods and the promise of change. The path ahead was still uncertain, but for the first time, it felt like an adventure waiting to unfold.

The air crackled with potential, a sense of urgency urging me to take action, yet I found myself clinging to the familiar comfort of my little town. The world outside my kitchen window buzzed with life, laughter spilling from the nearby café, the clinking of coffee cups mixing with the rustle of leaves. It was the kind of day that beckoned you outside, as if nature itself was calling me to step away from my turmoil and embrace the warmth of connection.

"Let's go for a walk," Sophie suggested, her voice light, almost musical, cutting through the fog of my thoughts. "You need to clear your head. Boston can wait, and besides, I promise the coffee shop has a new pumpkin spice latte that's worth the trek."

"Pumpkin spice? In October? How can I resist?" I feigned enthusiasm, rolling my eyes but unable to suppress a smile. Sophie had an uncanny knack for lightening my mood, even in the thick of my indecision.

As we strolled down the tree-lined street, the crisp air filled my lungs, and the earthy scent of fallen leaves mingled with the sweet aroma wafting from the bakery. Each step seemed to peel back layers of my anxiety, allowing for a sliver of clarity. "You know," I started, "I thought moving back here would mean stability, but it feels more like I'm treading water. I have this chance to dive back into the deep end, and yet—"

"Yet you're scared," she interjected, her pace slowing as she looked at me, genuine concern etched across her features. "And that's okay. Fear can be a helpful guide, you know. It tells you when something matters."

"It matters," I murmured, glancing at the ground, the rough pavement reflecting my turmoil. "But what if I'm not ready for that kind of responsibility again? What if I fail?"

"Then you fail, and you get back up. You're resilient, you know that, right?" Sophie paused, her eyes sparkling with the kind of certainty I envied. "Plus, you have me in your corner. Always. We'll start a support group: 'Former Bostonian's Anonymous.' I'll be the president."

I laughed, the sound echoing in the quiet street. "You're a terrible president. What would our meetings consist of? You handing out lattes and reminding me that failing is just part of the process?"

"Exactly! And I'd charge a fee, of course—free pastries included. You'd be rolling in the dough while we dissect your fears. It'll be a blast!"

Her playful banter offered a temporary reprieve, but as we reached the café, the aroma of freshly brewed coffee filled the air, pulling me back into reality. I watched as she ordered a couple of lattes, the barista smiling at her like an old friend. The warmth of familiarity enveloped me, grounding me in the moment, even as my mind swirled with thoughts of Boston.

When Sophie returned with our drinks, she raised her cup in mock salute. "To brave decisions and caffeine-fueled revelations!"

"To brave decisions," I echoed, taking a tentative sip of the rich, spiced latte, the flavors igniting something within me. It was as if with each sip, I was daring to acknowledge the possibilities. The café was lively, filled with chatter and laughter, yet my focus drifted back to the looming letter waiting at home. I had to confront it, like facing a stubborn ghost that refused to leave.

"Tell me," Sophie said, leaning in as if I might share a closely guarded secret. "What's the first thing that comes to your mind when you think of moving back to Boston?"

I hesitated, allowing the words to settle in my mind. "Opportunity. Excitement. But also... isolation," I admitted, my voice growing softer. "I remember the city's pulse, its relentless pace. Sometimes it felt exhilarating, and other times it was suffocating. Here, I know my neighbors, I have a life I've built. I don't want to lose that."

"Then don't. You're not leaving it behind, you're simply expanding your world." She paused, tapping her cup thoughtfully. "What if you make the move but return here often? You could create a life that combines both. You could be that Boston director with a second home in this town."

The idea took root, unfurling slowly, bringing a hint of warmth to my chest. "I could have it all, couldn't I? But what if it doesn't work out? What if I'm just chasing an illusion?"

"Nothing in life is guaranteed," she replied, the wisdom in her tone undeniable. "But wouldn't it be worse to always wonder 'what if'? Trust me, the worst regrets aren't the mistakes we make but the chances we don't take."

Her words hung in the air like a promise, settling into my heart with a gentle weight. Just then, a sudden gust of wind rattled the café door, sending a swirl of leaves dancing across the floor, echoing the turmoil of my thoughts. "Okay, you've convinced me to think about it. But if I move, you'll have to help me find a place that feels like home. No sterile apartments, only character!"

"Deal! I'll find you the coziest, quirkiest loft in all of Boston. Think brick walls, exposed beams, and a view of the skyline that makes your heart race," she said, her eyes sparkling with enthusiasm. "You'll have your Boston adventures and still be the charming small-town girl I know and love."

"I can see it now: my life as a city girl with small-town roots. What an oxymoron." I chuckled, the tension in my chest easing just a little.

As we finished our lattes and stepped back into the golden glow of the afternoon sun, I felt a shift within me, an acknowledgment that the fear that had paralyzed me for days was just a stepping stone on the path to something greater. Maybe it wasn't about choosing one life over the other but rather finding a way to harmonize them. With Sophie by my side, I felt emboldened to confront the letter, to unravel the threads of my life and weave them into a new tapestry.

As we walked back, laughter bubbling between us, I realized that maybe this crossroads wasn't just about a job. It was about redefining who I was and what I wanted, about finding the courage to embrace the unknown while holding onto the familiar. And perhaps, just perhaps, that journey was exactly what I needed to find my place in both worlds.

The evening settled around us like a velvet cloak, the fading light casting long shadows on the sidewalk as Sophie and I ambled back from the café. The thrill of our earlier conversation still buzzed in the air, mingling with the earthy scent of damp leaves and the distant murmur of laughter from a group of friends gathered at the local park. I felt lighter, as though the weight of the letter had been momentarily lifted, but a nagging uncertainty lingered, lurking just beneath the surface.

"I think I'll call them," I declared suddenly, surprising even myself. The thought had bubbled up like a fizzy drink, effervescent and undeniable. "Tomorrow. I'll call my old boss and at least hear him out."

Sophie's eyes sparkled with encouragement. "That's a step! Just make sure to keep the lattes flowing on your end. Maybe they'll sweeten the deal with free pastries for life."

I laughed, the image of a bakery brimming with pastries just for me dancing in my mind. "I'll hold you to that. Free pastries could be my secret weapon in negotiations."

As we reached my front porch, I felt the familiar tug of my surroundings—the warm glow from the lamp post flickered softly, and the comforting creak of the old wooden steps beneath my feet was a reminder of all the evenings I'd spent here, enveloped in the safety of home. But the letter sat there, waiting, still taunting me with its possibilities and pressures.

"Go on, open it," Sophie encouraged, leaning against the railing with a playful smirk, her arms crossed in that way that promised she wouldn't budge until I did. "You can't ignore it forever."

With a sigh, I picked up the letter, its crisp edges still as sharp as my indecision. "You know, you're really great at pushing people into uncomfortable situations," I said, half-jokingly. "Is that part of your job description as my friend?"

"It should be!" she quipped, nudging me playfully. "Besides, I'm here for emotional support and judgment-free zone status."

I inhaled deeply, savoring the comforting aroma of my home, and carefully unfolded the letter. The elegant script danced before my eyes, each word a siren call luring me back to a life that had once felt vibrant and full of promise. Yet now, it felt like a siren song echoing through an abyss, one I had just begun to climb out of.

Before I could succumb to the swirling thoughts, my phone buzzed in my pocket, jolting me back to the present. I pulled it out, expecting a message from one of my local friends, but my heart sank as I saw a name I hadn't expected—David, my former colleague from Boston. The last time we spoke, it had been a rushed farewell before my departure, punctuated by half-hearted promises to keep in touch. I hesitated, the gravity of the moment thickening the air around us.

"Answer it!" Sophie urged, peering at the screen with a curious glint in her eyes.

Taking a deep breath, I hit "Accept" and brought the phone to my ear. "Hey, David."

"Hey, wow, it's good to hear your voice! I wasn't sure if you'd pick up," he replied, his tone light yet tinged with an undercurrent of seriousness. "Listen, I heard about the offer. Congratulations! That's fantastic news."

"Thanks," I replied, feeling a mixture of pride and trepidation. "It's... a big decision."

"Yeah, I get that. But here's the thing," he continued, his voice dropping slightly, "I wanted to give you a heads-up about something. There's a lot happening with the project you were leading. The dynamics have shifted since you left, and I'm not sure the new director is handling things well. There are whispers about some major issues brewing."

My heart raced. "What kind of issues?"

"Let's just say there's some tension in the team. People are getting frustrated, and there are rumors that funding might be pulled if we can't get things back on track. You know how cutthroat it can be in that environment. I thought you should know, in case you're weighing your options."

I blinked, the implications of his words crashing over me like a wave. "Are you serious? That project was my baby. I can't believe it's in such disarray." My mind raced, spinning with thoughts of my potential role in fixing things, a pull I hadn't anticipated.

"Look, I'm not trying to pressure you or anything. Just... you're a valuable asset to the team. You know how to handle the chaos, and honestly, they could use your leadership right now. But it's your decision, obviously. I just wanted you to have all the information before you made any choices."

Sophie raised an eyebrow, her expression shifting from playful to serious as she listened intently. I could feel her energy shifting, sensing the weight of the conversation pressing down on both of us. "Thanks for the heads-up, David. I appreciate it. I'll think about what you said."

"Do that. And hey, I hope to see you back in Boston soon. We miss you over here." The warmth in his voice was palpable, but it only amplified the tightness in my chest.

After we hung up, Sophie turned to me, her eyes wide with a mix of excitement and concern. "What was that all about?"

I ran my fingers through my hair, the reality of David's words sinking in like a stone in my stomach. "The project is in trouble. Apparently, the new director isn't cutting it, and there's talk of funding being pulled if things don't improve. I... I didn't realize how much chaos awaited me back there."

"Chaos can be your playground, you know," she said, trying to coax a smile from me. "You thrive on that. And it could be an opportunity to step back into a role where you really shine."

"But what if I step into it and everything crumbles?" I protested, my voice rising with uncertainty. "What if I can't fix it? What if it's too late?"

Her eyes softened, the playful spark dimming as she regarded me seriously. "You can't think like that. You have to trust in yourself, and you have to decide what you truly want. This isn't just about the job; it's about what you want your life to look like."

As the night deepened, the shadows creeping up the walls of my cozy home, I felt the pressure mount, a brewing storm of decisions and emotions swirling within me. The letter loomed larger now, a gateway to the possibilities that lay ahead—both thrilling and terrifying.

And just when I thought I could grasp the direction I needed to take, the doorbell rang, cutting through the tension like a knife. Startled, I exchanged a look with Sophie, both of us frozen in place. Who could it be at this hour? I felt a shiver run down my spine, the night air suddenly thick with foreboding.

"Are you expecting anyone?" Sophie whispered, her playful demeanor returning with a hint of mischief.

"No," I replied, curiosity piquing along with the knot in my stomach. "Should I be?"

As I approached the door, the sensation of impending change washed over me, a flicker of unease entwined with the thrill of the unknown. With each step, I could hear the steady thump of my heart, the anticipation thickening the air around us. I reached for the doorknob, hesitating just for a moment before pulling it open, the hinges creaking ominously.

And there, framed by the glow of the porch light, stood a figure from my past, an unexpected arrival that sent my heart racing—a mix of exhilaration and dread intertwining in the air, pulling me toward a future I hadn't yet envisioned.

Chapter 16: A Heart Divided

The air was thick with the scent of pine and earth, the kind of freshness that wrapped around you like a warm blanket. Whispering Hills had always held a charm that made it easy to lose track of time. Here, the golden light of the setting sun filtered through the trees, casting dappled shadows on the ground. I wandered along the worn path leading to the edge of the lake, the gentle lapping of water against the shore a soothing symphony that contrasted sharply with the turmoil inside me. I had come here to think, to breathe, but every breath felt like a tether binding me to the life I had crafted in Boston.

I paused, crouching down to touch the water, cool against my fingertips, rippling gently as though it could sense my indecision. The lake shimmered like glass, reflecting my internal conflict with unsettling clarity. I was a woman split in two, caught between the dream I had nurtured in the bustling city and the unexpected warmth that had sprung up in this quiet town. I felt like a ship lost at sea, tossed between the waves of my ambition and the calming harbor of love. It was a dichotomy that gnawed at my insides, pulling at my heartstrings with every fleeting memory of Clayton.

Clayton. The name sent a rush of heat to my cheeks. I could still feel the way his lips brushed against mine, as if the world had stilled for those stolen moments. That kiss had ignited something deep within me, a spark that flickered to life every time I thought of him. His laughter echoed in my mind, rich and inviting, like the aroma of freshly brewed coffee on a rainy morning. How could I abandon that connection for the sterile skyscrapers and endless meetings that awaited me back in Boston?

"Hey, Earth to Eva!" A playful voice broke through my reverie, pulling me back to the present. I turned to find Clara, my best friend, jogging down the path, her curly hair bouncing with each step. She was a whirlwind of energy, always a step ahead in life, and today was no different. "You look like you just swallowed a lemon. What's going on in that pretty little head of yours?"

"Just contemplating life and the universe," I replied, forcing a smile. It felt brittle, like glass, ready to shatter under the slightest pressure.

"Right. And by life, you mean Clayton, don't you?" She plopped down beside me, uninvited but welcome. Her eyes sparkled with mischief, as if she could see right through my carefully crafted facade.

"I don't know what you're talking about," I deflected, though I knew my tone betrayed me. It always did when it came to him.

"Please, the entire town can sense the chemistry. You two might as well be on a reality show," Clara said, rolling her eyes dramatically. "I mean, have you seen the way he looks at you? It's like you're the last slice of pizza at a party—everyone wants a piece, but he's the only one who gets to have it."

I laughed despite myself, picturing Clayton's boyish grin and the way he often stole glances my way, as if trying to decipher the enigma I had become since I stepped back into his world. "It's complicated," I said, my voice trailing off. The weight of my decision pressed down on me like a heavy blanket.

"Complicated, or just terrifying? You're not one to shy away from a challenge, Eva. Why are you letting fear dictate your heart?" Clara's tone softened, and I could see the concern etched on her face.

I sighed, gazing out over the lake, where the sun's last rays danced upon the surface. "Because what if I choose wrong? What if I stay, and it doesn't work out? What if I leave, and I can't ever forgive myself for walking away from him?" My heart clenched as the words escaped me, raw and vulnerable.

"Or," Clara countered, nudging me playfully, "what if you stay and it becomes the best decision you ever made? Sometimes you have to leap into the unknown to find out what's waiting for you." Her encouragement was like a beacon, cutting through my doubts.

As if on cue, my phone buzzed in my pocket, pulling me back from the precipice of my thoughts. I fished it out, my heart skipping a beat when I saw Clayton's name flash on the screen. The message was simple, yet it felt like a jolt of electricity coursing through my veins.

Hey, Eva. You free tonight? There's something I'd like to show you.

"Speaking of leaps," Clara teased, peering over my shoulder. "What's that?"

"Just Clayton." The words slipped out before I could stop them, and suddenly the air felt charged, alive with possibility.

"Are you going to reply?" Clara nudged me with her shoulder, her eyes glimmering with excitement.

I hesitated, staring at the blinking cursor on the screen, the question gnawing at my resolve. The weight of my decision pressed harder, but beneath it all, a flicker of hope ignited. What if tonight was the moment everything changed? What if this was the step I needed to take, the leap that would define my future?

With a quick breath, I typed back a simple response, my heart pounding with anticipation. Sure. I'd love that.

As I hit send, I felt a strange mix of exhilaration and fear. Clara's grin widened, and I could see the wheels turning in her head. "Tonight could change everything," she said, her voice laced with a conspiratorial thrill.

I hoped she was right. I hoped tonight would finally show me which half of my heart I should follow.

The sun dipped lower, painting the sky in shades of orange and pink, as I made my way to the local café, a quaint little spot with rustic charm. It was where I had spent countless afternoons, sipping on the rich aroma of freshly brewed coffee while indulging in Clara's relentless musings about love and life. As I approached, I could see the warm light spilling from the windows, flickering like a beacon of comfort amid my growing unease.

Clayton was already there, seated at our usual table by the window, his tall frame slouched casually, but his eyes sparkled with anticipation. The moment he spotted me, his expression shifted, a smile breaking through the otherwise laid-back demeanor. It was as if he had been waiting for this very moment, and suddenly, the weight of my earlier doubts felt lighter, if only for a heartbeat.

"Hey there, wanderer," he greeted, his voice smooth like the whiskey I had watched him sip at the bar last weekend. "You look like you've been on an adventure. I hope it involved more than just contemplating your life choices."

I chuckled, sliding into the chair opposite him. "Well, the scenic route to existential dread is pretty picturesque, I must say." My attempt at humor didn't fully mask the tension simmering beneath my surface, but he rolled with it, effortlessly.

He leaned forward, resting his chin on his hand, a teasing glint in his eyes. "You know, it's only the second time I've seen you in this café, and I'm starting to think it's become your unofficial therapy spot. What is it about this place that draws you in?"

"The coffee, the atmosphere, and the subtle reminder that life can be sweet," I replied, my gaze drifting to the chalkboard menu. "Plus, it's the perfect backdrop for analyzing every single detail of my life."

He let out a soft laugh, a sound that both soothed and stirred my heart. "Then allow me to be your therapist for the evening. Let's dissect whatever's gnawing at you, and I promise to charge you half of what you'd pay at a real office."

I raised an eyebrow, intrigued and slightly wary. "What are your credentials? Did you take a course in coffee shop psychology?"

He feigned deep thought, running a hand through his tousled hair. "Well, I do have an impressive collection of self-help books.

And I've been known to give great advice—at least, that's what my mother tells me."

"Okay, Dr. Clayton," I teased, settling into the banter that had always flowed easily between us. "What do you prescribe for someone torn between two worlds?"

"Hmm, I'd say a generous dose of honesty." He leaned back in his chair, his expression shifting slightly. "But honestly, Eva, it sounds like you're facing a pretty monumental choice. What's really holding you back?"

I hesitated, the words swirling in my throat like autumn leaves caught in a gust of wind. "It's not just about the choice, Clayton. It's about what I stand to lose either way. If I stay, I risk my dreams. If I leave, I might lose… well, you." The last part came out softer, tinged with vulnerability.

He was silent for a moment, studying me with an intensity that made my heart race. "I won't lie; I'd miss you if you left. But I also want you to be happy. The last thing I want is to be the anchor that drags you down."

His honesty was refreshing, a cold splash of water that jolted me awake. "You're not an anchor. You're… a possibility," I said, the admission surprising even me.

He chuckled softly, his eyes glinting with a mix of amusement and something deeper, something that resonated with my own burgeoning feelings. "I like being a possibility. Sounds way more appealing than being an anchor."

Our laughter filled the small café, momentarily drowning out the world outside. It felt as if we were in our own little bubble, where the complexities of my life faded away, and all that remained was this electric connection sparking between us.

But as the laughter died down, reality crept back in, heavy and suffocating. I leaned back, the smile fading from my lips as I took in the warmth of the café juxtaposed against the chilling weight of my choices. "What if my decision is the wrong one? What if staying here is a mistake?"

"Eva, life is about risks," Clayton said, his tone suddenly serious. "Every choice we make comes with its own set of consequences. You could stay and find happiness, or you could leave and wonder what might have been. Either way, you're the one who has to live with your choice."

His words struck a chord, reverberating in the silence that enveloped us. "It's just... I've worked so hard for everything in Boston. I can't help but feel like leaving would be a betrayal to all I've sacrificed."

"Or it could be the best thing you've ever done for yourself," he countered gently. "Have you ever thought that maybe the career and the city don't define you as much as you think they do? You're more than just your job."

I bit my lip, considering his perspective. "But who am I without all of that? I've built a life, a future I thought I wanted."

"Maybe you need to build something different," he suggested, his gaze unwavering. "You could be building a future with me, with us." His honesty caught me off guard, the weight of his words lingering in the air between us.

I took a deep breath, feeling the weight of everything I had been avoiding. "You make it sound so easy."

"Nothing worth having is easy, but sometimes it's worth the fight," he replied, his voice low and sincere. "You're strong enough to navigate this. I believe in you, Eva."

In that moment, the walls I had carefully constructed began to crumble. The laughter, the connection, and the warmth of his words filled the empty spaces in my heart. Perhaps it was time to stop letting fear dictate my choices and start embracing the possibilities that lay ahead.

The café buzzed with life around us, but in our little corner, it felt as though time had slowed to a crawl. The air was rich with the scent of coffee beans and baked pastries, but all I could focus on was the deep, steady rhythm of Clayton's voice as he spoke. Each word seemed to wrap around me, warming the chill that had settled deep in my chest. I wanted to absorb every detail—the way the light caught the edges of his jaw, the subtle laugh lines that formed around his mouth when he smiled, the intensity of his gaze that seemed to read my very soul.

"I appreciate your belief in me," I said, the honesty behind my words catching me off guard. "But sometimes it feels like I'm standing on a precipice, ready to jump without knowing what's waiting below."

Clayton leaned closer, and for a moment, the chatter of other patrons faded away. "That's where the adventure lies, isn't it? You'll never know until you take that leap. And besides, you've always been the one to dive into the unknown."

A laugh escaped me, one part disbelief and another part admiration. "Only when I'm forced to, and usually under duress."

"Then I'll just have to make sure it's a fun dive," he said, his eyes twinkling with mischief. "Let's turn this decision-making session into an adventure. How about a night under the stars? I know a place that'll make you forget every worry you have."

His suggestion hung in the air, tempting and intriguing. "You think stargazing will cure my existential crisis?"

"Maybe not cure, but it'll definitely help. The universe is a great place to ponder life's big questions. Plus, if I'm lucky, I might get to see your face light up as bright as those stars."

The sincerity in his tone tugged at my heartstrings. It was a moment suspended in time, where hope flickered just beyond my reach. "Okay," I relented, feeling a spark of excitement mixed with apprehension. "Lead the way."

As we stepped outside, the cool evening air enveloped us, a refreshing contrast to the café's warmth. Clayton's presence beside me felt natural, as if we were two pieces of a puzzle that had finally clicked together. We strolled down the winding paths, our conversation flowing effortlessly from one topic to another. Laughter punctuated our dialogue, each shared joke drawing us closer.

"Do you ever miss the city?" he asked, his voice a low murmur as we passed under a canopy of trees.

"Sometimes. But it feels different now," I admitted. "I've spent so long chasing success that I forgot how to simply... enjoy life."

"Whispering Hills has a way of doing that." He glanced sideways at me, his expression serious for a heartbeat. "But that doesn't mean you have to choose one over the other. You can blend the two—find a way to make both parts of your life fit together."

"Easy for you to say," I replied, nudging him playfully. "You're already here, content in your little slice of paradise. I'm the one stuck in the middle, trying to figure out how to balance my heart and my head."

"Maybe it's less about balance and more about harmony. You can be a city girl who loves a quiet life in the hills." He paused, taking my hand in his, and for a moment, the world around us faded away. "You're stronger than you realize, Eva. You can do this."

A soft rush of warmth spread through me as I glanced down at our intertwined fingers. The simple connection ignited something within—a flicker of courage amidst the shadows of uncertainty. As we continued walking, I felt the tension that had gripped my heart start to ease, replaced by the comfort of companionship.

Eventually, we reached a clearing, a hidden meadow that opened up to the sky above. The stars glittered like diamonds scattered across velvet, and I felt a sense of wonder wash over me. "This is beautiful," I breathed, stepping further into the space, absorbing the vastness of it all.

"Not as beautiful as you," Clayton said, his voice low and sincere. The way he looked at me sent a thrill through my veins, igniting every nerve ending as if I were standing on the edge of something extraordinary.

I tried to keep my heart steady as I met his gaze. "Flattery will get you everywhere, you know."

"Just speaking the truth," he replied, taking a step closer. "You're a force, Eva. And the world deserves to see that."

We stood there, a heartbeat away, the energy crackling between us. The moment felt heavy with unspoken words, promises hovering just out of reach. "So, what do we do now?" I asked, my voice barely above a whisper.

He stepped even closer, his breath warm against my skin. "We embrace the unknown."

And then, in an impulsive moment that felt preordained, he leaned in and kissed me. The world around us melted away as I lost myself in the warmth of his lips, the sweetness of the connection electrifying my senses. It was everything I had imagined and more, a merging of dreams and desires that painted my thoughts in vibrant hues.

But just as I began to surrender to the moment, a sudden rustling in the bushes nearby shattered the intimacy like glass breaking against the floor. We pulled apart, confusion etched across both our faces.

"What was that?" I asked, my heart racing for reasons I couldn't quite articulate.

Clayton's expression shifted, alertness sharpening his features. "I don't know. Stay here." He moved toward the sound, his posture tense. I hesitated, torn between fear and concern, wanting to follow him yet sensing a wave of danger in the air.

"Clayton, wait!" I called out, but he was already moving, a protective instinct guiding him.

I took a step back, uncertainty flooding my thoughts. What if it was just a deer or a rabbit? But what if it was something more sinister? The tension thickened, and I could feel the atmosphere shift, as if the very stars above were holding their breath.

Just then, a figure emerged from the shadows, cloaked in darkness. My heart raced, and I instinctively reached for Clayton, but he was already blocking my path, his body taut with readiness.

"Who's there?" he demanded, his voice steady yet firm.

I held my breath, every instinct screaming that we were no longer alone in this serene, star-studded world. The figure stepped forward, revealing a familiar silhouette. My heart sank, confusion warring with disbelief.

"Clayton, it's me!" The voice rang out, slicing through the tension like a knife. And as the figure stepped fully into the light, the truth hit me like a cold wave—someone I had never expected to see again was standing right there, ready to change everything.

Chapter 17: The Space Between

The sun hung low in the sky, casting a golden hue over the sprawling fields that stretched behind the farmhouse. I took a deep breath, letting the sweet scent of wildflowers mingle with the crispness of the approaching autumn air. Each step I took crunched softly underfoot, the ground yielding to my weight as if it were reluctant to let me go. I found myself at the edge of the old barn, its wooden beams weathered and grey, standing as a silent witness to the countless memories we had created here. I pressed my fingertips against the rough texture of the door, tracing the grooves carved by time and neglect.

Clayton was everywhere, his laughter echoing in the corners of my mind like a favorite song I couldn't forget. I recalled the afternoon we spent building makeshift kites, laughter spilling from our lips as they soared high into the sky, dancing like carefree spirits above us. His competitive nature had come alive, and the way he'd challenged me to see whose kite could fly the highest still made me smile, even now. But the memory twisted like a knife in my gut. Those moments felt like they belonged to another lifetime, one that was slipping away as I prepared to return to Boston.

I strolled toward the tree line, the leaves rustling softly in the wind, whispering secrets I longed to know. The world around me was so vibrant, so alive, yet my heart felt heavy and suffocating. Each breath seemed to pull me deeper into the chasm of my indecision. Was I really ready to abandon everything I had here, everything Clayton and I had built together in the fleeting summer days? I thought of my small apartment in the city, filled with the scent of coffee and the soft hum of urban life, where opportunity awaited. But here, in this rustic paradise, I felt grounded. I felt whole.

The sky deepened, turning shades of violet and indigo, and I knew I had to make a choice. I could practically feel Boston tugging at my heartstrings, promising new adventures, but it felt selfish to leave. And what if Clayton was my adventure? What if everything we had experienced was merely the beginning of something greater? The mere thought of it sent a shiver down my spine, and I paused, half-tempted to turn back and call him, to tell him I needed to see him one more time.

Just then, a sound broke through my reverie—a rustling in the bushes nearby. I turned, my heart racing, half-expecting a deer to leap into view, but instead, it was Clayton himself, stepping out from behind a thick cluster of brambles. The shock of seeing him made my breath hitch. His hair was tousled by the wind, and his eyes sparkled with that familiar mischief I had grown to adore. "What are you doing out here, all alone? Trying to escape the rest of us?" His voice was teasing, but beneath it lay a genuine concern.

"Maybe I am," I replied, crossing my arms defensively, though the playful smirk tugging at my lips betrayed my feigned annoyance. "Or maybe I just needed some air away from your incessant chatter."

He stepped closer, and the air between us crackled with a tension I hadn't expected. "I see. Well, if you're planning to run away, you should know that I'm a pretty good tracker." His grin widened, revealing the boyish charm that had melted my resolve more times than I could count.

"I'm sure you are," I shot back, though my heart raced at the thought. "But what if I don't want to be found?"

"Then I guess I'll have to lure you back with something irresistible." He moved closer, the warmth radiating from him wrapping around me like a comforting blanket. "What's it going to take to convince you to stay?"

I opened my mouth to respond, to deflect with something witty, but the words died on my lips. Instead, I looked into his eyes, searching for something—anything—that would indicate what he was thinking. Was he feeling the same pull that I was? The moment felt suspended in time, electric, as if the universe held its breath in anticipation of what might unfold.

"What if I told you I'm leaving?" I finally managed to say, my voice barely above a whisper. The words felt like lead in my mouth, heavy and irrevocable.

He paused, the light in his eyes dimming slightly. "You don't mean that." It was more a statement than a question, and I could see the conflict etched across his features.

"Do I?" I challenged, my heart racing. "This life—it's not what I planned, Clayton. Boston is calling me. It's where my dreams are."

"And what about us?" His voice was steady, but I could sense the underlying tremor of fear, the way his vulnerability shone through the bravado. "You can't just walk away from everything we've built, everything we could still build together."

I inhaled sharply, the truth of his words hitting me like a wave. The weight of our shared moments—the late-night talks, the lazy afternoons spent on the porch—pressed down on me, and I suddenly felt a tidal wave of emotions crashing over my carefully constructed walls. I wanted to tell him everything, how torn I felt, how the thought of leaving him gnawed at my insides like a relentless parasite. But how could I say that without making it worse?

"I don't know what to do," I admitted, my voice trembling. "I wish I could just—"

"Just what?" he prompted, leaning in closer, his gaze intense and searching.

"Just figure it all out without hurting you," I finished, my heart racing with the weight of my confession.

He stepped back, running a hand through his hair, his expression shifting to one of resolve. "Then let's figure it out together. No more running. Let's face it. Together."

The warmth of the sun dipped lower in the sky, casting long shadows that stretched like fingers across the grass. The air was thick with the scent of earth and fading blooms, and I felt anchored to this place, as if the very soil had wrapped itself around my heart. Clayton stood before me, his expression shifting from concern to determination, each passing moment a delicate dance of unspoken words and shared memories. I took a shaky breath, grounding myself against the rush of emotions swirling inside me.

"Together," I repeated, tasting the word as it left my lips, feeling the weight it carried. It seemed so simple yet impossibly complex. "You make it sound easy, like we can just sweep everything under the rug and call it a day." I couldn't mask the edge of doubt in my voice, the fear of entangling our lives further when my own felt so precarious.

He shrugged, a casual gesture that belied the seriousness of our conversation. "Maybe we can't just sweep it all away. But ignoring it won't help either. I'd rather face the chaos with you than pretend it doesn't exist." His eyes sparkled with the kind of sincerity that made my heart skip. "What's the worst that could happen? We fall apart?"

"Good point. Falling apart does sound like a blast," I replied, feigning nonchalance, though the truth was I was terrified. But his smile, bright and earnest, cut through the tension like sunlight breaking through clouds.

"We could also figure it out," he pressed. "You might be heading to Boston for the life you've always wanted, but I can be part of that life too. Just think about it. Why can't we try?"

"Because you have roots here," I argued, shaking my head. "You have a community, friends, this place. I can't just drag you away because I'm having a crisis." My words were meant to be decisive, but even I could hear the uncertainty creeping in.

"And you're not dragging me anywhere," he countered, stepping closer, his warmth radiating like a beacon in the gathering dusk. "I want to be there for you. Besides, if Boston is where your dreams take you, then that's where I want to be too. We've got time."

His earnestness tugged at something deep inside me. The prospect of leaving felt heavy, but the thought of leaving without trying was unbearable. "What if I can't make it work?" I asked, a whisper of vulnerability slipping through my defenses. "What if I drag you into a life that isn't what you want?"

"Then we'll figure that out when we get there. Isn't that how life works? Jumping into the unknown?" He chuckled, shaking his head. "Or at least it is for you. You're not one to back down from a challenge."

"I'll have you know I have a knack for running away from them, too," I replied, crossing my arms with mock seriousness. "I could teach a master class in that."

"Ah, but I see through your sarcasm," he shot back, a playful glint in his eye. "You're just scared. And you know what? That's okay. But running away isn't your style, not really."

There it was—the truth, as hard as a rock, and I felt its weight settle in the pit of my stomach. I wanted to believe that I could face this head-on, that I could take this leap with him. But doubts crept in, whispering insidious thoughts about failures and heartbreak. "You make it sound so easy. But life is messy. People get hurt."

"True," he said, tilting his head thoughtfully. "But they also find joy, laughter, and love in unexpected places. Life can be beautiful if you let it be. And we've got to let ourselves explore that. Trust me."

I searched his face, seeking the reassurance I desperately craved. The earnestness etched in his features pushed me closer to the edge of decision. "Okay," I finally said, my voice steadying. "Let's say we try. What does that even look like?"

His smile broadened, as if I'd just handed him the keys to the kingdom. "For starters, you'll take me to Boston, and we'll spend a weekend there together. You can show me your world, and I'll show you mine."

A rush of warmth filled my chest at the thought of sharing my life with him, the city that pulsed with opportunity and ambition. But doubt quickly followed, fluttering like a trapped bird in a cage. "And then what?" I asked, my voice trailing off. "What happens when the weekend is over?"

"Then we'll figure it out, as you said," he replied, his gaze unwavering. "But I'm willing to try for you. Just think—what if you could have the best of both worlds? Boston and this place, all in one life?"

I blinked, trying to process the enormity of his proposition. The blend of our two lives felt both exhilarating and terrifying. "You really think we can do this?"

"I know we can," he insisted, his tone firm and sincere. "Life is too short to live with 'what ifs.' We'll make memories, even if it means stumbling along the way."

We stood there, the world around us dimming into twilight, but my heart felt ablaze. The air was electric with possibility, and for the first time in what felt like forever, I believed we could bridge the gap between what was familiar and what lay ahead.

"Alright, Clayton. Let's give it a shot," I said, my voice steady with newfound conviction. "But don't blame me when we're knee-deep in chaos."

He laughed, a sound that echoed in the stillness of the evening, wrapping around us like a warm embrace. "I wouldn't have it any other way. Now, how about we celebrate this moment with ice cream?"

"I don't think I can take that kind of pressure," I replied, my heart lighter than it had been moments before. "But I suppose I could be persuaded."

"Great! We can make it a two-scoop kind of celebration," he grinned, already taking a step back toward the farmhouse. "After all, we're jumping into the unknown here. Might as well indulge, right?"

And with that, I fell in step beside him, my heart soaring as we walked into the darkness, armed with laughter and a promise—a promise to navigate the space between what was and what could be, together.

The ice cream shop was a little slice of heaven, a quaint establishment painted in pastel colors, with vintage posters peeling slightly on the walls. The air was filled with the sweet scent of waffle cones, swirling together with laughter and the cheerful jingle of the bell above the door as we entered. I couldn't help but smile at the sight of families gathered around small tables, kids giggling as they tried to keep their cones from toppling over.

Clayton stepped up to the counter, his eyes scanning the array of flavors like a kid in a candy store. "Okay, what's your poison?" he asked, grinning as he gestured to the overwhelming selection of ice creams. "I think I'm feeling adventurous today."

"Adventurous? In an ice cream shop?" I laughed, shaking my head. "That's a bold claim. I stick to my favorites—mint chocolate chip, classic but effective."

"Mint chocolate chip? You're playing it safe," he teased, tapping his chin in mock contemplation. "What if I suggested something wildly exotic, like lavender honey? Or how about black sesame? That could really shake up your world."

"Black sesame?" I raised an eyebrow, feigning horror. "What am I, a food critic? That sounds like something my grandmother would've insisted was good for my soul. I'll pass."

He leaned closer, eyes dancing with mischief. "But think of the stories you'd tell! 'I once had a very enlightening experience with black sesame ice cream.'"

"Or 'I suffered a culinary trauma and have sworn off ice cream for life,'" I shot back, laughing. "I'm not falling for that. You're on your own with the weird flavors."

"I'll take that as a personal challenge," he said, ordering a scoop of something pink and mysterious. "Now you can watch me broaden my horizons while you cling to your safe choices."

As we settled into a corner booth, the soft light from the hanging fixtures casting a warm glow around us, I took a moment to simply absorb the scene. Clayton was animated, gesturing dramatically as he recounted a story from his childhood about an epic water balloon fight gone awry. His eyes sparkled with life, and the way he leaned forward, as if the world around him had faded away, made my heart flutter.

"But the best part," he concluded, a wide grin plastered on his face, "was when Aunt Edna slipped on a rogue balloon and fell into the kiddie pool. I thought I'd never stop laughing!"

"That does sound like a classic," I replied, unable to suppress a laugh. "Your poor aunt must have been traumatized for life."

"She took it like a champ, I promise. She just came out of the water, wringing her hair, and yelled, 'That was the most refreshing thing I've experienced!'" His laughter was infectious, and it drew me in, wrapping me in the warmth of our shared moment.

We spent the next hour in a delightful ebb and flow of conversation, the barriers between our lives slowly dissolving. I found myself sharing stories of my own awkward childhood moments, moments that painted a picture of who I was beyond the girl who was torn between two cities. Every laugh, every shared secret stitched us closer together, but with each word, the reality of my upcoming move loomed larger.

"I can't believe we're really doing this," I said suddenly, breaking the easy rhythm of our banter. "I mean, jumping into the unknown like this... it's kind of wild, isn't it?"

Clayton leaned back, a thoughtful expression crossing his face. "It is. But sometimes, wild is where the magic happens. What's the alternative? Staying safe and never knowing what could be?"

"I guess you're right," I conceded, though a pang of anxiety tightened in my chest. "But it's not just about me. What if it doesn't work? What if you hate Boston? What if I end up hating it?"

He reached across the table, his fingers brushing mine, sending sparks of warmth through me. "We won't know until we try. And if it doesn't work, we'll figure it out together. That's what we agreed, right?"

"Together," I echoed, the word feeling both like a promise and a threat. The deeper I fell into this connection, the harder it would be to untangle our lives if it all fell apart.

"Now, let's focus on the immediate problem," he said, breaking through my spiraling thoughts. "You've got a serious ice cream dilemma on your hands. You have to try at least one adventurous flavor, or I'll feel personally betrayed."

"You really won't let this go, will you?" I groaned, but laughter bubbled beneath my feigned annoyance.

"Not a chance," he replied, leaning in with an earnestness that made my heart flutter. "You owe it to yourself to step outside your comfort zone. Come on, I'll even share my pink mystery ice cream."

I sighed, knowing I was fighting a losing battle. "Fine, but if I hate it, I'm blaming you for the rest of our lives."

He grinned widely, his excitement palpable. "Deal! If you don't like it, I'll make sure to order you mint chocolate chip for the rest of eternity."

"Now that's a punishment," I laughed, playfully rolling my eyes. "Alright, let's do this."

He waved the server over, and we ordered an extra scoop of the pink concoction. When it arrived, I looked at it with the same mix of fear and intrigue one might feel before jumping into an icy lake. "Here goes nothing," I murmured, taking a tentative bite.

Surprisingly, it was delightful—a swirl of flavors that danced across my palate, a sweet tang that felt refreshing. I turned to

Clayton, my eyes widening in surprise. "Okay, I might have underestimated this one."

"Told you!" he beamed, victorious. "See? It's not so scary after all. Next time, I'm thinking garlic chocolate."

"Please don't ruin this moment," I shot back, laughing again. But I felt lighter, as if the burdens I had been carrying were slowly dissipating.

As we savored our ice cream, I allowed myself to entertain the thought of us navigating Boston together. Maybe we could forge a path that felt right, a life that blended our dreams and aspirations into a beautiful tapestry. I could almost picture it—long walks along the Charles River, coffee dates in cozy cafes, and laughter echoing in the halls of my apartment.

But just as I felt a glimmer of hope, my phone buzzed violently against the table, shattering the moment. I glanced down, my heart dropping at the sight of a text message from my boss. "Need you back in Boston ASAP. There's an emergency."

Clayton's smile faded as he noticed my expression. "What is it?"

"It's work," I replied, my voice strained. "They need me back. Like, right now."

His brow furrowed with concern, and I could see the wheels turning in his head. "Can't they wait? This is... this is a big moment for us."

"I know, but if I don't go, I'll lose my job. They don't care about my personal life." I felt a knot tighten in my stomach, the familiar pressure of duty battling against the burgeoning excitement of the unknown.

He leaned closer, his voice softening. "Hey, whatever happens, this isn't over. We'll still have our plans. You just need to handle this. I'll be here when you get back."

I swallowed hard, the bittersweet taste of his words lingering in the air. "I really want to make this work, but I didn't think it would be this complicated."

"We'll figure it out," he reassured me, but his eyes revealed a flicker of uncertainty. Just as I opened my mouth to respond, my phone buzzed again, this time with a call. I answered, hearing the urgency in my boss's voice on the other end, the weight of responsibility crushing down.

"I have to go," I said, standing abruptly, the urgency of the situation forcing me into action. Clayton stood too, his expression a mix of support and worry.

"Okay," he said, his voice steady but tinged with an undercurrent of concern. "I'll be here waiting."

"I'll be back as soon as I can," I promised, but as I turned to leave, the sense of impending change hung thick in the air, and the reality of my decision loomed like a storm cloud overhead. The sweetness of ice cream quickly soured in my mouth as the tension surged between us.

And just like that, I stepped out into the night, uncertainty trailing behind me, the echo of our laughter swallowed by the darkness. The world felt impossibly vast, filled with both opportunity and impending chaos, and I had no idea what awaited me on the other side of this moment.

Chapter 18: Bound by Fate

I found him at the old barn, the one we used to sneak into as kids, long before life got complicated. The scent of hay and aged wood mingled in the air, a familiar aroma that whispered secrets of our youth. Sunlight filtered through the cracked wooden slats, casting golden stripes across the floor like a well-loved quilt, and in that moment, I was twelve again, my laughter echoing through the rafters as we dared each other to climb higher, to jump farther. He was hunched over a rusted tractor engine, his hands stained with grease, utterly engrossed in his task. The sight of him, so focused and determined, tugged at a part of my heart I thought had grown calloused over the years.

For a moment, I just watched him, the way his brow furrowed in concentration, how he occasionally wiped his hands on his faded jeans, the soft blue fabric brushing against his strong thighs. It was mesmerizing, and my heart danced to a rhythm of memories, both sweet and sour. The summer days we spent here had been filled with dreams of the future, of endless possibilities. But that was before high school and heartaches, before we drifted apart, pulled by the relentless tide of adult responsibilities.

He didn't see me at first, and I almost wished he wouldn't. My chest tightened at the thought of what I had to tell him, the words threatening to bubble over and spill into the quiet space between us. But when he finally looked up, there was something in his eyes—something that stopped me in my tracks. Those deep brown irises were flecked with hints of gold, shimmering like sunlight caught in autumn leaves, a mixture of warmth and intensity that made me feel both comforted and terrified.

"Hey," he said, his voice rough like gravel yet wrapped in a familiar warmth that sent shivers down my spine.

"Hey," I managed to reply, my throat dry as the barn's wooden beams.

"You leaving?" he asked, and I nodded, fighting the lump forming in my throat. "I got the job," I admitted, the words tasting bittersweet on my tongue. The air between us thickened, heavy with unspoken feelings and memories, all swirling like dust motes caught in the light. I waited for him to say something, anything that might make this easier, a lifeline to pull me back from the precipice of uncertainty.

But instead, he just looked at me with those steady, dark eyes, and I knew. Whatever this was, it wasn't going to end the way I'd hoped. I could see it in the way his jaw tightened, the slight flaring of his nostrils as he absorbed the weight of my news. A thousand unsaid words hung in the air, thickening the silence like the lingering scent of hay.

"I thought you were going to stay," he said finally, his voice low, almost a whisper, as if he were afraid to shatter the fragile moment we shared.

"I did too," I confessed, my heart racing in a futile attempt to bridge the distance that had grown between us. "But this is what I've worked for. It's a chance to start fresh, to do something big." The words slipped out, tinged with desperation as I fought to justify my decision.

"Starting fresh," he echoed, his tone laced with a bitter twist that made me wince. "And what about us? What does that leave us with?"

The question hung there, the unrelenting tension palpable, a rope taut between us. My stomach twisted in knots, and I searched for an answer that would wrap around my heart and squeeze it tight. But the truth was, I didn't have one.

"I... I don't know," I finally admitted, my voice barely above a whisper. "Maybe this is just what we need—a clean break?"

He straightened, a flicker of anger flashing across his face before it was quickly masked by something unreadable. "A clean break? Or are you just running away?"

His words cut deep, and I felt a wave of shame wash over me, mingling with the hurt that flared in my chest. "I'm not running away. I just need to figure things out for myself."

"By leaving everything behind?" he shot back, the frustration in his voice rising like the storm clouds that often rolled over the fields in summer, dark and ominous. "You think that's going to solve anything?"

"I thought it would give me some space," I countered, my own anger igniting. "Space to breathe, to figure out who I am without all of this." I gestured to the barn, the place where our dreams had once seemed limitless.

He stepped closer, the tension crackling like electricity in the air. "And what if you realize that you don't want to come back? That you're happier away from here?"

The question hung between us, laden with the weight of possibilities. My heart raced at the thought. "Is that what you think? That I wouldn't want to come back?"

"I don't know what to think!" he snapped, running a hand through his tousled hair in frustration. "You're acting like leaving is going to be some grand adventure when all it really is... is a goodbye."

"Maybe it is a goodbye," I said, my voice softer now, the fight ebbing away as the reality of our situation settled in. "But it doesn't mean I want it to be. It doesn't mean I want to lose you."

Silence enveloped us, heavy and suffocating. His gaze flickered away for a moment, and I could see the struggle etched across his face, the battle between anger and the undeniable bond we still shared. My heart ached, torn between the path I felt compelled to follow and the anchor I feared I would leave behind.

The silence between us felt like a chasm, the kind that could swallow us whole if I didn't find a way to bridge it. I took a tentative step closer, the crunch of gravel beneath my shoes breaking the tension like a well-placed joke, but it wasn't enough to dispel the gravity of our conversation. He didn't flinch at my approach; instead, he remained as still as the barn itself, a silent fortress, his expression a mix of hurt and anger that I desperately wished I could wipe away with a mere touch.

"Did you really think I'd just be okay with this?" he asked, his voice low but sharp, like a blade hidden in velvet. There was a raw honesty in his words that struck me, cutting through the fog of uncertainty that had clouded my mind. "You've been talking about this job for weeks, but did you even think about what it means for us?"

"Of course I thought about it!" I snapped, a burst of frustration spilling over. "But it's not like I'm leaving just to get away from you. I need this for me." I crossed my arms defensively, wishing I could fold myself into a neat little package and disappear into the shadows. "I need to feel like I'm more than just... this." I gestured around, at the dilapidated barn, at the dusty memories that clung to the air like the scent of old hay.

He clenched his jaw, and I could see the muscles twitch beneath the surface, a physical manifestation of his inner turmoil. "And what if you find out you're happier without all this?" He was trying to sound rational, but the hurt in his eyes told a different story.

"I don't want to be happier without you!" I shouted, the words erupting from me like a dam breaking. The admission hung there, suspended in the thick air, pulsating with unrestrained emotion. I felt a rush of vulnerability, an acknowledgment of how deep my feelings for him ran.

His gaze softened momentarily, and I caught a glimpse of the boy I once knew—the one who used to tell me I could conquer the world as long as I had him by my side. "Then why do you keep pushing me away?" he asked, his voice barely above a whisper, and I could see the flicker of hope mixed with despair dancing in his eyes.

"I'm not trying to push you away," I said, my tone shifting, the fight draining from my words. "I'm scared. Scared of what's out there and what it means for us." My heart raced, pounding against my ribs like a frantic drum, desperate to be heard.

For a moment, we stood there, caught in the web of unspoken words and what-ifs, and I felt the weight of our shared history pressing down on me. The laughter of our childhood rang in my ears, the whispered secrets exchanged in the moonlight, and the countless times we had planned our futures in this very barn. Memories that should have felt comforting now twisted painfully in my chest.

He took a step closer, his hands now resting on the edge of the workbench, the space between us shrinking but still palpable. "Maybe what you need is here, not out there."

"Or maybe what I need is to find out what I can become without this place hanging over my head." I met his gaze, defiance simmering beneath the surface. "I can't live in a memory forever."

The tension crackled again, and I watched as he struggled with my words. "You think leaving means moving on? You can't outrun the past, you know." His voice was steady, but I could hear the undercurrent of pain beneath it, a chord strummed too hard.

"I'm not trying to outrun it," I said, my voice softening again. "I'm trying to grow. Don't you want me to grow?"

"Of course I do," he said, the words tumbling out like a secret. "But it feels like you're trying to do it without me."

"What if I can't do it with you?" I blurted, the question surprising even me. "What if we're just holding each other back?" The implication settled between us, a weighty truth that neither of us could ignore.

His expression hardened again, and I could see him processing my words, calculating the implications. "So that's it then? You just want to cut ties and see how far you can fly?"

"No!" I shouted, my voice rising again. "I want to explore what's out there, but I don't want to lose you in the process."

"Then fight for it!" he exclaimed, the frustration bubbling to the surface like lava threatening to erupt. "If this matters to you, if we matter to you, then fight for us."

I blinked, taken aback. The sheer intensity of his plea washed over me like a cold wave, a mixture of hope and desperation. "Fight how?" I asked, the question escaping me before I could think.

"Show me you want this," he said, his voice now almost pleading. "Don't just walk away like it's nothing. Don't walk away like I'm nothing."

I took a step back, the weight of his words crashing down on me. "I can't promise anything," I said quietly, feeling the familiar sting of tears prick at the corners of my eyes. "This is what I need to do for me."

"Then maybe you don't really want this," he said, his voice hardening again, and a part of me recoiled at the accusation. "Maybe you're just scared of facing what we could be."

"Maybe you're right!" I shot back, the anger flaring up again. "Maybe I am scared. But isn't it better to admit that than to pretend everything's perfect?"

He looked away, frustration etched on his features as he took a deep breath, the air between us thick with unfulfilled desires and the sharp edges of unresolved tension. "I don't know if I can be here while you figure this out," he finally admitted, his voice low, tinged with an emotion I couldn't quite place—sadness, perhaps?

"Then what are we doing here?" I asked, my heart racing as the truth settled heavily within me.

"I guess we're figuring it out," he said, his voice barely above a whisper, and I could see the light flickering in his eyes, dimming with each passing second.

"Together?" I ventured, the question hanging in the air like a fragile promise.

"Maybe."

In that single word, everything shifted. The air grew heavy with the enormity of uncharted territory, and I could sense the world around us vibrating with possibilities, each moment stretching out like the horizon at dawn. And just like that, we stood on the precipice of something new, something terrifying yet exhilarating, and I realized that whatever lay ahead, we would navigate it together, one unsteady step at a time.

"Maybe I don't want to fight for something that feels like it's slipping away," he said, his voice steady despite the tremor of vulnerability that lay beneath. Each word was a stone thrown into a still pond, creating ripples that echoed through the silence that had wrapped around us.

I took a deep breath, the air heavy with the scent of rust and wood, and I struggled to gather my thoughts. "You think it's easy for me?" I shot back, the heat of my frustration simmering just beneath the surface. "You think I haven't lain awake at night, questioning everything? I didn't come here to hurt you, but it feels like I'm stuck in a loop I can't break free from."

"Then let's break it together," he said, stepping closer again, the distance between us evaporating like morning mist under the sun. "Stop pretending this is about the job. It's about us, about what we could be if you just opened your eyes and let yourself see it."

I shook my head, uncertainty clawing at me. "But what if I can't?" My voice wavered, and I cursed myself for letting the vulnerability seep through. "What if I never want to come back? What if I discover a life that doesn't include you?"

He paused, his expression a mix of hope and desperation. "Then I guess we'll cross that bridge when we get to it," he said, his tone softening. "But you owe it to yourself to at least try. You're chasing something, but I'm right here, ready to chase it with you."

A flutter of something—hope, perhaps—stirred within me, but I crushed it down, unwilling to let it take flight just yet. "I can't promise you I won't get swept away. I don't want to put you through that."

"Maybe you don't have to decide right now," he said, his voice laced with an unexpected gentleness. "Maybe we can just... take it one day at a time."

His suggestion hung in the air like a delicate thread, binding us together in the softest of ways. "One day at a time?" I echoed, my heart racing at the possibility. "What does that even look like?"

"It looks like us," he replied, his lips curving into a wry smile that ignited a spark of warmth in my chest. "I'll be here, and you'll be out there, and we'll figure it out as we go. We can have our own adventures and share our stories when you come back."

I studied him, his earnestness radiating from him like the sun breaking through a cloudy sky. "You really think that can work?"

"I don't know," he admitted, his honesty refreshing. "But what's the alternative? You just walk away and never look back? I'd rather take a chance on you than let you go without a fight."

His words sank deep into my soul, and for the first time in what felt like an eternity, the weight of my decision felt a little lighter. "Okay," I whispered, the word slipping past my lips like a secret. "I'll think about it. One day at a time."

"Good." He nodded, a flicker of hope igniting in his eyes. "That's all I ask."

As the sun dipped lower in the sky, casting a warm glow through the barn's wooden beams, I felt the tension between us shift, morphing from desperation into a tentative bond. I could almost hear the threads of our shared history weaving back together, forming a tapestry that held memories of laughter and warmth. But as the shadows grew longer, a new realization washed over me—a question that nagged at the back of my mind.

"What if I can't come back?" The thought spilled from my lips before I could stop it, a haunting echo that reverberated through the stillness.

He stepped back, the light dimming in his eyes as he processed my words. "Then we'll deal with that when we get there," he said, but the confidence in his tone faltered, and I could see the cracks beginning to form in his resolve.

"Promise me something," I said, my voice trembling slightly. "If I'm out there and it feels right, promise me you won't wait for me forever."

"Why would you even ask that?" His brow furrowed, and I could see the hurt flickering behind his eyes. "I want to be here for you, no matter what that looks like."

"Because I can't let you get stuck in a limbo waiting for me to figure things out," I insisted, my heart pounding. "You deserve more than that."

"I'll decide what I deserve," he shot back, frustration lacing his voice, but there was an undercurrent of understanding, a flicker of resignation that told me he understood my intentions.

"I'm being selfish," I whispered, the weight of my choices pressing down on me like a lead blanket. "I want to have it all—freedom and you—but that's not fair to either of us."

He opened his mouth to respond, but the words died in his throat, and I watched as uncertainty clouded his expression. "Maybe you should just go," he said, his voice strained. "If you think it'll help you find clarity, then maybe you should."

The abruptness of his words struck me like a cold wave crashing over me. "You don't mean that," I said, fear tightening my chest. "You don't really want me to leave."

"I want you to be happy," he said, his tone softer but still carrying an edge of frustration. "But if it means you have to leave me behind, maybe it's the only choice you have."

"Don't say that!" I exclaimed, desperation creeping into my voice. "You're not just a choice. You're a part of me."

His gaze held mine, a storm of emotions swirling within. "Then don't make it a goodbye," he said, his voice barely above a whisper, a plea wrapped in a question.

Tears threatened to spill over, and I blinked them back, my heart aching at the thought of leaving him, of walking away from everything we had built together. "I don't want to lose you," I admitted, the words slipping out with a raw honesty that felt like tearing open a wound.

"You won't lose me," he assured me, his voice steady now, wrapping around my heart like a lifeline. "But you have to trust that I'll be here, no matter what."

In that moment, a flicker of something akin to hope ignited within me. Maybe he was right. Maybe this was just a detour rather than a dead end.

But as I searched his eyes, ready to solidify our unspoken promise, a sudden noise shattered the fragile moment—a loud bang followed by the unmistakable sound of footsteps crunching through the gravel outside. My heart raced as I exchanged a glance with him, confusion and alarm washing over us both.

"Who's that?" I whispered, the sudden urgency making the hairs on the back of my neck stand on end.

"I don't know," he murmured, shifting into a protective stance, and I could see the tension in his body, the instinct to shield me from whatever was coming.

We stood frozen, the silence that had enveloped us moments before now replaced by an electric anticipation that crackled through the air. As the door creaked open, revealing the darkening sky beyond, I felt a sense of dread wash over me, a premonition that whatever came next could change everything.

And just as I braced myself for the unknown, a shadowy figure stepped into the barn, the light behind them casting an ominous silhouette that filled the space with an uneasy tension. My heart pounded wildly, and I could feel the weight of the moment pressing down on us as I whispered, "Who are you?"

But before I could catch my breath, the figure stepped closer, revealing a face that sent shockwaves through my heart, a ghost from my past that I had never expected to see again.

Chapter 19: The Goodbye That Wasn't

I sank into his embrace, letting the warmth of his body wrap around me like a favorite blanket. Clayton's scent was a mix of fresh cedar and something uniquely him, a comforting reminder of the moments we had shared in the woods and beside the rushing river. I had thought this would be a straightforward farewell, something simple and clean, but standing there in the dim light of his living room, I realized how naive that notion had been. The unspoken words hung heavily between us, as palpable as the autumn air outside, crisp and electric with the promise of change.

"I didn't think you'd come," he finally murmured, his voice low and gravelly, as if he had just woken from a deep sleep. The shadow of confusion crossed his face, battling with something deeper—a glimmer of hope that I could almost taste. I didn't answer; instead, I buried my face in the crook of his neck, letting the warmth seep into my bones. I felt like I was teetering on the edge of a precipice, the only thing holding me back from falling into the abyss of uncertainty was his strong arms.

We stayed like that for a moment, wrapped in silence, the kind that spoke volumes more than any words could convey. I pulled back slightly to look into his eyes, those deep pools that had seen me at my best and my worst, and I could feel the weight of my indecision pressing down on both of us. My heart raced, a cacophony of emotions vying for my attention. Fear of leaving this place, this man, clashed violently with the desire for freedom, the yearning for something beyond the hills that had sheltered me for too long.

"I just—" I began, but the words slipped away again, a wisp of smoke disappearing before I could grasp it. I shook my head, willing myself to speak, to clarify my chaotic thoughts, but all that came was the steady rhythm of my heartbeat echoing in the silence.

"Tell me what you're feeling," Clayton urged, his hands gently cradling my face as if I were something precious, something fragile. "You don't have to go if you don't want to."

His words stirred something inside me, an unsettling mix of hope and fear. What did I want? The question echoed in my mind like a stubborn refrain, relentless and cruel. I wanted to scream, to throw my hands up and admit how terrified I was of what lay ahead. I wanted to tell him how much I would miss the way his laughter rolled over me like a summer wave, how the simple act of watching the sun dip below the horizon had become an art form in his company.

Yet, there was a part of me, the part that craved adventure and the unknown, that whispered that leaving was the right thing to do. I had come to Whispering Hills to find myself, or at least to escape the life I had left behind, and now that I was so close to stepping into that future, the thought of clinging to him felt like chains binding me to the very place I had sought to escape.

"I can't stay, Clayton. I have to go," I finally said, the words tasting bitter on my tongue. "There's so much out there that I need to see, to experience. I can't just... linger."

His expression hardened for just a second, a flicker of something close to anger or maybe disappointment shadowing his features. I held my breath, waiting for him to lash out or, worse, to give up on me altogether. Instead, he stepped back slightly, creating a distance I hadn't realized I needed. "And what if you discover that what you're looking for has been right here all along?"

It was a fair point, and one that cut deeper than I expected. I swallowed hard, shaking my head as if I could physically shake off the truth of his words. "But you can't hold me back," I insisted, desperation creeping into my voice. "I need to find out who I am outside of this place. Outside of us."

"Us?" he echoed, the weight of that word lingering in the air like the last notes of a song. "So you see us as something, then? More than just fleeting?"

His vulnerability pierced through my own defenses, and I felt the tears threatening to spill over again. I could almost see the wall he was building, brick by brick, and it made my heart ache. "It's not that simple, Clayton. I didn't come here to fall in love. I came here to heal, to rediscover myself. You've helped me with that, but it doesn't change the fact that I have to move on."

He was silent for a long moment, his gaze intense and searching, and I felt exposed under the weight of it. "You think I'm just going to let you walk away without a fight?" he finally said, a fire igniting in his eyes that made my heart flutter. "I'm not ready to give up on what we have."

"Maybe it's not about giving up," I countered, stepping back, needing to reclaim some of that space he had created. "Maybe it's about understanding that sometimes love means letting go."

The tension between us crackled like dry leaves underfoot, sharp and electric. I turned away, willing myself to breathe through the aching tension in my chest. The world outside was darkening, the stars beginning to twinkle like distant memories waiting to be made.

"Let me take you somewhere," he said suddenly, his voice cutting through the quiet. "Somewhere that will make you see just how beautiful this place is. Just one last adventure before you go."

I hesitated, weighing my options like a tightrope walker teetering on the edge of a choice that could change everything. The lure of one final escapade tugged at my heart, but I also felt the weight of impending departure pressing down on me like an iron hand. The clock was ticking, and I could feel the sand slipping through my fingers, but a part of me wanted to hold on to this moment, to linger just a little longer in the warmth of his presence.

"Let me take you somewhere," he insisted, his grip on my hand steady, as if anchoring me in a sea of uncertainty. I could see the spark in his eyes, the same spark that had ignited our adventures since the moment I'd arrived in Whispering Hills. Curiosity clashed with the rational part of my brain, but as I looked at him, the decision started to feel inevitable.

"Okay," I finally replied, a cautious smile breaking through the remnants of my tears. "But where are you taking me? The last time you said 'somewhere,' we ended up knee-deep in a creek looking for that 'legendary' fish that turned out to be just a really big stick."

Clayton chuckled, the sound deep and warm, chasing away the last of my sadness. "Trust me. This is a real place. You'll love it." He flashed me a grin that felt like sunlight breaking through a thick fog, and I couldn't help but return it.

As we stepped out into the cool night, the sky was a canvas of stars, twinkling with a clarity that felt almost otherworldly. I breathed in the crisp air, feeling alive in a way I hadn't in weeks. He led me down a narrow path, the gravel crunching softly beneath our feet. The woods wrapped around us like an embrace, the faint rustle of leaves creating a melody that played against the backdrop of our quiet conversation.

"What's this place like?" I asked, glancing up at him, eager to see the boyish excitement that danced in his eyes.

"It's a secret spot," he replied, a hint of mischief coloring his tone. "Only the locals know about it. I stumbled upon it years ago, and it became my refuge. Just a small pond, but at night, when the moon hits it just right, it's like magic."

He led me deeper into the woods, and soon the trees parted to reveal a shimmering body of water, the moonlight reflecting off its surface like a thousand scattered diamonds. I gasped, taking a step closer, the sight captivating me. "It's beautiful," I breathed, marveling at the tranquility that enveloped us. The pond glistened under the stars, the gentle ripples distorting the moon's reflection, making it look as if the sky had spilled its secrets into the water.

Clayton stepped beside me, his presence a comforting weight. "Told you. It's my favorite place to come when I need to think," he said, his voice barely above a whisper. "It has a way of putting everything into perspective."

"I can see why," I replied, unable to tear my gaze away from the serene surface. "It feels... peaceful here. Like the world just melts away."

"Exactly." He turned to me, the intensity of his gaze sending butterflies fluttering in my stomach. "And it's the perfect place for a little last adventure, don't you think?"

I nodded, a mix of excitement and sadness flooding through me. I couldn't ignore the irony that while I had been planning my escape, here I was, standing at the edge of the world with the man who had made me feel more alive than I had in years. "What do we do now?"

"I thought we could have a little picnic," he said, reaching into his backpack and pulling out a blanket, a couple of sandwiches, and what appeared to be a thermos of hot chocolate. "I didn't know if you'd want to eat, but I figured it wouldn't hurt to bring some snacks."

"Hot chocolate and sandwiches? You really went all out." I laughed, the sound echoing across the water. "Are we five years old again?"

He shrugged, his grin infectious. "Sometimes, it's the simple things that matter most."

We spread the blanket out on the grass, sitting side by side, the warmth from his body mixing with the chill of the night air. As we dug into the sandwiches, our conversation flowed freely, punctuated by laughter and teasing. Clayton's stories about the local wildlife made me laugh until my sides hurt, and I found myself sharing tales from my life, each one revealing pieces of who I was, as if we were weaving a tapestry of shared memories under the watchful eyes of the stars.

"So, what's your plan when you leave?" he asked, his tone suddenly more serious. "I mean, besides the road trip to find yourself?"

I hesitated, the question landing heavily between us. I had rehearsed my answer in my mind a hundred times, but now it felt daunting. "I don't know," I finally admitted, pushing my hair behind my ear. "I guess I want to explore. Maybe travel a bit. I've always dreamt of seeing the ocean, feeling the waves crash over me. But it's more than that; I want to learn who I am without the baggage of my past."

His expression softened, and for a moment, the weight of unspoken words settled over us again. "And what if you find out you don't want to come back?"

The question lingered, and I felt the air thicken with unfulfilled possibilities. "What if I do?" I shot back, trying to mask the uncertainty creeping into my voice. "What if I find that I want to return? That Whispering Hills becomes a part of my story, not just a chapter I'm closing?"

"Then you'd come back, and I'd still be here," he said, the conviction in his voice wrapping around my heart like a promise. "But if you decide to stay away, I won't hold that against you. I want you to have your adventures, even if it means leaving me behind."

I turned to him, searching for any sign of resentment, but all I found was sincerity shining through his deep blue eyes. "You make it sound so easy," I replied, my voice barely above a whisper.

"It's not easy," he admitted, his gaze locking onto mine, "but sometimes, we have to be selfish for our own happiness."

His honesty cut deep, forcing me to confront the reality of my choices. I reached out, brushing my fingers against his, the spark of connection igniting again. "I don't want to lose this," I confessed, a tremor in my voice. "Whatever this is."

Clayton leaned closer, the space between us disappearing. "Then don't. Let's make this moment count."

In that instant, surrounded by the beauty of the night and the whispers of nature, I felt a shift. The weight of my impending departure hung in the air, yet somehow, it no longer felt like an ending. Maybe, just maybe, it was the beginning of something new, a promise wrapped in uncertainty, waiting to unfold.

The air was thick with unspoken words and raw emotions as we sat together, our knees almost touching, the blanket still nestled around us. The peacefulness of the pond enveloped us, a stark contrast to the tempest of feelings swirling within me. I could hear the distant croak of frogs and the soft rustling of leaves, but they felt far removed from the chaos brewing in my heart.

"Do you ever think about what it would be like if we hadn't met?" Clayton's voice broke the silence, his eyes reflecting the stars above us, their brilliance mirrored in the depth of his gaze. "What if you'd left without coming here? Without me?"

The question hung between us like a phantom, stirring an unsettling mix of gratitude and dread within me. "I try not to," I admitted, the confession slipping out with surprising ease. "But every time I think of it, I feel like I'd be missing a piece of myself. You've changed me, Clayton, and I'm not sure I can walk away from that."

His lips quirked into a half-smile, but it didn't quite reach his eyes. "You're a lot tougher than you think. I get it, though. We all have those moments that define us, that shape our future." He paused, letting the weight of his words sink in. "But you also need to decide what's more important—staying here with me or chasing what you think you want out there."

The honesty in his words was both a balm and a burn, igniting a flicker of resolve deep within me. "What if I don't want to choose?" I challenged, my tone sharper than intended. "What if I want to have both?"

"That would be ideal, wouldn't it?" He leaned back on his hands, a gesture of mock defeat. "Unfortunately, life is more like a choose-your-own-adventure book where every choice leads to a different ending. You have to pick one and hope for the best."

I scoffed, rolling my eyes dramatically. "Wow, thanks for the life advice, Yoda. Next, you'll be telling me to meditate under a waterfall or something."

His laughter rang out, bright and genuine, cutting through the tension like a knife. "Hey, if that's what it takes to find your path, I'm all for it. I'll even carry the towels."

As our laughter faded, the weight of reality settled back around us. "You make it sound so easy, but I feel like I'm standing at a crossroads, and every direction looks like a dead end," I said, my voice quieter now, the humor slipping away.

Clayton turned serious, his expression thoughtful. "Then maybe you need to stop looking at it as a dead end and start seeing it as an opportunity for new beginnings. What if there's more out there than you ever imagined?"

I let his words sink in, mulling over the possibilities. The idea of adventure, of embracing the unknown, began to spark something inside me, a flicker of excitement and fear intertwined. "You know, it's funny," I said, taking a sip of the hot chocolate, savoring its warmth. "When I first arrived in Whispering Hills, I thought it would just be a stopover. I never expected to find something... someone... who made me want to stay."

"Maybe that's exactly what you needed," he replied, his voice low, drawing me in. "To find a piece of yourself you didn't even know was missing. But remember, discovering who you are doesn't mean you have to abandon the people who matter to you."

A silence settled between us, heavy with the weight of that truth. I glanced up at the stars again, their shimmer filling me with a sense of longing and wonder. "I wish I could bottle this feeling," I said, glancing sideways at him, "the magic of this moment, so I could revisit it whenever I needed a reminder of why I came here in the first place."

"Then let's make a pact," Clayton said, suddenly animated, his eyes lighting up with mischief. "Every time you feel lost or uncertain, you think of this night, of us, and it'll guide you back to what's important."

"I like that," I smiled, my heart swelling at the thought of our bond transcending distance. "A sort of emotional compass, but a little less cheesy."

"Exactly! Less cheesy, more focused on the adventure of life," he replied, and his laughter felt like a warm embrace.

As the night wore on, we shared stories and dreams, our words weaving an invisible thread that pulled us closer. I could feel the pull of dawn approaching, a reminder of the ticking clock of my departure, and yet, in that moment, I allowed myself to be fully present, living in the magic of now.

Then, just as I thought the evening couldn't get any more perfect, a sudden rustle from the underbrush snapped my attention back to reality. My heart raced as I strained to hear, half-expecting a raccoon or maybe a deer. But what emerged from the shadows sent an unexpected jolt of tension through the air.

A figure stepped into the clearing, silhouetted against the moonlight, and my breath caught in my throat. "Well, well, what do we have here?" a familiar voice drawled, smooth and confident, cutting through the intimacy of our moment.

I turned, my heart plummeting as I recognized him—Derek, my ex-boyfriend. The last person I wanted to see, especially now. "What are you doing here?" I demanded, my pulse quickening.

Derek chuckled, the sound devoid of warmth, his eyes scanning the scene before landing on Clayton, whose jaw clenched, tension radiating from him. "Looks like I've interrupted a little rendezvous. Didn't think you'd be so easy to find, especially after the drama you pulled when you left."

"Drama?" I echoed, disbelief lacing my words. "You mean the decision to leave an unhealthy relationship behind?"

He stepped closer, an arrogant smirk plastered on his face. "Right. Because running away is the solution to everything. But you didn't really think you could escape your past, did you?"

Clayton shifted beside me, a protective presence, and I felt the urge to lean into him, to find comfort in his strength. "This isn't the time or place, Derek," I said firmly, trying to keep my voice steady.

"Ah, but it is, isn't it?" Derek retorted, leaning against a tree, his posture casual but the threat underlying his words evident. "You're about to leave town. I just came to remind you of what you're leaving behind. You think you can just erase me?"

The air crackled with tension, and I glanced at Clayton, whose expression was a mix of confusion and anger. "I think it's time for you to leave," he said, his voice low but steady.

"Or what?" Derek challenged, a glimmer of amusement in his eyes. "You'll protect her? How sweet."

I felt my heart race, caught between the two men in my life, their contrasting energies colliding. I could sense the potential for conflict bubbling just beneath the surface, and the anxiety threatened to choke me.

"Derek, this isn't about you anymore," I said, forcing my voice to stay calm. "You don't get to dictate my choices."

"Oh, but I think I do," he said, stepping closer, his gaze unyielding. "You made a mistake when you left me, and I think it's time you realized it."

A chill swept through me as the implications of his words sank in, the night suddenly feeling darker, more ominous.

Clayton shifted, stepping between us, a barrier of defiance. "You need to back off," he warned, the tension in his voice crackling like the electricity in the air.

For a moment, the three of us stood there, the weight of choices and unresolved emotions pressing down like a thick fog. The world around us faded, and I could almost hear the silent ticking of my heart, each beat a reminder that everything was about to change.

And then, as if summoned by my fear, the darkness crept closer, and the weight of the night settled heavily upon us, leaving me to wonder just how far I would have to go to reclaim my freedom—and at what cost.

Chapter 20: The Road Not Taken

The sun hung low in the sky, casting a golden hue over the asphalt as I maneuvered the car along the familiar yet foreign roads. Each passing mile felt like a step away from home and a step deeper into uncertainty. The chatter of the radio faded into a soft hum, its words muffled by the cacophony of my thoughts. I could almost hear the echoes of laughter from the diner—Kathy's hearty chuckle as she poured coffee, the way she would scold the regulars for their late-night shenanigans, and the warmth that wrapped around the place like a favorite old quilt.

Yet it wasn't just the diner that haunted me. It was the way Clayton's eyes sparkled when he spoke about his dreams, a light I couldn't quite capture or comprehend. He had wanted me to stay, to help him chase those dreams under the starry skies of our small town, but I had chosen the city instead. My heart ached at the thought of that choice, like a bruise that refused to heal, thumping in rhythm with the tires rolling over the uneven pavement.

A soft sigh escaped my lips as I took a deep breath, trying to fill my lungs with the air that tasted of nostalgia. The scent of pine and earth lingered in the wind, reminding me of summer afternoons spent hiking through the woods, laughter mingling with the rustling leaves. Those woods held secrets and whispers, dreams forged under their expansive canopies, and they beckoned me to return. I could almost see Clayton standing by the old oak tree, his hand brushing against its rough bark, waiting for me to come back, to feel rooted again.

But I kept driving, my knuckles white on the steering wheel as I navigated the road that seemed to stretch infinitely before me. With every bend, I fought the urge to veer off and turn back, to retrace the path to the life I had left behind. Just one more look at the familiar landscape, one more taste of home, and I would be okay. I could feel the tug of that longing deep in my chest, a relentless whisper that urged me to reconsider.

And yet, Boston waited for me—its chaotic energy, the promise of opportunity, the chance to rediscover myself in a city that pulsed with life. The allure of galleries and coffee shops, the possibility of falling back in love with the art world that had once cradled me. I yearned to dive into the city's embrace, to find inspiration amidst its bustling streets, but the lingering shadows of my decision kept me company, reminding me of what I was leaving behind.

As I approached the highway, the towering trees gave way to sprawling fields, golden and green, stretching endlessly like a painter's canvas. The transition was jarring, a sharp reminder that I was straddling two worlds—one filled with comfort and familiarity, the other shrouded in the unknown. I turned the radio dial, searching for a song that would drown out the clamor of my thoughts, but instead, I was met with the sweet strains of a ballad that twisted the knife in my heart. The singer's voice wrapped around me, a haunting melody that spoke of lost love and second chances, and I couldn't help but choke on my emotions.

"Great, just great," I muttered to myself, trying to rein in the swell of tears that threatened to spill over. "What a way to start a new chapter."

Suddenly, the sudden blare of a horn jolted me back to reality. A car shot past, its driver glaring at me as if I had personally offended him. I glanced at my speedometer—just under the limit, but the unexpected surge of adrenaline made my heart race. "Well, at least someone is in a hurry," I said aloud, attempting to lighten my mood. I could almost hear Clayton's teasing remark about my tendency to daydream, something he had often called 'getting lost in the clouds.'

The road twisted ahead, and I gripped the wheel tighter. I was almost at the exit for the highway, the one that would lead me away from everything I knew. But something—perhaps it was intuition, perhaps it was sheer defiance—tugged at me to take a different path. A sudden urge to detour flooded through me, an impulse that whispered of possibilities I hadn't yet considered.

"Okay, let's see what's down this road," I announced, my voice steady despite the turmoil within. I turned the wheel sharply, veering off onto a narrow country road. Trees lined the path like sentinels, their leaves whispering secrets as I drove deeper into the heart of the landscape. It felt reckless, thrilling, and terrifying all at once. The city could wait a little longer, and perhaps I could find what I was looking for in these uncharted territories.

As I drove on, the road narrowed, flanked by wildflowers that danced in the breeze. The air was fresher here, infused with the scent of blooming honeysuckle and damp earth. With every mile, I felt a strange kind of liberation, as if I had shed a layer of my old self and was becoming something new, something more in tune with the world around me.

Then, almost out of nowhere, a sign appeared, its faded letters promising a local festival just a few miles down the road. I felt a flutter of excitement. The thought of laughter, music, and perhaps even a fleeting moment of joy pulled me in like a moth to a flame. What if I found a reason to smile, a reason to reconnect with the life I was leaving behind? What if this detour led me to something—or someone—I didn't know I needed?

With a newfound determination, I pressed the accelerator, my heart racing not just from the speed but from the thrill of the unknown that lay ahead. Perhaps it was time to embrace the unexpected, to allow fate to guide my journey instead of clinging tightly to my carefully laid plans. After all, the road not taken was still out there, waiting for me to explore its winding paths and hidden treasures.

The road narrowed, twisting through lush greenery that wrapped around me like an embrace, the trees leaning in as if to catch a glimpse of my burgeoning resolve. Each bump and curve rattled my nerves in an invigorating way, awakening a sense of adventure that I had buried beneath layers of practicality. A flicker of laughter bubbled in my chest, urging me to let go of my worries, at least for a moment. "Who knew the back roads could be this lively?" I murmured, chuckling at the absurdity of my own thoughts as the car rocked gently over the uneven terrain.

The festival loomed closer, a splash of color against the backdrop of the sprawling fields. Bright tents and fluttering flags danced in the wind, and I felt an involuntary smile tugging at my lips. I parked the car under the shade of an ancient oak, its branches stretching wide, welcoming. As I stepped outside, the sounds of laughter and music drifted toward me, wrapping around me like a warm blanket. The earthy smell of freshly popped popcorn mingled with the sweet scent of cotton candy, awakening a nostalgic hunger that surged through me.

"Not too shabby for a last-minute detour," I remarked, squaring my shoulders as I approached the entrance. The moment I crossed the threshold, I was hit with a wave of vibrancy. Children ran past, faces painted with the smudged remnants of their morning adventures, and couples wandered hand in hand, their eyes sparkling with the thrill of the festival atmosphere. My heart lightened, the weight of my earlier decisions momentarily forgotten.

I paused, taking in the scene. A group of teenagers stood near a makeshift stage, laughing as one of them strummed a guitar. Their easy camaraderie reminded me of summer nights spent with friends, playing music under the stars until dawn slipped in, tired and forgiving. The melody floated through the air, and I found myself swaying slightly, lost in the rhythm of the moment.

Just then, a familiar face emerged from the crowd—Sarah, my old high school friend, her dark curls bouncing as she made her way toward me. "Is that really you?" she exclaimed, her voice rising over the din. "Look at you, all grown up and fleeing the scene!"

I laughed, the tension in my shoulders easing. "You know me, always on the run from responsibility."

"Right, and straight into the arms of adventure, I see." Her eyes twinkled mischievously, and I could feel the years melt away as we embraced. "What brings you back to our little corner of paradise?"

"A bit of a spontaneous detour, I suppose. I was heading back to Boston, but then I saw the festival sign and thought, why not?"

She clapped her hands in delight, her enthusiasm infectious. "Perfect! You must stay and have some fun! You won't believe how crazy this place gets when the sun sets."

I hesitated, a flicker of doubt creeping in. "I don't know, Sarah. I shouldn't linger too long. I have a life waiting for me back home."

"Life? Or just a set of responsibilities that keep you from living?" She raised an eyebrow, a teasing grin spreading across her face. "Just tonight. Promise me you'll stay, at least until the fireworks."

"Fine," I conceded, unable to resist her infectious energy. "But only for a couple of hours. I really need to get back on the road."

She grabbed my wrist, pulling me toward the heart of the festival. "That's the spirit! Let's grab something to eat. You look like you could use a funnel cake and some fun."

As we wandered through the vibrant stalls, my senses were overwhelmed. The laughter of children, the distant strumming of guitars, and the tantalizing aroma of grilled corn and warm pastries blended into a symphony of delight. We snagged a plate of fries topped with gooey cheese and ranch dressing, sitting on a weathered bench that had seen better days.

"Tell me everything," she urged between bites, her eyes wide with curiosity. "What's life like in the big city? Is it as glamorous as they say?"

"Glamorous? More like chaotic," I replied, unable to keep a straight face. "The subway smells like a mix of regret and bad coffee, and the people move like they're in a constant state of caffeinated frenzy. I feel like I'm always dodging tourists and taxi cabs. Not exactly the dream."

She giggled, her laughter bright against the backdrop of the festival. "Sounds charming. And what about Clayton? Are you two still... whatever it is you were?"

A lump formed in my throat at the mention of his name. "We were never really anything defined. Just... two people trying to figure things out." The admission felt heavy on my tongue, and I took a deep breath, the laughter fading slightly. "I think I needed to break free, to find my own path without being tied down."

"And how's that working out for you?" she asked, her gaze piercing yet compassionate.

"Honestly? I'm still not sure. I thought leaving would give me clarity, but all I feel is... lost." I looked around, at the joyous faces and the laughter that surrounded us. "It's like I'm in a limbo, you know? I'm supposed to be excited about the future, but instead, I'm haunted by what I left behind."

"Maybe you're just not ready to let go." Her voice softened, but her eyes sparkled with mischief. "But tonight is about fun. We're going to dance, eat too much sugar, and watch the stars explode in the sky. You need this—an escape."

"Fine! Let's escape," I declared, throwing my arms up in mock surrender, and her laughter rang out again, rich and warm.

Just then, a commotion broke out nearby. A group of festival-goers had gathered around a dunk tank, and I turned to see a familiar face perched above the water. It was Tom, the high school heartthrob, grinning widely as he teased the crowd. "Come on, folks! Let's see who's brave enough to take me down!"

I couldn't help but laugh. "I forgot how much he loved the spotlight."

"Oh, he's always been a performer. Let's see if anyone has the courage to knock him in," Sarah said, nudging me forward. "What do you think? Care to give it a try?"

A sudden surge of confidence rushed through me. "Why not?" I replied, my voice a bit louder than intended, drawing the attention of those nearby.

"Alright, then!" Sarah cheered, pushing me toward the line. "Let's show him what we're made of!"

I took a deep breath, the atmosphere buzzing with anticipation as I picked up a ball, my fingers gripping it tightly. Tom flashed a cocky grin as I stepped up to the platform. "You think you can take me down, huh?" he called, and the crowd roared in laughter.

I met his gaze, a spark igniting within me. "Just watch me!" I threw the ball with all my might, and in a split second, it hit the target. Tom tumbled into the water with an exaggerated splash, and the crowd erupted in cheers. Laughter bubbled up inside me as I basked in the moment, feeling more alive than I had in days.

"Now that's what I call a welcome back," Sarah laughed, clapping her hands in delight as the crowd cheered. For a fleeting moment, all my worries faded, and I felt like I was exactly where I needed to be—caught in the exhilarating rush of the now, surrounded by friends and laughter. I could taste the freedom on my lips, sweet like cotton candy, and in that moment, I understood what it meant to truly let go.

The sound of splashing water echoed in my ears as I stepped away from the dunk tank, a newfound thrill coursing through me. Tom resurfaced, his laughter mingling with the cheers from the crowd, and the lightness in my chest blossomed into something beautiful—perhaps joy, or the spark of connection I'd been missing for far too long. I grinned at Sarah, who was practically bouncing with excitement. "That was amazing! I feel like I could conquer the world right now!"

"Just wait until the fireworks," she replied, her eyes twinkling as she nudged me toward the next booth. "Let's grab a drink to celebrate your victory over Mr. Heartthrob."

The air was thick with anticipation as we strolled through the festival, absorbing the kaleidoscope of colors and sounds. We stopped at a stall selling homemade lemonade, its icy sweetness beckoning like an oasis. I took a long sip, letting the cool liquid wash over me, and as I savored the flavor, I felt the weight of my earlier choices begin to lift, even if just a little.

As we made our way past stalls of handwoven crafts and laughter, I noticed a corner of the festival where people had gathered around a makeshift stage. A woman in a flowing dress sang softly, her voice weaving through the air like a gentle breeze. The atmosphere shifted, becoming more intimate, as if the music had wrapped around us, inviting us to pause and reflect.

"Wow, she's incredible," I murmured, drawn to the warmth of the performance.

"Isn't she?" Sarah replied, her gaze fixed on the singer. "That's Lily. She used to play at the diner on Fridays. She moved to the city for a bit but came back to her roots. Seems like she's found herself again."

"Maybe I need a little of that," I said lightly, though the words hung heavy in my mind. The thought of reclaiming my own self felt like a distant dream, something I could only watch from the sidelines.

After a while, Sarah leaned closer. "Want to join her? I know she's always looking for backup singers, and you have that lovely voice of yours."

"Me? No way!" I laughed, though my cheeks flushed at the compliment. The idea of stepping into the spotlight, of being seen and heard, sent a thrill down my spine. "I haven't sung in ages."

"Then tonight is the perfect night for a comeback!" She nudged me with her shoulder, and before I could second-guess myself, she pulled me toward the stage.

The singer finished her set with a flourish, and the crowd erupted into applause. Sarah and I joined in, clapping enthusiastically, and as Lily stepped off the stage, Sarah caught her attention. "Hey, Lily! My friend here is an incredible singer. You should let her join you for a song!"

"Me? No, I—" I stammered, suddenly feeling very much like a deer caught in headlights.

Lily smiled warmly, her dark hair swaying as she approached us. "Oh, I'd love that! You should definitely sing with me. It's all about having fun."

Before I could backtrack, Sarah was shoving me forward. "Come on! Just one song. What's the worst that could happen?"

The crowd parted as I stepped onto the stage, the lights shining down and illuminating the swirling doubts in my mind. My heart raced, thumping wildly against my ribcage. I glanced back at Sarah, who was grinning like a Cheshire cat, and then at Lily, who radiated confidence and warmth.

"Alright," I said, trying to summon a bit of bravado. "But you're going to have to bear with me."

Lily laughed lightly, and before I knew it, the music started, the notes swirling in the air like whispers of encouragement. I closed my eyes, letting the melody wrap around me, and I began to sing, my voice rising with the tune.

At first, my nerves threatened to overwhelm me, but as I listened to Lily's harmonies weave with my own, something shifted inside. The fear receded, replaced by a rush of exhilaration. The crowd swayed, lost in the moment with us, and I couldn't help but smile, feeling a spark of the old me—the one who dreamed of performing and felt alive under the spotlight.

When we finished, the applause erupted like fireworks in my chest, and I stood there breathless, the thrill of the performance flooding through my veins. "That was amazing!" I exclaimed, turning to Lily, who was beaming back at me.

"You were fantastic! You should do this more often," she encouraged, her voice warm and genuine.

"I don't know about that," I replied, still riding the wave of adrenaline. "I've got a whole life to get back to in Boston."

"Oh, come on," Sarah chimed in, throwing her arm around my shoulders. "Don't think about it right now. Just enjoy the moment!"

As we stepped down from the stage, I felt an unfamiliar sense of belonging wash over me. The laughter and cheers of the crowd faded into the background, but the warmth lingered, weaving a thread of connection to this place, to the people, and most importantly, to myself.

Just then, as the sun dipped lower in the sky, the first firework exploded overhead, painting the evening with brilliant colors. "Wow," I breathed, tilting my head back to watch the spectacle unfold. The bursts of light reminded me of the dreams I'd tucked away, igniting a flicker of hope.

"Are you feeling that?" Sarah asked, her voice slightly muffled as she leaned in closer. "Like everything is about to change?"

I nodded, my heart racing as I caught the eye of someone in the crowd. It was Clayton, standing there, a shadow in the vibrant light, his gaze locked onto mine. My breath caught, the warmth of the moment replaced with a chill that swept through me like a sudden storm.

"What is he doing here?" I whispered, my heart pounding with a mix of surprise and apprehension.

"Is that...?" Sarah followed my gaze, her eyes widening. "Oh wow, he looks good. You should go talk to him!"

"Talk to him? Are you insane?" The weight of a thousand emotions crashed over me, pulling me back into the whirlwind of memories I thought I'd escaped. "I can't just walk up to him like everything is fine!"

But there was Clayton, standing in the glow of the festival lights, the last remnants of the sunset framing him in a way that made my heart ache with longing. For a heartbeat, time stretched, and the laughter faded into a hushed silence, the world narrowing down to just the two of us.

"Why not?" Sarah nudged me gently. "You've come this far. Just go say hi."

As I stood there, frozen between past and present, the sky exploded again with light, brilliant and blinding, and for a moment, I was lost. The colors danced above us, a cascade of possibilities—and yet, all I could focus on was the man who had once held my heart, now standing before me like an unanswered question.

With the firework's final boom echoing in the night, I took a step forward, uncertainty twisting in my stomach. Would this moment change everything, or would it simply confirm what I already knew? Before I could decide, another voice broke through the haze—a low, firm tone cutting through the laughter and the chaos.

"Hey, there you are!" A stranger stepped in front of me, blocking my view of Clayton. "I've been looking for you."

I blinked, taken aback by the intrusion, my heart racing as I tried to make sense of the new arrival. The festival lights flickered around us, and the path before me shifted in an unexpected direction, leaving me to wonder if I was truly ready for whatever lay ahead.

Chapter 21: Unraveling

The sound of heels clicking against the polished marble floors echoed in my ears, a rhythm that felt foreign in the sprawling expanse of my once-familiar office. I paced the halls like a caged animal, eyes darting to the frosted glass doors of my colleagues, half-listening to their animated conversations. Their laughter seemed to float above me, an ethereal reminder of a world I no longer inhabited. I could feel the weight of my promotion—an achievement celebrated with confetti and champagne—resting heavily on my shoulders. It was as if I was wearing a crown forged from thorns, the glittering jewels cutting into my skin.

"Hey, are you okay?" Tara, my bubbly colleague with a penchant for brightly colored cardigans and a never-ending supply of enthusiasm, caught me mid-spiral. Her voice was a warm melody that danced through the sterile atmosphere. I forced a smile, the kind that reached my lips but never quite touched my eyes.

"Yeah, just... you know, getting used to the new role," I replied, waving my hand dismissively as if that gesture could erase the jagged edges of my reality. "All good!"

She raised an eyebrow, not quite buying it, but she was too polite to press. I envied her, the way she threw herself into her work, her laughter ringing like bells. I wondered if she felt the weight of expectations too, the gnawing sensation of something vital slipping away.

With a sigh, I retreated to my office, where the familiar scent of fresh paper and overpriced coffee provided a stark contrast to the chaos of my thoughts. The walls were adorned with motivational posters—quotes promising success and happiness—but they felt hollow, echoing my own discontent. I sank into my chair, the leather cool against my skin, and pulled up the reports that had piled high in my inbox. The words blurred together, dancing mockingly on the screen.

As I stared, lost in a fog of numbers and figures, my phone buzzed. A message from Clayton. My heart flipped, a traitorous spark igniting a flicker of hope. I opened it, the familiar warmth of his words crashing over me like a wave. "Thinking of you," it read, simple yet profound. It was a lifeline thrown into the tempest of my solitude.

I couldn't resist typing back, my fingers trembling slightly as I fought the urge to unleash all the bottled emotions swirling inside me. "I miss you." It was honest, raw, and so unlike the professional facade I wore every day. I hit send before I could second-guess myself, a rush of adrenaline washing over me.

The seconds ticked by, each one stretching into eternity. I could almost hear the echo of his laughter, the way it made the corners of my world feel bright and full. But when my phone lit up again, it wasn't a reply. Instead, it was a news alert, flashing across my screen with all the subtlety of a marching band. "Local Businessman Charged with Fraud."

I clicked on the headline, my heart sinking as I read the details. There it was—Clayton's name. My pulse quickened, confusion threading its way through my chest like a needle pulling tight the seams of my heart. I had seen the signs, the whispers of financial troubles, but this? I felt as though the ground beneath me had cracked open, and I was teetering on the edge.

With a resolve I didn't quite understand, I grabbed my coat and headed out into the vibrant pulse of the city. The autumn air was crisp, wrapping around me like a reminder of life beyond the sterile walls of the office. I navigated the streets, the kaleidoscope of colors blurring as my thoughts spiraled out of control. The hustle of Boston swirled around me, but I felt detached, as if I was watching the world from behind a glass wall.

"Hey! You okay there?" a voice called from a nearby café. It was an older gentleman with a beard that looked like it had seen a few winters too many. He was standing at the door, coffee cup in hand, concern etched on his weathered face.

"Yeah, just… processing," I managed to reply, forcing a smile that felt like a mask. He nodded, his eyes kind and understanding, before retreating back inside.

I walked, my feet moving of their own accord, until I found myself in front of the building where Clayton had his office. My heart raced as I stood there, staring at the sleek glass façade. Memories flooded my mind—late nights filled with laughter, dreams woven into the fabric of our lives. But that was before the rumors, the whispers that hung in the air like fog, threatening to swallow us whole.

Taking a deep breath, I pushed open the heavy door and stepped inside. The receptionist glanced up, her smile faltering as she recognized me. "He's not in today," she said, her tone sympathetic yet distant. I felt the weight of her gaze, like a spotlight shining on my vulnerabilities.

"Do you know when he'll be back?" I asked, my voice steadier than I felt.

She hesitated, glancing at her computer screen. "I think he's dealing with some… personal matters." The way she said it made my stomach twist, an unspoken understanding lingering in the air.

I thanked her and turned to leave, but the gravity of the situation pulled me back. I needed to know more. I needed to understand. My heart thudded in my chest, each beat echoing my determination as I pulled my phone from my pocket, scrolling through news articles that painted a picture I couldn't quite grasp. Each headline was like a punch to the gut, sharp and unforgiving.

As I stepped back into the bustling streets of Boston, a sense of urgency surged within me. I had to reach Clayton, to untangle this web of confusion before it ensnared us both. The city buzzed around me, unaware of my internal chaos. I wasn't just searching for answers; I was clawing my way back to the life I had almost lost, to the man who had filled my world with light. The journey would be anything but straightforward, but I was ready to unravel the truth, no matter where it led.

The sun hung low in the sky, casting a golden hue over the cobblestone streets of Beacon Hill, igniting the bricks with a warmth that felt at odds with my frigid heart. I drifted past boutique shops, their windows displaying delightful trinkets that caught my eye but failed to stir any joy within me. A pashmina caught in the breeze danced like a specter at the edge of my vision, reminding me of Clayton's laughter, the way it filled the room, wrapping around us like a cozy blanket on a chilly night. I almost reached out to touch it, but the memory slipped away, leaving me with the heavy cloak of reality.

I turned the corner and found myself in front of the coffee shop where we used to frequent, a quaint little place with brick walls adorned with local art. The scent of freshly brewed coffee wafted through the door, pulling me in like a moth to a flame. I stepped inside, greeted by the familiar barista, a cheerful young woman with vibrant purple hair and an infectious smile. She was already in the process of crafting a cappuccino, expertly foaming the milk with the precision of an artist.

"Hey there! The usual?" she chirped, her voice brightening the air.

"Actually, I think I'll try something different today," I replied, forcing a smile that felt more like a mask than an expression of genuine cheer. "How about a mocha?"

"Coming right up! It's like a hug in a cup!" she exclaimed, and as she turned to prepare my order, I caught my reflection in the mirror behind the counter. The face staring back was familiar yet foreign—eyes a touch too haunted, lips set in a line that was more of a frown than a smile.

I took a seat at a small table by the window, absently fiddling with the napkin holder, lost in thought. My mind churned with images of Clayton, his laughter ringing in my ears, his touch igniting fires that flickered out as quickly as they ignited. What was happening to him? The headlines had painted a picture of chaos, of a man on the verge of collapse. It felt surreal, like a plot twist in a novel that had taken a dark turn. I sipped my drink when it arrived, the warmth spreading through me, yet it did little to melt the ice encasing my heart.

"Here you go!" The barista placed the mocha in front of me, her smile unwavering. "Let me know what you think!"

I took a tentative sip, the sweetness a comforting contrast to the bitterness of my thoughts. "It's perfect," I said, genuinely impressed. "I might have to switch it up more often."

"Life's too short for the same old thing, right?" she replied, a glimmer of mischief in her eyes.

"Exactly. I should take a page out of your book," I laughed lightly, though the sound felt foreign. "Try something new every once in a while."

"Just remember to let me know when you find something you love! I want to be in the know," she grinned, moving to the next customer.

I returned to my thoughts, the warmth of the mocha a temporary reprieve from the swirling storm inside me. I needed answers, a direction to steer my muddled emotions, and that meant confronting the chaos. I had to reach out to Clayton, to bridge this unsettling distance that felt more like a chasm every day.

As I stepped back onto the street, the chill air nipped at my skin, sharpening my resolve. I fished out my phone, my fingers hovering over his name. Would he even answer? The last few exchanges had felt like texts thrown into a void, unanswered and lingering like ghosts. I took a deep breath, my heart racing as I tapped the screen.

"Can we talk? Please."

I sent the message, my finger hovering over the "send" button for longer than I cared to admit. The moment I let go, an exhilarating wave of fear and hope crashed over me. What if he was too far gone, too mired in whatever mess he was tangled in? I needed to know, but the prospect of hearing his voice again sent a thrill through me, tangled with dread.

Minutes felt like hours, the bustling streets of Boston blurring into a backdrop of noise as I waited. I paced back and forth, my mind a cacophony of memories and fears, until finally, my phone buzzed with a reply.

"I'll be at the park in an hour."

A simple response, yet it sent my heart racing. The park was our spot—a haven where laughter and warmth mingled with the scent of blooming flowers and freshly cut grass. I could picture him there, hands shoved in his pockets, looking like a tempestuous storm wrapped in a man's form, both thrilling and daunting.

The walk to the park was a blur, my mind consumed with anticipation and dread. I could feel the air shift around me, the sky deepening into twilight as I approached the familiar archway of branches that marked our sanctuary. The world outside faded, replaced by the vibrant hues of sunset spilling across the horizon, a canvas of oranges and pinks that reminded me of better days.

When I arrived, I found him seated on our favorite bench, a slight frown etched across his brow. The sight of him stirred something within me—a mixture of warmth and worry. His hair, usually neatly styled, was tousled, as if he had run his hands through it in frustration. I approached cautiously, unsure of what to expect.

"Hey," I said softly, my voice barely above a whisper as I took a seat beside him.

He turned to me, his eyes darkened by shadows that had nothing to do with the fading light. "Hey." The word fell between us, heavy with unsaid things.

"I saw the news…" I started, but he cut me off, a wave of frustration crashing over him.

"Don't." The word was sharp, an edge that sliced through the air. "I don't want to talk about that right now."

I nodded, feeling the chill creep back into our space. "Then what do you want to talk about?" I was probing, testing the waters.

He sighed, leaning back against the bench, the tension in his body palpable. "Honestly? I don't know." His vulnerability was a dagger that lodged itself in my heart.

"Clayton, you're not alone in this," I urged, reaching out to touch his arm gently. "Whatever's happening, we can face it together."

His gaze met mine, a mix of frustration and longing swirling in the depths. "I don't want to drag you into my mess. You deserve better."

"Better than what? Better than caring?" I shot back, my voice sharper than intended. "You think I can just turn my back on you?"

The air between us crackled with tension, and I held my breath, waiting for his response. He turned away, staring out at the park, where the leaves rustled in the gentle breeze, dancing in their autumn glory. I felt a knot of helplessness tightening in my chest as I fought to keep my voice steady.

"I came here because I'm worried about you," I said, my tone softer now. "I want to help. But you have to let me in."

Silence enveloped us, thick and suffocating. The moments stretched on, filled with unspoken words and emotions bubbling just below the surface. Finally, he turned to me, the fight leaving his eyes.

"I don't know if I can," he admitted, his voice barely above a whisper.

"Then let's figure it out together," I replied, my heart pounding. "Just give me a chance."

He hesitated, the weight of the world pressing down on him, but I could see a flicker of hope behind the storm. Perhaps it was just the fading light playing tricks on my eyes, but I clung to it fiercely, willing it to grow. In that moment, as the sun dipped below the horizon, I realized this wasn't just about unraveling; it was about weaving the threads of our lives back together, one conversation at a time.

The air was thick with unspoken words, an invisible weight pressing down on us as we sat on that familiar park bench. The flickering twilight cast long shadows, mirroring the uncertainty that danced between us. I could see the gears turning in Clayton's mind, a mix of worry and defiance crossing his features as he struggled with his next move. I wanted to bridge the distance, to reach out and pull him back to the vibrant life we once shared.

"Listen, whatever you're dealing with, we can face it together," I pressed, my voice steady but soft, trying to create a safe space for him to spill his fears. "You're not the only one who's had their life turned upside down."

He turned his gaze from the park's fading beauty, his eyes locking onto mine with an intensity that sent a shiver down my spine. "What if it's too late for that?" he asked, vulnerability cracking the surface of his bravado.

"Too late? For what?" I countered, leaning in closer. "For you to let me in? For us to be honest with each other?"

He exhaled, a long, weary sound that seemed to resonate with the weight of the world. "You don't know what I'm caught up in," he replied, his tone edged with a mix of frustration and fear. "It's not just about me anymore. There are consequences, and I'm worried they'll spill over into your life too."

"Is that what this is about? You're trying to protect me?" I asked, my heart swelling with a mixture of gratitude and frustration.

"Because if you think that shutting me out is going to keep me safe, you're mistaken."

He looked away again, his hands fidgeting with the frayed edges of his jeans. "It's complicated," he mumbled, almost to himself.

"Complicated? I've read enough romance novels to know that complicated is just a euphemism for 'I'm terrified of what comes next.'" My attempt at levity hung in the air, a fragile bridge between us, but Clayton didn't respond. His eyes were distant, lost in thought.

I watched him, this man who had once been my anchor, now adrift in a sea of uncertainty. My heart ached to reach out, to pull him back from whatever brink he teetered on. "What if we could start untangling the mess together?" I suggested, my voice a gentle coaxing. "You've been carrying this alone for too long. Let me help."

He turned his head sharply, surprise flashing across his face. "You think it's that easy?"

"Easy? No. Worth it? Absolutely."

There was a flicker of hope in his eyes, the tiniest spark that made my heart race. "You're talking about risking everything. I can't do that to you."

"Clayton, I'd rather take the risk and fight for you than let you walk away into this dark hole alone," I replied, leaning closer, desperate to bridge the gap between us. "You matter to me more than you realize."

Silence enveloped us once more, but this time it felt charged with possibility. I held my breath, waiting for him to say something—anything—that would shatter the distance between us. But instead, he simply stared ahead, the shadows deepening around us.

Suddenly, his phone buzzed on the bench between us, vibrating with urgency. He grabbed it, his face paling as he read the message. I leaned in, curiosity piqued, my heart racing with concern.

"What is it?" I asked, sensing the shift in his demeanor.

"It's... my lawyer," he said, his voice tight as he scrolled through the message. "There's a meeting tomorrow morning."

"A meeting about what?" I pressed, but his eyes were fixed on the screen, his expression shifting from worry to outright dread.

"They found something," he murmured, his voice barely above a whisper. "Something that could change everything."

"What do you mean?" Panic flared inside me, sharp and fierce. "Clayton, you need to explain this to me!"

"I can't. I can't explain anything right now." His voice was thick with frustration, and the tension between us escalated. "You need to go."

"Go? Are you serious?" I shot back, my heart pounding in my chest. "I'm not going anywhere. I'm here for you!"

He shook his head, his expression darkening. "No, you don't understand. This isn't just about us anymore. I'm in too deep, and I don't want to drag you down with me."

His words hit me like a punch to the gut. I felt the ground shift beneath me, a whirlpool of emotions threatening to pull me under. "Clayton, please, just tell me what's going on!" I pleaded, my voice rising in desperation.

Before he could respond, his phone buzzed again, a series of rapid notifications that seemed to shake him further. He looked at the screen, his expression shifting to one of alarm. "They're moving faster than I thought," he muttered, more to himself than to me.

"What does that mean?" I demanded, frustration boiling over.

"It means I have to handle this alone," he snapped, suddenly defensive.

"Handle what?" I pushed back, unwilling to let him retreat behind his walls.

"The investigation. It's getting messy, and I don't want you involved in any of it," he replied, his voice hardening. "You don't deserve this."

"You're right, I don't deserve it," I shot back, my temper flaring. "But I'm not going to just stand by while you self-destruct! You're throwing away everything we've built—everything we could still build—because of some ridiculous notion of protecting me!"

He stood abruptly, the bench creaking beneath him. "You don't get to dictate how I handle my life!" he retorted, his voice rising.

"Then why the hell are we even having this conversation?" I shouted back, the tension crackling in the air like static electricity.

"Because I care about you!" he shouted, his frustration mingling with something softer, something raw that hung in the air between us. "And I don't want to see you hurt."

"I can take care of myself!" I replied, but my voice faltered, the weight of his concern pressing down on me like a physical force.

"Can you? Can you really?" His gaze bore into mine, a challenge wrapped in desperation.

I opened my mouth to respond, but my words faltered. Suddenly, a shadow passed over us—a figure loomed at the edge of the park, watching us with an intensity that sent a shiver down my spine. My heart raced as I caught sight of a man in a dark coat, his face obscured by the growing darkness.

"Clayton," I whispered, my voice trembling.

He turned to look, his expression shifting from anger to concern in an instant. "What is it?"

"That man... he's been watching us," I said, a sense of unease crawling up my spine.

The figure stepped forward, and the world around us faded as tension spiraled in the air. Clayton's jaw clenched, a flash of recognition crossing his features.

"Get back!" he shouted, pushing me behind him, his body a shield against whatever threat lay ahead.

"What's happening?" I asked, fear coursing through me.

But as the figure approached, his intentions became chillingly clear, and I realized that the night held more danger than I could have ever anticipated.

The man stopped just within earshot, a cold smile playing on his lips as he locked eyes with Clayton. "I believe we need to have a chat."

My heart thundered as I felt the ground beneath me shift once more, reality spiraling into chaos, and I knew we were on the brink of something far more dangerous than any of us could have prepared for.

Chapter 22: The Phone Call

The rain pattered against my window, a steady rhythm that matched the rapid beating of my heart. Each droplet danced down the glass, tracing paths I couldn't help but follow with my eyes, lost in thoughts of what could have been. Clayton's name blinked on my phone, a lighthouse in the fog of my loneliness, and for a moment, the world around me faded into the background. I took a deep breath, feeling the familiar tension coil in my stomach, a blend of anxiety and excitement that I hadn't felt in months. I almost convinced myself to let it go to voicemail, to shield myself from the vulnerability of this unexpected connection.

But the memory of his laughter, bright and teasing, pulled me in. How long had it been since we shared those moments, the easy banter that felt as natural as breathing? I tapped the screen and answered, the sound of his name on my lips stirring something deep within me. "Hey, it's me," I said, my voice soft, almost afraid to disrupt the fragile atmosphere we had created in this shared silence.

"Lana." His voice, smooth as dark chocolate, enveloped me. I could picture him there, probably leaning against the counter in his small kitchen, coffee cup in hand, just like he used to when we'd spend lazy Sunday mornings discussing everything from the universe to the best flavors of ice cream. "I didn't expect you to pick up."

"I almost didn't." I smirked, even though he couldn't see me. It felt good to play with that old spark, to flirt with danger. "But here we are, defying expectations. What's up?"

There was a slight hesitation on his end, a pause that stretched into a moment of uncertainty. I could almost see him running a hand through his tousled hair, the way he always did when he was wrestling with something difficult. "I... I just wanted to see how you've been."

I leaned against the wall, the cool paint a comfort against my skin. "You know, the usual. Rain, work, a lot of binge-watching terrible reality TV. I've become quite the expert on the lives of strangers." I chuckled, my tone light, but the truth was more complex. My life felt like a series of carefully arranged dominoes, all teetering on the edge, waiting for a nudge to send them tumbling.

"Sounds thrilling." He laughed, and I could feel the warmth of it wrap around me. "But really, how are you doing? I mean it." His sincerity cut through the casual chatter, grounding me.

I opened my mouth to answer, but the truth hung in the air, an unspoken weight between us. "I'm managing. Some days are harder than others, you know?" The words slipped out before I could filter them, honest and raw. "But I'm trying. I guess that's all we can do, right?"

"Yeah, it is." He paused again, and I imagined the countless thoughts racing through his mind. "I was thinking about that time we got caught in the rain at the park. You remember?"

"Who could forget? You insisted we could outrun it." I laughed, picturing us, soaked to the bone, running through puddles and shrieking with laughter, the world around us blurring into a backdrop of laughter and joy. "I think you might have been wrong on that one."

"I'll take my share of the blame." He sighed, his voice shifting to something deeper, more contemplative. "I just... I wanted to reach out because I miss those moments. I miss you."

Each word felt like a pebble dropped into the depths of my heart, sending ripples through my carefully constructed façade. I fought the urge to let that vulnerable side of me peek through. "It's easy to miss the good times when you're stuck in the rain." I said lightly, but my heart twisted at the reality behind my words.

"Lana, it's not just the good times," he said softly, the shift in his tone pulling me closer, drawing me into his world, a world that felt both familiar and terrifying. "I miss the way we talked about everything and nothing. I miss you."

My stomach tightened. "You know we can't just pick up where we left off." The words slipped from my lips, sharp and bitter, like an unripe fruit. The past loomed over us like a shadow, dark and heavy with unspoken grievances and hurt feelings.

"I'm not asking for that," he replied, urgency creeping into his voice. "I just want to be in your life again, even if it's just as friends. I don't want to lose you completely."

The honesty in his words struck a chord, resonating within me. "You think it's that easy?" My voice trembled, caught between anger and sorrow. "We can't just sweep everything under the rug and pretend we're fine. Things happened, Clayton."

"I know." His admission hung in the air, raw and unpolished. "But I've thought about it. I've thought about us. I've realized I don't want to live in a world where you're not a part of my life."

I closed my eyes, trying to stifle the flood of emotions he had stirred. The memories surged forward—our laughter echoing through the quiet streets, late-night talks under the stars, and the deep connection that had bound us together even when the world had threatened to tear us apart.

"You're making it hard for me to breathe," I confessed, my voice barely a whisper. The thought of opening that door, of letting him back in, felt like standing on the precipice of a cliff, staring into the abyss below. Would I fly, or would I fall?

"Then don't breathe. Just listen." His voice was steady, a balm against my chaos. "Let's just start with a conversation. One that doesn't involve any past mistakes. Let's build something new, together."

The invitation hung in the air, tempting yet terrifying. Could we truly reshape the narrative of our lives, rewrite the chapters that had been marred by regret? I was lost in thought, the rain continuing its soft symphony outside, when a single thought broke through the tumult: I missed him too.

The conversation lingered like the scent of rain-soaked earth, familiar yet unsettling, weaving through my thoughts long after I hung up. I cradled my phone in my hand, staring blankly at the screen, wondering if the connection we had felt was real or simply a mirage created by loneliness. The rain continued to tap a steady rhythm against my window, but instead of feeling confined by the weather, a peculiar thrill danced within me. It was a feeling I hadn't experienced in far too long—a blend of hope and fear that hinted at the possibility of something new.

A thought wormed its way into my mind: what if I invited him over? The idea rolled around, gathering strength like the storm clouds overhead. I could brew a pot of coffee, light some candles, and we could talk face-to-face, diving deeper into the choppy waters of our past without the safety net of a phone call. It was reckless, and a part of me hesitated at the brink, warning me of the potential fallout. But the allure of seeing him again, of feeling that electric charge between us, was too tempting to resist.

After a few moments of indecision, I dialed his number, my heart racing as I listened to the rings echoing in the silence of my apartment. It felt surreal, as if I were playing a role in a movie, with the script unwritten and my heart leading the way.

"Hello?" His voice, slightly breathless, danced through the receiver.

"Clayton, it's me," I said, biting my lip to suppress a smile. "How about we continue our conversation in person? I could use some company, and I think you could, too."

There was a brief pause before he responded, a hitch of surprise that made me giddy. "You want me to come over? Right now?"

"Yes. The rain makes everything feel cozy, and I have a killer stash of coffee that's just begging to be brewed. Plus, I could use a good laugh. You still owe me for that awful attempt at cooking I had the last time you were here."

He laughed, a warm sound that sent butterflies fluttering through my chest. "Okay, I'm in. Just give me a few minutes."

As I hung up, anticipation bubbled within me, filling the empty spaces that had felt so heavy for months. I rushed to tidy up, throwing a stray blanket over the back of the couch and shoving a few dishes into the sink. The clock ticked ominously as I glanced out the window, watching the rain blur the world outside into a watercolor painting of muted colors.

I put on some music, soft and soothing, to break the silence in the room, while my heart raced with the thought of seeing him again. Each beat seemed to echo louder than the last, urging me to embrace this moment. The doorbell rang, jolting me from my reverie, and I took a deep breath before opening the door.

Clayton stood there, a little drenched but undeniably charming, his hair slightly tousled and a sheepish grin on his face. "I promise I didn't mean to bring the rain with me," he said, shaking droplets off like a dog just out of a pool.

"Just an added ambiance," I quipped, stepping aside to let him in. "Besides, it gives me an excuse to cuddle under a blanket later."

His laughter filled the small entryway, and as he stepped over the threshold, it felt like a barrier had been lifted between us. We settled into the living room, the atmosphere charged with an undercurrent of unspoken feelings. I busied myself in the kitchen, pouring coffee into mugs while he slumped onto the couch, looking both relaxed and slightly anxious, as if the walls of our shared past were closing in around us.

"Did you bring any of your infamous conversation starters?" he teased, propping his feet up on the coffee table, a playful spark in his eyes.

"Infamous? You make it sound like I'm an interrogator." I rolled my eyes, handing him a steaming mug. "But no, today we'll just wing it. I'm feeling spontaneous."

"Ah, spontaneous. The perfect setup for disaster." He sipped his coffee, the rich aroma wafting between us, making the moment feel more intimate.

"Speaking of disaster, remember the camping trip?" I asked, a mischievous smile creeping onto my face. "When you tried to start a fire using just two sticks? I thought we were going to freeze to death that night!"

He groaned, leaning back against the couch. "Don't remind me! I swear the wilderness was conspiring against me. I even had a 'firestarter' playlist, and it didn't help."

We shared a laugh, the kind that felt like sunlight breaking through clouds. As we reminisced, the air shifted subtly, charged with the electric possibility of rekindling what we once had. Each story pulled us closer, the distance that had felt insurmountable gradually dissolving with every chuckle and exchanged glance.

But as the laughter faded, a heaviness crept back in, tugging at my heart. "So, what are we doing here, really?" I asked, my voice quiet but steady, meeting his gaze. "Are we just two friends reminiscing, or is there more to this?"

He set his mug down, leaning forward with an intensity that made my heart race. "I don't know. I want to say I've thought about it a lot since our last conversation. I just... I want you in my life, Lana. Not just as a friend, but more. I've missed you in ways I didn't realize until you weren't around."

The vulnerability in his voice sent a shiver down my spine. My pulse quickened, excitement and fear mingling in a chaotic dance. "But what if we end up back where we started?"

He shrugged, his eyes unwavering. "That's the risk, isn't it? But isn't it worth it to try? We can't change what happened, but we can build something new, together. Isn't that what you want?"

I felt the weight of his question settle in my chest, both thrilling and terrifying. Did I want to take that leap of faith, to plunge into the unknown with him? The thought of opening myself up again was daunting, yet the prospect of forging a new path with him was equally tantalizing.

"Okay," I said finally, the word tumbling from my lips before I could second-guess myself. "Let's try. Let's see where this goes."

His grin widened, lighting up the room, and in that moment, the past melted away, leaving space for the promise of what was to come. I felt lighter, almost buoyant, as if the rain had washed away the heaviness I had carried for too long. The air crackled with unspoken possibilities, and I knew that whatever came next, I was ready to face it—together with him.

The atmosphere between us shifted, a palpable tension humming in the air as I adjusted to this new dynamic. Clayton leaned closer, a glimmer of mischief sparking in his eyes as he tucked a loose strand of hair behind his ear. "So, how do you feel about adventure?" he asked, the corners of his mouth twitching up in that infuriatingly charming way.

"Adventure? You mean like camping and trying to start fires with sticks?" I shot back, my own lips curling into a smirk. "Or are you suggesting a daring escape from the monotony of my current Netflix binge?"

"Honestly, both sound equally appealing," he replied, his grin widening. "But I was thinking of something a bit less rustic and more... urban."

"Urban adventure?" My curiosity piqued, I tilted my head, intrigued. "Are you talking about a midnight pizza run or something more clandestine, like sneaking into an art gallery after hours?"

His eyes sparkled with excitement. "How about we start with the gallery idea? I've heard there's a late-night exhibit opening, and rumor has it they're serving free wine."

"Free wine? Now you're talking my language," I said, the prospect of a little escapade igniting a fire within me. The idea of stepping out of my comfort zone, of indulging in spontaneous fun, felt liberating. "But what if we get caught? Do we have a getaway plan?"

He laughed, a sound that filled the room with warmth. "We'll just act like we belong. Confidence is key, right? Plus, I'll take the fall if we get nabbed. You can always say you were just following my lead."

"Ah, so I'm the innocent bystander, huh?" I raised an eyebrow, both amused and tempted. "What if you're the one who gets us into trouble?"

"Then I'll be your charming accomplice," he quipped, leaning back with an exaggerated flourish. "Besides, I think we could both use a little trouble in our lives."

As we exchanged banter, I felt the old sparks between us reignite, pulling me closer to him. It was as if time itself had folded around us, erasing the heartache and complications of our past. Suddenly, the idea of stepping out into the world didn't seem so terrifying.

"Alright, Mr. Charming Accomplice," I said, a determined smile on my face. "Let's see if you can really pull this off."

With a shared glance that spoke volumes, we leapt into the adventure. Clayton took the lead, guiding us through the rain-slicked streets, the city alive with a pulse that mirrored our excitement. The scent of damp asphalt and the faint hints of roasted coffee filled the air as we wandered through familiar neighborhoods transformed by the night. The galleries, usually locked tight, glimmered in the soft glow of street lamps, casting shadows that danced with possibility.

"Here we are," Clayton said, stopping in front of a small, unassuming building with a modest sign that read "Gallery Now Open." I felt my heart race at the thought of what lay beyond those doors.

As we stepped inside, I was struck by the atmosphere—soft music enveloped us, mingling with the hushed conversations of art enthusiasts sipping wine from delicate glasses. The walls were adorned with vibrant paintings, each one a story begging to be told.

Clayton squeezed my hand gently, a reassuring gesture that grounded me in the midst of the chaos. "See? We belong here," he whispered, his breath warm against my ear.

"Right, because we totally look like we belong in an art gallery," I retorted, trying to mask my nerves with humor. "I mean, I can barely tell the difference between a Monet and a watercolor painting done by a toddler."

"Don't sell yourself short," he replied, a twinkle in his eye. "You could totally pull off the role of a sophisticated art critic."

"Only if my critique includes the words 'pretty' and 'wow,'" I shot back, and we both burst into laughter, drawing curious glances from nearby patrons.

As we wandered deeper into the gallery, I found myself captivated by the art—bold strokes and intricate details that seemed to speak to me in ways I didn't quite understand. The colors swirled and danced before my eyes, igniting memories I had long buried. I found myself standing in front of a piece that echoed the chaos of my own heart, an explosion of colors that mirrored my own tangled emotions.

"What do you think?" Clayton asked, standing beside me, his gaze intent.

"It's beautiful and chaotic," I admitted, my voice barely above a whisper. "Like it's caught between something wonderful and something painful."

He nodded, studying my expression. "You've always had an eye for the deeper meaning, haven't you? It's what I love about you."

I turned to him, surprised by his sincerity, the warmth of his words wrapping around me like a blanket. "You're not so bad yourself, Mr. Firestarter."

He chuckled, but there was something deeper in his gaze, a flicker of emotion that made my heart flutter. Just as I opened my mouth to respond, a sudden commotion at the entrance drew our attention. A group of people had gathered, their whispers rising to a crescendo as two figures burst through the door.

"Is that...?" I whispered, squinting to get a better look.

Clayton's expression shifted, the color draining from his face. "No way. It can't be."

But it was—there stood Amanda, my former roommate, and her new boyfriend, Max. Their arrival felt like a tidal wave crashing into our intimate moment, pulling me under with an unsettling force. Amanda's gaze swept across the gallery, her eyes landing on us, a smirk dancing across her lips.

"Well, well, if it isn't the dynamic duo," she called out, her tone dripping with sarcasm. "Out on the town, are we?"

Clayton stiffened beside me, a shadow of discomfort passing over his features. "We should—"

But I interrupted, my cheeks flushing with embarrassment. "We're just enjoying the art," I said, forcing a casualness I didn't feel. "What brings you here?"

"Oh, you know, just mingling with the elite," Amanda replied, waving her glass as if to emphasize her importance. "Unlike some people, we actually have connections."

The barbs in her words sliced through the air, and I felt an uncomfortable tension creep in. Clayton stepped closer, a protective instinct igniting. "We're here to have a good time, Amanda. No need for the attitude."

"Look who's getting all defensive," she mocked, her laughter echoing in the gallery. "What's next? A poetic declaration of love in front of everyone?"

The air crackled with the fallout of her taunt, and I could see the heat rising in Clayton's cheeks. "This isn't about you," he said, his voice firm.

Amanda shrugged, feigning innocence. "But it seems to be a theme. So tell me, how does it feel to rekindle an old flame?"

A knot formed in my stomach as I glanced at Clayton, uncertainty flooding my mind. Could we really navigate the labyrinth of our past with distractions like Amanda lurking nearby?

Before I could respond, Max stepped forward, grinning widely. "We should all do a group photo! Capture this moment of nostalgia."

"Right, because nothing says 'great time' like a forced smile next to the ex," I muttered under my breath.

Clayton took a breath, his eyes locking onto mine, and in that moment, I saw the flicker of determination behind his uncertainty. "Let's not give them the satisfaction," he said quietly. "We came here to enjoy ourselves, not to entertain the gallery gossip."

But as I turned to tell him that I wanted to leave, a loud crash echoed through the gallery, followed by startled gasps. All eyes turned to the front, where a painting had toppled from the wall, shattering glass scattering across the floor.

"What the—" I started, but before I could finish, I felt a surge of panic. In that chaotic moment, Clayton's hand found mine, a lifeline amidst the turmoil.

"Stay close," he murmured, his voice steadying me as the atmosphere shifted, a palpable tension wrapping around us like a dark cloud.

We were caught in a web of chaos, and I couldn't shake the feeling that our night of adventure had just taken a turn into the unexpected. My heart raced as I wondered if this was merely a clumsy accident—or if something far more sinister was at play.

Chapter 23: Return to Whispering Hills

The dawn had barely broken, casting a muted glow over Whispering Hills, as I stood at the barn door, my fingers trembling slightly on the weathered wood. The air was thick with the scent of damp earth and fresh hay, the sweet undertone of morning dew mingling with the faint whiff of leather from the saddle hooks hanging nearby. I had always found solace here, in the rustic embrace of the barn, where the world felt expansive yet intimate, as if every beam and nail held a piece of my heart.

Clayton was leaning against the corral fence, his dark hair tousled, with sleep still lingering in his gaze. He looked up as I approached, and for a moment, time hung suspended between us, thick with memories and unspoken words. The last few years had been a turbulent sea of emotions, but standing here now, under the watchful gaze of the old barn owl perched above, I felt the first flickers of hope igniting within me.

"Didn't think you'd come back," he said, his voice low and rough, like gravel rolling down a hill. He straightened, shoving his hands into the pockets of his faded jeans, as if trying to conceal his own vulnerability. I could see the way the sunlight brushed against his cheek, illuminating the boyish charm that had always drawn me in.

"I wasn't sure I would either," I admitted, a shaky laugh escaping my lips, a nervous dance of sound in the stillness. "But I figured I had to face the music eventually. And I can't quite shake the feeling that this is where I belong."

He studied me, his piercing blue eyes searching for the truth behind my words, and the intensity of his gaze sent a shiver down my spine. The barn, once filled with our laughter and whispered dreams, suddenly felt charged with unspoken tension. "What's changed?" he finally asked, his brow furrowing slightly.

I took a deep breath, inhaling the comforting scent of hay and wood, a stark contrast to the sterile office building I had escaped. "Life, I suppose. Sometimes it takes a little distance to realize what you truly want. I thought I needed to prove something to the world, to myself, but I only ended up losing sight of what was really important."

Clayton remained silent, but the tightening of his jaw suggested he was wrestling with his own demons. I took a tentative step closer, the sun rising higher, spilling golden light into the barn like a promise. "I miss this," I continued, gesturing around. "I miss you. I don't want to just let that slip away."

He uncrossed his arms, leaning forward slightly as if the gravity of my words was pulling him in. "You think it's that simple? You waltz back in after everything that's happened, and I'm just supposed to forget the hurt?"

The edge in his voice stung, but I understood. I had made my choice all those years ago, a choice that had sent ripples through both our lives. "I don't expect you to forget, Clayton. But can't we at least talk about it? I'm not the same person I was when I left."

His silence was deafening, punctuated only by the soft nickering of the horses inside the stalls. I could feel the weight of my admission hanging in the air, a fragile thread that bound us together, yet also threatened to snap under the pressure of unacknowledged pain. "What are you afraid of?" I asked, my voice softer now, laced with urgency. "What if we could find a way back to what we had?"

He ran a hand through his hair, the sunlight catching the faint flecks of gold in it, making him look almost ethereal. "You think it's easy for me? Seeing you again after all this time? After how we ended?" His eyes narrowed slightly, and I could see the tumultuous storm brewing beneath his calm exterior.

"Nothing worth having is easy," I countered, emboldened by the rush of adrenaline coursing through me. "You taught me that. You always said that love was a choice, a commitment. So, let's commit to figuring this out, together."

He shook his head, a flicker of something—a memory, perhaps—dancing across his features. "What if it's not there anymore? What if it was all just a fleeting moment?"

"Then we'll make new moments," I said firmly, stepping even closer until the familiar warmth radiating from him wrapped around me like a blanket. "We can start from scratch, learn all over again. I'm willing to take that chance if you are."

In that moment, the barn seemed to hold its breath, the air thick with the tension of possibilities. I could see the conflict flickering in his eyes, a battle between the hurt of the past and the hope of a new beginning. As the sun broke free from the horizon, casting golden beams through the slats of the barn, it illuminated a spark of something deeper within him—a glimmer of desire and connection, nearly lost but not yet extinguished.

Clayton shifted slightly, his gaze drifting to the horses, then back to me. "You really think we can just pick up the pieces?"

"Why not?" I urged, my heart racing. "Life is messy, but it's also beautiful. We've already navigated the mess; let's not shy away from the beauty waiting to unfold."

He inhaled deeply, the breath filled with the scents of earth and hay, the promise of renewal. "Alright," he said slowly, his voice gaining strength. "Let's see if we can build something from the ashes."

My heart leapt at his words, a rush of exhilaration coursing through me as I realized the path we were embarking on was fraught with uncertainty, yet infused with possibility. This was the moment I had yearned for, the chance to reclaim what had been lost, to redefine our narrative in the tapestry of life that was Whispering Hills.

As we stood there, the sun casting a warm glow over the barn, I could feel the weight of the past beginning to lift, replaced by a flicker of hope that whispered of the love and laughter we could still share. Together, we would face the unknown, step into the light, and let the winds of change guide us toward a new beginning.

The sun spilled through the barn's windows, casting long shadows that danced playfully on the hay-strewn floor as Clayton took a step closer. The air around us was electric, charged with the weight of all the unsaid words lingering between us like dust motes caught in the sunlight. My heart thumped in rhythm with the distant thuds of hooves, a quiet reminder that life carried on, even amidst the chaos of emotions swirling around us.

"Okay, then," Clayton finally said, the corners of his mouth twitching into a half-smile that almost shattered the tension. "What's the first step in this rebuilding process? A few yoga sessions? Or maybe a group therapy retreat?"

I chuckled, feeling the knot in my stomach loosen just a bit. "Let's skip the yoga. I can barely touch my toes. How about we start with coffee instead? I'd wager that's the best therapy we could ask for."

He raised an eyebrow, a hint of mischief in his gaze that reminded me of our late-night debates over the best coffee blend. "Coffee? Isn't that a bit too casual? Shouldn't we be discussing our feelings over artisanal lattes or something equally pretentious?"

"Pretentious? Please," I scoffed, waving my hand dismissively. "You know I'm a simple black coffee kind of girl. Let's not complicate things."

His laugh was a warm balm, easing the lingering tension like sunlight melting morning frost. "Alright, black coffee it is. But we'll brew it right, no shortcuts. You do remember how to make it, don't you?"

"Excuse me?" I shot back playfully, hands on my hips. "I'll have you know I've been making coffee like a barista. I can even froth milk now. Next, I'll be opening a café right here in the barn."

"Let's not get ahead of ourselves," he replied, mock seriousness taking over his features. "But I could see the sign now: 'Whispering Hills Café: Specializing in Black Coffee and Regrets.'"

"Oh, the perfect tagline!" I laughed, and for a moment, the air between us felt lighter, infused with the warmth of shared memories. "But I think we'd need a few pastry options. Nothing says healing like a flaky croissant."

"Agreed. But first, we need to figure out how to brew this coffee." He motioned toward the back of the barn where a small kitchenette had been set up, an odd addition to the rustic charm of the place.

As we moved to the kitchenette, I couldn't help but admire the way the morning light illuminated Clayton's features, the way the years had carved new lines of experience into his face but had failed to diminish his inherent charm. There was a deep warmth in his laughter, the same warmth that had always made me feel safe.

"Grab the beans," he instructed, his voice slipping into a comfortable rhythm. "I'll get the water going."

I opened the cupboard, inhaling the earthy aroma of the coffee that seemed to promise warmth and comfort. As I poured the dark, glossy beans into the grinder, I felt the familiar stirrings of a connection—intangible yet palpable, like the bond we'd forged long ago, now rekindling in the simplest of tasks.

"Remember that time we tried to brew coffee in the old pot and it exploded all over the kitchen?" I asked, a grin spreading across my face as the memory unfurled.

Clayton chuckled, his eyes sparkling with the mirth of shared nostalgia. "How could I forget? We ended up smelling like burnt coffee for a week. I still think the universe was punishing us for being too ambitious."

"Ambitious? More like reckless," I teased, reaching for a mug that had been tucked in the corner. "But look at us now. Full-fledged adults who know better than to mix coffee with questionable machinery."

"Speak for yourself," he replied, leaning against the counter. "I'm still questioning half of my life choices."

"Are we really going to dive into that?" I shot back, raising an eyebrow. "Because I've got a list."

"Please don't," he laughed, shaking his head. "I'd prefer my existential crises to remain unexamined, thank you very much."

With the coffee brewing, I took a moment to observe him, my heart swelling at the sight of the man I had once loved so deeply. The years had etched their story into his skin, each line a testament to the journey we had taken apart. Yet, the essence of who he was—the humor, the warmth, the way his eyes crinkled at the corners when he smiled—remained unchanged.

The coffee gurgled, a rich, dark stream pouring into the pot, filling the air with a deep, familiar aroma that wrapped around us like an old, cherished blanket. I poured two steaming cups, the liquid swirling like our lives—complex, rich, and sometimes a little messy.

"Cheers," I said, raising my cup toward him, my heart pounding in my chest.

"Cheers," he echoed, clinking his mug against mine with a sound that felt like a promise.

We sipped, letting the warmth spread through us, and the conversation flowed easily, punctuated with laughter and gentle teasing. Yet, beneath the surface, an undercurrent of tension simmered, a reminder that this was just the beginning of something far more complicated than a simple cup of coffee.

As we moved outside to sit on the porch, the morning sun brightened the sprawling fields, painting them in shades of gold and green. The hills rolled in the distance like soft waves, and the soft sounds of nature surrounded us—a gentle rustle of leaves, the distant call of a bird, the peaceful whinny of a horse in the barn.

"Tell me about your life," he said, settling into the creaky porch swing, his eyes fixed on mine, expectant. "What's been going on in the big city?"

I took a sip of coffee, the warmth grounding me as I considered my response. "It's a whirlwind, really. I dove into my career, thinking it would fill the void. And for a while, it did. I spent late nights at the office, attended more meetings than I care to remember, and networked my way through endless social events."

"Sounds glamorous," he said, his tone teasing. "Did you rub elbows with any famous coffee connoisseurs?"

"More like burnout experts," I replied, rolling my eyes. "But I learned a lot about what I don't want. I thought chasing success was the answer, but it turns out, I was just running away."

Clayton studied me, and I could see the wheels turning in his mind. "Running away from what?"

"From myself, I suppose," I admitted, the truth hitting me like a wave. "I wanted to escape the memories, the pain of losing you. But it only left me feeling more lost. I realized that I had built a life on shaky ground, one that didn't feel like home."

He nodded slowly, understanding evident in his gaze. "And coming back here, you think it'll change everything?"

"I don't know," I confessed. "But it's a start. I need to reconnect with what matters, and that's you, this place."

Silence enveloped us, heavy and poignant, as we both processed my words. The world around us faded into a backdrop of color and sound, leaving only the two of us suspended in our shared history. The past was a landscape filled with both beauty and hurt, a mosaic of our lives that deserved acknowledgment.

"What if I told you that coming back doesn't mean you have to leave everything else behind?" Clayton said suddenly, a hint of something new in his voice—curiosity, perhaps, or hope.

"What do you mean?"

"Maybe you can have both—the city and Whispering Hills. They can coexist."

The idea sparked something within me, igniting a flicker of excitement. "You think so? Could I really balance my life here with my ambitions there?"

"Why not?" he encouraged, his eyes dancing with encouragement. "If anyone can manage it, it's you. You've always had a knack for defying expectations."

I laughed lightly, the weight of the world momentarily lifted. "You make it sound so easy, but it's complicated, Clayton. There's so much to figure out."

"Complicated? Maybe. Worth it? Absolutely."

As we shared our laughter, the sun climbed higher in the sky, illuminating the possibilities that lay ahead. The past might linger like a shadow, but with each sip of coffee, I could feel the promise of a new chapter unfurling before us, filled with uncertainty and hope, ready for us to write it together.

The sun climbed higher in the sky, its golden rays illuminating the landscape in a warm embrace, as I savored the coffee's rich aroma. Clayton leaned back in the creaky porch swing, his fingers lightly brushing against the weathered wood, as if drawing strength from the familiar surroundings. There was a comfort in our shared silence, a gentle rhythm that spoke of unspoken words and layered emotions. I could sense that we were on the precipice of something significant, something that demanded courage from both of us.

"You know," he began, breaking the stillness, "the last time we sat here, we were plotting how to take on the world. Remember? You wanted to travel the globe, and I was convinced I could become a famous rodeo star."

I laughed, the sound bubbling up like a clear spring. "Yes, and you insisted on wearing that ridiculous cowboy hat, even in the dead of summer. I think I have pictures somewhere."

"Oh, please don't," he groaned, mock horror painted across his face. "The world does not need to see that."

"Too late. I already have the evidence stored in a very safe place," I teased, my eyes dancing with mischief. "It's going right next to your famous pancake recipe that almost burned down my kitchen."

"Hey, my pancakes are legendary," he shot back, a playful grin spreading across his lips. "If it weren't for the smoke alarms, they would've been award-winning."

We fell into a comfortable banter, the familiar rhythm of our friendship intertwining with the uncharted territory of our present. Yet, beneath the laughter, I could feel the weight of what lay ahead pressing on us, a specter of unresolved emotions and lingering feelings. The lightness of the moment made me brave enough to ask, "What do you really think of me being back? Is it too much?"

He tilted his head, considering my words with the seriousness they deserved. "I think it's complicated. You returning means revisiting the past, and that brings its own set of challenges."

"True, but isn't it worth it? The possibility of rebuilding what we had?" I pressed, the need for honesty thrumming beneath my skin.

Clayton's expression softened, the sunlight catching the contours of his face. "You know I'd like that. But it's not just about us. There are other pieces to this puzzle. Things have changed since you left. I've changed."

"Changed how?"

He hesitated, the shadows of uncertainty flickering across his features. "Well, for starters, I've taken over the family farm. It's not just a hobby anymore—it's a full-time commitment."

"I know," I said gently. "I've heard bits and pieces. But how does that affect us?"

"Because it means I have responsibilities now. People depend on me. If this doesn't work out between us, it's not just my heart on the line. It's the whole farm."

The reality of his words hung heavy in the air, weaving an intricate tapestry of risk and reward that I hadn't fully considered. "But what if it could work? What if we could make this all fit together? Maybe I could help—"

"Help?" he interrupted, a hint of surprise lacing his voice. "You think you can just jump in and take over the reins?"

I leaned forward, my heart racing. "Not take over, but support. I mean, I have ideas. I've been working in marketing, and I could help bring the farm into the modern age. Attract tourists or create a community event—"

He shook his head, an incredulous smile tugging at his lips. "You want to turn this place into a tourist attraction? With my luck, we'd end up with more selfie sticks than cows."

"Maybe it wouldn't be so bad. Imagine the stories we could tell. 'Come to Whispering Hills and sip coffee with a cowboy!'"

He chuckled, but there was a hint of uncertainty in his laughter. "I'm not sure it's that simple. I need to keep the focus on the farm—"

"While keeping yourself locked in the past?" I challenged, unable to hide the urgency in my voice. "You've been carrying the weight of this place for too long, Clayton. Maybe it's time to share that weight instead of pushing me away."

He fell silent, contemplating my words as the birds flitted above us, darting in and out of the branches. The soft rustle of the leaves painted a backdrop of life, the world moving forward even as we stood still. "I don't want to hurt you again," he finally said, the raw honesty in his voice a dagger to my heart.

"But you're already hurting me by holding back," I replied, the truth ringing clear. "Let's not let fear dictate our choices. Life's too short for that."

As I watched the sun inch higher, I could see the walls around him begin to crack, a flicker of something hopeful sparking behind his eyes. "Maybe we can try," he conceded slowly, his voice a fragile whisper. "But we take it one step at a time. I won't promise the moon if I can't even guarantee the stars."

"Fair enough," I said, relief flooding through me. "One step at a time sounds good. We'll start with coffee and work our way to cows."

He laughed again, and I felt the tension ease just a little more. "Cows first, coffee later? You've got a strange ordering system."

"Well, what can I say? I'm an unconventional thinker," I retorted, crossing my arms playfully.

But just as the moment began to feel comfortable, the tranquility shattered with the sound of tires crunching gravel. I turned my head, spotting a familiar old pickup truck rumbling down the driveway. My heart sank when I recognized the silhouette behind the wheel.

"What's that?" Clayton asked, following my gaze.

"Uh-oh," I murmured, my heart racing. "That looks like trouble."

As the truck came to a stop, the engine sputtered into silence, and the door swung open to reveal Jess, a blast from the past who had always been a thorn in our side. Her hair was a wild halo of curls, a smirk dancing on her lips as she approached, clearly enjoying the unexpected reunion.

"Well, well, well," she called out, her voice dripping with mock sweetness. "Look what the cat dragged back to town! The prodigal daughter has returned."

Clayton stiffened beside me, the warm glow of our conversation instantly overshadowed by Jess's arrival. "What does she want?" he whispered, the unease radiating from him palpable.

I shrugged, feigning nonchalance, but my stomach twisted in knots. "No idea, but it can't be good."

"Surprise! I came to check on my favorite cowboy and see how things were going in the old neighborhood," Jess said, leaning against the porch railing with an air of casual defiance.

"Since when do you care about the neighborhood?" I shot back, unable to hold back the edge in my voice.

She laughed, a sharp sound that cut through the air. "Oh, I've got my reasons. You know how it is—keeping up with old friends is just good business."

"Right," Clayton replied, stepping forward slightly. "What business are we talking about?"

Jess's eyes sparkled with mischief, her demeanor suddenly shifting from friendly to calculating. "Let's just say I have a proposal that could change everything. For both of you."

The way she leaned in, her gaze flitting between us, sent a chill down my spine. I could sense the air grow thick with tension, a storm brewing just beyond the horizon of our fragile truce. Whatever Jess had in mind, it wouldn't be anything simple.

And as she opened her mouth to speak, the weight of the world shifted once more, teetering on the edge of a revelation that could very well change the course of our lives forever.

Chapter 24: The Beginning

The air hung thick with the scent of pine and freshly turned earth as I stepped into the clearing, the remnants of the late afternoon sun casting long shadows that danced like ghosts among the trees. Each breath I took filled my lungs with the crispness of autumn, mixed with the lingering warmth of summer that was reluctant to fade. Whispering Hills had always been a magical place, a vibrant tapestry of colors and sounds that seemed to sing with life. It was here, in this sacred ground where my heart had first learned to flutter, that I found the courage to return.

Clayton stood before me, a rugged silhouette against the backdrop of golden foliage. His dark hair tousled by the breeze, he looked like the embodiment of the wilderness that surrounded us. I had forgotten how striking he was, his features sharp and yet softened by a hint of vulnerability. But his eyes—those stormy depths—held a tempest of emotions I could scarcely comprehend.

"I'm back," I whispered, my voice barely breaking the silence that had enveloped us. My heart raced, thumping against my ribcage like a wild creature desperate to escape. There was so much I wanted to say, to explain, but all I could manage was that simple declaration.

He stepped closer, the space between us shrinking as he searched my eyes with an intensity that made my breath hitch. It was in that moment, the world around us faded away, leaving only us suspended in time. I could feel the weight of unspoken words and past decisions hanging in the air, heavy and poignant. And then, just like that, he pulled me into his arms.

The warmth of his body wrapped around me, solid and grounding, and I melted against him, feeling like a puzzle piece that had finally found its home. "I knew you'd come back," he murmured against my hair, his voice low and raspy, sending a shiver down my spine. I inhaled deeply, trying to memorize this moment, the scent of cedar and him, something uniquely Clayton, something I had missed more than I had ever realized.

Relief washed over me in waves. In that embrace, I felt the walls I had built around my heart begin to crumble, brick by brick, and with it came a surge of hope that surged through me like electricity. This wasn't just a reunion; it was a promise—a silent agreement that we would face whatever had kept us apart head-on. I closed my eyes, savoring the feeling of belonging that wrapped around me like a warm blanket.

We stood like that for what felt like an eternity, lost in each other, until the coolness of the evening air nudged us back to reality. I pulled away slightly, enough to see his face, his expression a mixture of relief and something deeper, something that set my pulse racing. "You look different," he said, his thumb brushing lightly against my cheek, a gentle caress that ignited sparks in its wake. "Stronger."

I chuckled softly, feeling the warmth rise to my cheeks. "Maybe a little. Life has a way of toughening you up when you least expect it." I was surprised at my own honesty, the words flowing freely as if they were merely the natural course of a river.

He grinned, a slow, easy smile that made my heart flip. "Or maybe you just missed my rugged good looks."

I rolled my eyes playfully. "Please. You know I'm not that easily swayed."

"Are you sure about that? Because the last time I checked, you were rather fond of my 'rugged good looks' and—"

"Okay, okay!" I interrupted, laughing, feeling the tension ease between us. "Point taken. You've got the looks, but I've got the brains."

"Brains, huh?" He raised an eyebrow, amusement dancing in his eyes. "So what's your grand plan now that you're back?"

The question hung in the air, heavy with possibilities. What was my plan? The truth was, I had returned seeking closure, but now it felt like the beginning of a new adventure. "I want to find out what I've missed, what this place has become without me," I said, my voice steady. "But more than that, I want to see if we can pick up where we left off. If you're willing."

His expression shifted, seriousness clouding his playful demeanor. "I've always been willing. I just didn't think you would come back."

"Neither did I," I admitted, my voice softening. "But life has a funny way of leading you where you need to go."

A comfortable silence settled between us, a shared understanding unspoken but palpable. As the last rays of sunlight dipped below the horizon, the air grew cooler, a reminder that time was not on our side.

"What about all those dreams you had?" Clayton asked, his gaze steady. "The ones that took you away from here?"

I hesitated, the weight of that question pressing against my heart. Dreams. They felt so distant now, like echoes of a life I had nearly forgotten. "Some dreams were worth chasing, but they led me to a dead end. I thought I could outrun my past, but it always found a way to catch up to me."

His eyes softened, and I saw the flicker of understanding there. "Maybe it's time to create new dreams, together. Right here."

The idea sent a thrill through me, a spark of hope igniting my spirit. I nodded slowly, my heart swelling with possibilities. "Together." The word tasted sweet on my tongue, like honey mixed with freedom.

Clayton stepped closer again, our bodies almost touching, and I could feel the warmth radiating off him. "What if I told you that Whispering Hills still has secrets waiting to be uncovered? Things you wouldn't believe."

My curiosity piqued, I leaned in slightly. "Secrets? Now you've got my attention."

He chuckled, a low, rumbling sound that reverberated through me. "Oh, just wait. You're in for a surprise."

As we stood there, bathed in the golden glow of the fading day, I realized that this was more than a return; it was a resurrection. I was no longer the girl who had run away from this place. I was ready to embrace it, with all its imperfections and mysteries. And with Clayton by my side, I felt a fierce determination bubbling within me. Whatever lay ahead, I was ready to face it. Together.

The sun dipped lower, painting the sky in hues of amber and lavender, and for a moment, the world outside our embrace blurred into an impressionistic masterpiece. As Clayton's arms tightened around me, a rush of emotions surged through my veins, rekindling the warmth of memories I thought I had buried. Each heartbeat echoed with a sense of belonging, of returning to the place where my roots intertwined with the very soil beneath us.

"Did you really miss this place?" Clayton asked, pulling back just enough to look into my eyes, his expression an intriguing mix of curiosity and vulnerability.

"Like you wouldn't believe," I replied, finding my voice steadier now. "There's a magic here, isn't there? A certain... something that makes you feel alive."

He chuckled softly, the sound like a warm breeze rustling the leaves around us. "It's the air, I think. Or maybe it's just the ridiculous amount of coffee I drink."

I laughed, the tension easing between us, but beneath the lightness lingered an unspoken challenge. "Coffee? Are you still brewing that awful dark roast?"

Clayton feigned offense, placing a hand over his heart. "That 'awful dark roast' is a carefully crafted blend of beans, thank you very much. You just have no appreciation for the finer things in life."

"Finer things?" I scoffed, shaking my head in mock disbelief. "The only fine thing about your coffee is the way it feels like a punch in the gut."

He grinned, a flash of mischief lighting up his eyes. "Well, if you're back for good, maybe I can convince you to expand your palate."

"Or maybe I'll just bring my own supply," I countered, feeling a warmth bloom in my chest. It felt good to bicker, to fall back into this rhythm that felt as natural as breathing.

A shift in the wind brought a chill, and I shivered involuntarily. Clayton noticed, his brow furrowing in concern. "Let's get you inside before you catch a cold," he said, and I followed him through the winding path that led to the cabin.

The wooden structure loomed ahead, its weathered exterior speaking of stories etched into its very bones. A place that had seen laughter, tears, and the passage of time like the rings of an ancient tree. As we stepped inside, the familiar scent of cedar and pine enveloped me, wrapping around me like an old friend's embrace.

"Home sweet home," I murmured, glancing around. The cozy interior was a hodgepodge of memories—photos adorning the walls, each framed moment a whisper of laughter and love. "You've kept it just as I remember."

"Of course," he replied, leaning against the counter, arms crossed. "I figured if you ever decided to grace us with your presence again, you'd want a piece of home."

"Flattery will get you nowhere, you know."

"Noted," he said, pretending to jot down notes on an imaginary notepad. "But just so you know, it's not all flattery. The roof needs fixing, and I've been meaning to redo the bathroom—"

"Right, right. Let me just pull out my toolkit," I interrupted with a grin. "It's not like I left all my skills behind."

His laughter rang out, brightening the dim corners of the cabin. "Maybe we could tackle a few projects together. You know, team bonding."

"Or just an excuse to spend more time with me," I teased, unable to hide the hope lacing my words.

"Hey, I'm not opposed to a little home improvement—especially with your dazzling charm to motivate me," he shot back, his eyes sparkling with mischief.

Before I could respond, a sudden noise echoed from the porch, a thud followed by a muffled yelp. Our banter evaporated as we exchanged startled glances, and instinctively, we moved toward the sound, curiosity piquing our interest.

Clayton opened the door, and we stepped out onto the creaky wooden steps. What we found nearly made me burst out laughing. A scruffy golden retriever, muddy and wagging his tail like a metronome, was enthusiastically attempting to play tug-of-war with an old, tattered welcome mat.

"Bandit!" Clayton exclaimed, bending down to scratch the dog's ears, his earlier bravado replaced with affection. "What are you doing, you little menace?"

The dog, oblivious to the world around him, yanked at the mat, pulling it free from the porch and rolling onto his back, tail wagging furiously. I couldn't help but smile, the sight so delightfully ridiculous that it warmed my heart.

"He's a good boy," I said, kneeling to join the playful chaos. "Though I think he needs a bit of training."

Clayton chuckled, looking at me sideways. "Funny you should say that. He was the only thing keeping me company when you left."

I shot him a quizzical look. "So you're saying I was replaced by a dog?"

"Not replaced. Just... diversified my companionship portfolio."

"Ah, so now you're an investment banker for furry friends?"

"Precisely. And Bandit here has given me a solid return on investment."

I laughed, my heart lifting as I scratched Bandit behind the ears, and the dog leaned into my touch, eyes sparkling with canine joy. "How long have you had him?"

"About a year. Found him wandering near the old mill, and it was love at first sight. Can you blame me?"

"Not at all," I replied, glancing between them. "I think you two make quite the pair."

"Let's just say he's got a knack for keeping me in line," Clayton said, standing up and throwing a playful glance at Bandit. "I could use that in my life."

"Don't worry. I'm back now to keep you both in line," I declared with mock seriousness, standing with a sense of newfound purpose.

Just then, the wind picked up, sending a shiver down my spine. A strange sense of anticipation hummed in the air, like the calm before a storm. The sky darkened ominously, casting a shadow over the landscape, and I could feel the shift, as if the very earth beneath our feet was bracing for something.

"Looks like we might get a storm," Clayton said, glancing at the horizon, where dark clouds loomed.

"Perfect weather for a cozy night in," I suggested, trying to quell the rising tension within me. "What do you say to some hot cocoa and a movie?"

He considered this, a thoughtful expression crossing his features. "Only if you promise not to pick one of those cheesy romantic comedies."

"What's wrong with a little romance?"

"Nothing, unless it's one of those where the girl chooses the wrong guy—"

"Alright, how about something with a twist?"

"Deal. But let's hope Bandit doesn't chew through the remotes in the process."

The dog yelped, as if in agreement, and I couldn't shake the feeling that the storm brewing outside mirrored the shifting tides within me. It was time to face whatever secrets Whispering Hills held, but for now, I would relish this simple moment—together with Clayton and our rambunctious new friend, ready to uncover the mysteries waiting just beyond the horizon.

As the clouds gathered ominously overhead, a palpable electricity filled the air, making the hairs on my arms stand on end. Bandit, still recovering from his dramatic welcome, pawed at my leg as if sensing the change. I glanced at Clayton, who was already looking out toward the horizon, his expression suddenly serious.

"Are you sure we should be out here?" I asked, my voice a mixture of concern and curiosity. "Storms around here can sneak up fast."

"Trust me," he replied, confidence lacing his tone. "I've lived through more than a few of them. Besides, I've got the world's best watchdog at my side." He ruffled Bandit's fur, who seemed to puff up with pride at the compliment.

As we retreated into the cabin, the wind picked up, howling through the trees and sending a shiver down my spine. I pulled the door shut behind me, sealing out the encroaching chill and the darkening sky. The cozy interior felt like a refuge against the chaos outside, and I sighed, trying to shake off the tension that had begun to creep into my bones.

Clayton moved to the kitchen and began rummaging through cabinets. "Let's get that cocoa going. I promise not to burn it this time."

"Your culinary skills leave much to be desired," I teased, leaning against the doorframe, watching him with amusement as he searched for the cocoa powder. "I'd think you'd want to impress me."

"Impress you?" He turned, holding a half-empty bag of cocoa like it was a trophy. "I'm already winning, and I haven't even started cooking yet."

"Winning?" I laughed. "You're not exactly competing against Gordon Ramsay here. You should see my pasta skills. I can whip up a mean carbonara."

"Pasta? Now we're talking! Is that a challenge?"

"Absolutely," I replied, stepping further into the kitchen, letting the scent of cedar mingle with the chocolate as it began to warm on the stove. "Loser has to clean up after dinner."

"I'll take that bet, but I'll warn you, I've got a reputation for being undefeated in the kitchen."

"Then it's a good thing you didn't go pro," I shot back, savoring the playful banter. It felt like the threads of our old rhythm were weaving back together, stitching up the gaps that had formed over the years.

As the cocoa bubbled and foamed, I stole glances at Clayton, who was trying—and failing—to hide his grin. This was the side of him I had missed: the easy confidence paired with an undercurrent of warmth that made every moment feel significant.

"Do you think it'll storm?" I asked, glancing toward the window, where the first droplets of rain began to splatter against the glass, creating a symphony of sound that resonated deep within me.

"Definitely," he said, stirring the cocoa and watching the steam rise. "But I'd like to think it's just nature's way of giving us a dramatic backdrop."

"Or perhaps an excuse to huddle under blankets and binge-watch terrible movies?" I suggested, a playful glint in my eye.

"Now you're speaking my language. Just no rom-coms."

"No promises," I teased, knowing full well that I had a stash of cheesy love stories at the ready.

We poured the cocoa into mismatched mugs, a testament to his questionable taste in dinnerware, and settled onto the worn couch, Bandit sprawling contentedly at our feet. The room was bathed in the soft glow of a single lamp, and the rain began to drum against the roof, creating a rhythm that was almost hypnotic.

"Okay, your pick for the first movie," Clayton said, taking a sip from his mug.

I pretended to ponder, tapping my chin in mock seriousness. "I'm feeling something adventurous. How about a classic heist movie? Nothing beats clever plots and witty dialogue."

His eyebrows shot up, a mischievous smile breaking across his face. "Ah, so you're challenging my intelligence now?"

"More like testing your patience," I replied, scrolling through the list of movies on the screen. "Let's see what we've got here..."

Just as I made my selection, a sharp crack of thunder roared outside, causing us both to jump. Bandit, in his usual dog-like fashion, barked at the sound, adding to the already charged atmosphere.

"Calm down, buddy," Clayton said, scratching Bandit behind the ears. "It's just a little thunder. Nothing to worry about."

"Easy for you to say," I replied, feeling a knot of anxiety tighten in my stomach. "You're not the one who freaks out every time the skies rumble."

"Okay, fair enough. Maybe I should have you cuddle with Bandit while I protect you from the big, scary storm."

"Ha! As if that would help."

The movie started, and the screen flickered to life, immersing us in a world of action and suspense. I tried to focus, but every crack of thunder outside sent my heart racing. I curled up on the couch, Bandit nudging against me, seeking comfort.

Halfway through the film, I felt Clayton's gaze on me, his expression contemplative. "You okay?"

"Just... the storm," I admitted, biting my lip. "It's a bit unnerving."

He reached over, his fingers brushing against mine, and I felt a jolt of electricity shoot through me. "You're safe here. Trust me."

"I do." The truth rolled off my tongue easily, and I found myself looking into his eyes, caught in the warmth of his reassurance.

Another crack of thunder echoed outside, louder this time, and the lights flickered, causing us both to pause. A heartbeat later, the power went out, plunging us into darkness.

"Perfect," I said, trying to inject humor into my voice, but my heart raced at the sudden quiet. "I guess this is what they call ambiance."

"Don't worry, I've got a flashlight somewhere," he said, standing up and fumbling in the dark. "Just... stay right there."

As he moved toward the kitchen, I heard a strange noise outside—a low growl, a sound that didn't belong to Bandit. My pulse quickened, and I strained to hear through the chaos of the storm.

"Clayton?" I called, my voice shaking slightly.

"Just a sec," he replied, his voice muffled as he rummaged through drawers.

The growl came again, louder this time, sending chills down my spine. I stood up, straining to see through the darkened windows. "I think we've got company," I whispered, my heart thudding in my chest.

"What do you mean?"

I felt a rush of adrenaline as I approached the window, peering into the storm. The wind howled like a creature, but then, just beyond the treeline, I saw a pair of glowing eyes staring back at me. They were unlike anything I'd seen before—piercing and unyielding, a haunting reminder that the wild wasn't just a backdrop to our cozy night.

"Clayton!" I shouted, my voice rising above the storm. "You need to see this!"

He came rushing back, the flashlight beam cutting through the dark like a lifeline. As he joined me at the window, we both froze, the realization of what we were looking at sending shockwaves through the air.

"What is that?" he breathed, his voice low and tense, as if speaking too loudly would provoke whatever was lurking outside.

I opened my mouth to respond, but before I could, the creature moved closer, revealing a massive silhouette. It wasn't just a figment of the storm; it was real and looming, a shadow of something primal and fierce.

In that moment, as the storm raged and the creature drew nearer, I realized that we were standing on the precipice of something far more significant than a reunion. The wilds of Whispering Hills had secrets, and they were finally ready to be unleashed.

www.ingramcontent.com/pod-product-compliance
Lightning Source LLC
Chambersburg PA
CBHW021944120726

47992CB00001B/131